Elysian Fields

J. L. Perrigo

CONTENTS

1   Chapter 1: The Book of Revelations   1

2   Chapter 2: The Exodus   16

3   Chapter 3: Wormwood   42

4   Chapter 4: Out of the pan   79

5   Chapter 5: The Reaping   113

6   Chapter 6:The calm before   160

7   Chapter 7: House of Storms   193

8   Chapter 8: Genesis   238

9   Chapter 9: The burning man   285

10   Chapter 10: There came a pale horse   341

11   Chapter 11: Sounding of the seventh   376

Chapter 1: The Book of Revelations

Part 1

Pastor Jimmy Clark woke the same way he had for three days, in a cold sweat, shaking like a child. He looked at the clock on the nightstand. The digital light showed 3:26 in blazing red, like it had the last three nights.

He slung the covers aside and planted his feet on the floor. Jimmy had come to accept its cold comfort. He knew deep down that he wasn't still dreaming. Yet as he stared into the infinite darkness of his own room, the visions still haunted him.

He reached up and ran his hand through his salt and pepper hair. Each coming day, he wanted more time. The flooring creaked with his own weight as he made his way towards the kitchen. His wife used to complain about his nightly trips. Jimmy used to feel disdain as she would carry on about it. It seemed trivial compared to her absence now. He fetched a can of coffee out of the cabinet.

"There is something coming."

His words seemed to echo in every crevice and hole in the empty house. Jimmy shook off the morning's earlier visions. He finally believed he was right for a change.

Part 2

Henry Myers sat in the remains of a empty building. He listened to distant explosions and the occasional burst of gunfire. This mission had went to shit. The remnants of the crashed black hawk helicopter across the street was a good enough sign of that.

It was supposed to be a snatch and grab, but that wasn't going to happen. Henry hoped the evacuation chopper reached them before the pirates did.

He took the photo out of his ballistic armor and stared down at it. He smiled even though he knew he was a dead man. His wife and daughter meant the world to him. Henry had grown tired of this way of life a long time before now, but he wanted his daughter to have a good college fund.

"Psshh, hey Henry, want some chew?"

Travis McGee had been Henry's friend since high school. They signed up together thinking they would save the world. The only thing they had managed to save was each others lives. Other than that there was no saving this place. Henry snapped from his thought as he thought he heard footsteps. He took the can of tobacco from Travis and put a pinch in his lip.

" Thanks." Henry whispered to Travis as he handed the can back to him.

War was a terrible monster that had taken the best from him. Henry had thought he was a dead man many times before now. Yet, they had always managed to make it home. He had lost most of the hearing in his right ear from a mortar that had landed close to him. He had been awarded the purple heart several times; more times than he wanted to get it, that was for sure.

Henry was pretty sure he had a few cracked ribs from that rough landing they had an hour ago. Every time he took a breath in it felt like someone was stabbing him in the side.

"Our ride is on the way fellas. E.t.a. ten mikes." Captain Wilkes informed those of them that had survived the crash.

Henry looked around at all the faces. Each one looked in pain or just blank. Henry remembered his drill sergeant trying to drill that one in their heads. It's called a steel trap the man had said. You want to survive you take all your fear and trap it in the mental box in your head. **If you are afraid you hesitate, and when you hesitate**

you will die. Henry called it being a huge, emotionless robot capable of any amount of carnage. This way of life had no room for pity.

That's when Henry saw it. The shadows flashed quickly four times through the crack in the boards. If the moon hadn't been out he would have never seen it in time. Henry grabbed his assault rifle from its resting place on his chest. Henry aimed down the sight at the door.

Travis had seen it in his eyes. The man's action mirrored Henry's like they had when they played football together in high school. Travis had managed to get behind cover as the door exploded open. Henry squeezed the trigger as the first man came through the door. They piled in as he kept shooting. Henry heard a bullet crash into the wall beside his head as he shot the third one through the door.

"Door!" Travis had shouted as Henry continued to fire towards the door.

Everything had slowed down for him though. Henry could hear the clinking as the shell casings were bouncing along the paved floor. He watched as the muzzle flash from his barrel did a brilliant strobe of death to all those that entered his kingdom. Henry had claimed this run down abandoned building in Africa his lands. Intruders were scaling the castle walls. Henry watched as the tear gas grenade came spinning through the door. Its trail of smoke following its crash to the floor.

"Changing!" Henry cried and Travis started firing from his covered position.

Henry ejected the magazine and was replacing it. He saw something else come through the doors. Henry was already on his way to a standing position when he saw it roll into the room.

"Grenade!" Travis cried and dove on top of it.

Henry had screamed no at his friend but it was already too late.

Part 3

Henry Myers didn't realize that he was screaming. Not until the knocking at his door brought him to his senses. The explosions and screaming voices were still so familiar in his head.

"Daddy what's wrong?" the voice asked from the door.

Henry's heart was beating like a forgotten war drum as he glanced around the room. It was dark and empty. There were no dead bodies missing pieces of themselves. No enemies creeping through the night. Those red eyes eager for the blood of the sleeping. Sweat beaded up and raced in rivulets down his chest.

Henry took in a deep breath and tried to calm the shaking.

"Daddy?" the voice asked again hesitantly.

The thought came back to the knocking at the door he had completely forgotten for a second.

"I'm fine Abby, just another bad dream."

Part 4

Abigale Myers had been having the most peculiar dream when her father's screams had woken her. Now as she gently touched cold wood of his bedroom door; her dream seemed petty. He had been having night terrors for a while now. She knew they had something to do with the war. She could only imagine but never dare to ask. She thought that some things were best left alone.

She turned around and started back down the hall to her room. The coolness of the floor had chased away most of the grogginess from her head. Abigale was positive she would never be able to go back to sleep.

"I'll go for a run," she told herself as she stripped down.

The town was usually pretty quiet. It was still an hour before dawn. Abigale bet she could even get back and cook breakfast before Henry got up. She laced her running shoes with deliberate skill. Yet as her body responded to the remedial task of shoe tying with accuracy, her mind was back to the dream. The fields of dying flowers and all those red eyes in the dark. Abigale shivered at the recollection and left for her run.

Part 5

Sam Roberts cursed as he reached for the lamp beside his bed. Sleep was still heavy as a blanket in his mind. He found the switch and light flooded the darkness of the room. Sam closed his eyes with a scowl. It was way too early to be awake, and Sam knew it.

He glanced towards the bedside table. 3:40 a.m. the digital light showed on his alarm clock. He looked in a daze for his cell phone. Sam fumbling through the covers until he found it. He looked at the screen and realized it was his father. Sam closed his eyes and said a small prayer as he flipped the phone open.

"Hello?" he spoke into the receiver.

Sam tried not to hide the discontent in his voice. He propped himself up to be comfortable. His father had the bad habit of calling him from time to time to display his dissatisfaction. Jimmy Clark had never cared for his son's way of life. The man had always found a way to be displeased with his choice of work. Yet as the silence dragged on in the receiver, Sam sensed something was different.

"I miss you Samuel," his father said in a plain tone.

If there had been anyone else in the room with Sam Roberts they would have been awestruck. He had never been one for expressing his feelings. His agent had cautioned him about his robotic responses to clients. Now as he felt the shock spread in his own face at his father's words, Sam almost felt sad.

His father had made him the way he was. Sam couldn't remember a time when his father had shown even a remote emphasis on caring for him. The harsh beatings he had received as a child on his father's sense of disapproval had come without emotion. The silence dragged on as he searched for the words to say. Sam took in a deep breath and held it for a second.

"I love you too Dad," Sam said into the phone, and then his father began to tell him about his recent dreams.

Part 6

Sam Roberts touched the end key on his cell phone and let out a deep breath. He didn't have words for what his father had told him. Sam racked over his brain about red eyed children and angels consuming flesh. He felt the goosebumps creep across his arms.

Sam's father had been a patriarch among the Baptist community for as long as he could remember. Yet with all the melodrama he had to use before to prove a point, this seemed too horrific to fill the collection plate. If Pastor Jimmy Clark would have told his same story in a church sermon, the pews of Elysian Fields Baptist Church would have been empty the next Sunday.

Sam closed the phone and placed it on the nightstand. Maybe that big house without his mother had become too much for his father. It was possible the old man had finally bit too deep into the fruit of knowledge and had become lost in his book of evils. Either way, Sam's father had struck a chord in him. He hadn't since Sam was in grade school.

A dull familiar ache began to creep into Sam's head as he looked across the room. The faint light of the table lamp caught the empty bourbon bottle and cast eerie shadows through the room. The paint on the canvas he had been working on was still fresh. The field of buttercups with long jagged crisscrosses of black. Sam didn't know why he felt compelled to put the red dots in the shadows on the horizon. He had seen the same thing in a nightmare the night before.

He would go tomorrow and visit his father, he thought as he fell backwards into the cold sheets. Sam knew he needed to stop drinking while he painted. It always seemed to make his works so much darker. He thought about texting Abby, but sleep claimed him.

Part 7

Abigale Myers had managed to run, shower, and have breakfast almost cooked when she heard her father come down the stairs.

"Something smells good," Henry Myers said as he entered the kitchen.

Abigale beamed her best smile as she flipped the slab of bacon in the skillet. She had a lot on her mind. When she stepped into the shower, Sam had been a bit weird as in late; he had been drinking more. Her father's recurring nightmares were beginning to scare her. The anniversary of her mother's death was tomorrow. Abigale knew she had to remember to get flowers today.

"That's a deep train of thought, pumpkin," her father said as he pulled the container of orange juice from the refrigerator.

Abigale shook her head and snapped back to reality. Her father loomed over her in stature and build. She could smell the starch in his uniform. Henry was well built for his age, but as his large hand touched hers, she cringed. He pulled his hand back and began searching for a glass within the cabinet.

"Sorry daddy," she said, "still half asleep."

She could read in her father's eyes, he didn't believe her. Abigale had always been a horrible liar. Even all those times she had tried to hide the bruises from Brittney Carmack down the street. Henry had never believed her. He knew that Brittney was a bully and had tried to talk to her parents, but bullies come from bullies.

Sissy Carmack was a closet alcoholic, and Billie Carmack was a supposed pedophile. There had been several times Billie had been accused of being a peeping tom. Abigale's mother had insisted on Henry saying something. Henry had gone over, Brittney innocent faced and all, and had come home disappointed. Abigale had listened to the argument in her room. Her father, the gentle giant, took that beating with clenched jaws.

The next day he took her out into the backyard and showed her how to defend herself. The next week, Brittney's parents had come over for a talk. She sat innocent faced and all, and the battle was won. Abigale lifted the sizzling bacon from the skillet and sat it on a plate she had sat in the middle of the table. She sat down and had a wordless breakfast with her father. Henry Myers crunched on his bacon; she smiled.

Part 8

Frank Pearson sat at his kitchen table and sipped on his coffee. It was six in the morning by the clock on his the wall. The small two bedroom house was quiet. It was how he liked to start his day. He picked up the cigarette from the ash tray and took a long drag. He blew the smoke in swirls across his kitchen table like an ancient dragon.

The dream he had that morning had kept him from going back to sleep. It had brought back memories that Frank wished he had forgotten. The large African men with machetes. Those burning red eyes.

Frank had decided to get up and clean his forty caliber side arm before work. As he had sat there polishing the weapon he could still hear the women screaming. Those bodies piled in ditches waist high. The thoughts still haunted him as he took another drag off the cigarette. Today was going to be a bad day. It was one of those gut feelings Frank got from time to time. They were never wrong.

Part 9

Henry Myers had felt bad coming down the stairs. He could tell by the smell of eggs and bacon Abby was trying to make him happy. He had closed away all emotion from the night before away in a special place. He had been taught hard in boot camp that you always save your face. The enemy can always see weakness.

Yet Henry had never seen his little girl as the enemy. Yeah, he had seen her with a lot of those he didn't like. The newest of these was Sam Roberts. A drunk-wanna-be that didn't have the stomach to actually be something. As his hand touched the tip of the banister he put on his best happy face.

"Something smells good," he said as he came through the door.

Henry could tell the dreams were starting to get the best of him. The doctor down at the precinct had warned him of PTSD. Seemed like a bunch of letters she didn't understand. Henry had seen Mike Peterson sink his knife into a boy's throat that couldn't have even been fifteen years old. He had happened to be the wrong place at the wrong time. To see what they put their kids up to; things like that stuck with you for life.

"That's a deep train of thought, pumpkin," he said as he looked at

Abigale's face.

He knew that she worried about him. She was worried about what night he would kill her in her room. When he wouldn't understand the difference. Henry reached into the fridge and found the orange juice. He didn't much care for it, but didn't want to worry her. She had fixed this meal for him. Her mother had always worried for her. He still did sometimes. Henry touched her hand and for the first time since he had to discipline her as a child he saw fear. Henry hurt on the inside, something he hadn't felt in years.

"Sorry daddy," she said, "still half asleep."

He took the glass form the cabinet and sat down at the table. He could tell by her eyes she knew; and as she set the bacon onto the plate he felt something down low. Something was bad wrong with today. He lifted the first piece of crispy bacon to his lips and it crunched loudly. The watched as his baby girl smiled. Something was wrong.

Part 10

Doctor Phillip Rhodes had been the chief medical examiner in Jacob's Ladder for the last fifteen years. He was a tall feeble looking man with shaggy white hair. He started his day off the same way he had for the last twenty years. He got up and fixed a pot of coffee;

then sat on his porch and watched the sun come up.

This time of year was almost perfect. The leaves had already started to turn. Soon all these hills would look like rolling waves of fires. Grace had always liked this time of year. He could feel the corner of his mouth curve into a smile as he lifted the steaming black towards his face. It hadn't been two months since she had passed on. He never was sad like they told him he should have been. They had twenty seven good years. The sun's crimson brilliance splashed hues of color across the distant horizon. Phillip Rhodes lifeless body fell silently to the ground.

Chapter 2: The Exodus

Part 1

Revelation 18:11

"Then I saw heaven opened and there was a white horse! Its rider is called faithful and true and in righteousness he judges and makes war."

The headlines read around the world. 1.1 trillion people had dropped dead overnight. They were calling it an epidemic of mass proportions. Yet there was no trace of drug or biological weapon. Millions of Americans huddled around their television screens; praying for a sign. Yet as the news casts posed on and on no one had an answer. The questions kept mounting. Did I touch this person? Did I make sure to wash my hands? As the people fell into fear, the world stood still.

Part 2

Felix Cherry of the center for disease control had risen to his title from hours of tireless work. He had lost two wives to divorce because of his relentless work ethic. 7:00 A.M. call had woke him from his usual Mexican dream. Felix felt his head drop. Somehow he had hoped for a chance to shine his colors.

Felix's aide poured over the details of the attack on his portable phone. He felt ill equipped with purpose and determination for a task like this. He dressed heartily that morning.

The President wanted him on the eleven o'clock news. We need to be reassuring the American people they are safe. He pulled his tie tight with distinction. There was something that told him heroics were at a loss. He closed his briefcase and made his way towards the door.

Part 3

Sam Roberts sat straight up in bed. His stomach was rolling hard as he watched the sunlight creeping through his shades. He glanced at the watch on this wrist. It said 8:06 and he felt sick again.

Sam was still focused on the dream when his cell phone began to ring again. He looked around for it in a stupor when the vibration echoed through the room again. He snatched the phone violently for the nightstand with much discontent. Sam's eyes searching the display screen. He swallowed as he clicked open the phone.

"Mike this had better be good," he griped into the receiver.

He had to fight off the daze of sleep, as the voice on the end rattled on with pause. Half of what he had heard he didn't quite understand as he tried to clear his head.

"What do you mean dead?" he said.

Sam Roberts was still trapped in the grogginess. The voice on the line replied in almost complete hysterics. Mike Miller always got this way about everything.

"Turn on the television dude." Mike replied.

Sam reached for the remote, but he wasn't prepared for what he was about to see.

Part 4

Abigale Myers still vividly remembered the glass of orange juice exploding on the floor. Her father had got up to answer the phone; when she saw her father's face go white. Time seemed to almost stop as the glass tumbled to the floor. The expression on his face seemed to dissolve like it was never there as he hung up the receiver. He didn't even look at the mess in the floor as he turned and started up the stairs. He seemed almost robotic to her. Abigale felt a sick feeling in her stomach as she bent down to clean the mess. She hadn't realized she cut herself until she noticed the red dots in the orange pool.

"Those red eyes," she whispered to the empty kitchen.

Part 5

Frank Peterson had been the captain of Jacob's Ladder for the last three months. He replaced the older captain Henry Myers. Frank had served under Henry for years and deeply respected him. Something had been plaguing Henry. When the chief had wanted to suspend him Frank was the first to plead his case.

"I'll get him under control," he had told Chief Raines.

Frank had stuck to his word. Story down the grapevine had said Henry was showing signs of post traumatic stress. He had seen it in a lot of his friends in coming back from Somalia and Kuwait. Some of the shit you saw you couldn't forget. Night terrors and flashbacks usually was the start. Frank knew Henry was stronger than that. When the call came in about the possible terrorist attack he had called Henry first.

"I need you Henry," he said, "you're the best we got."

He knew back when times were rough a little morale went a long way. A little time to shine and Henry would be his old self again. Jacob's Ladder was a moderately small community compared to bigger cities like Houston. It still had people, and people needed protection. Word from brass had said only fifty in town had fallen to the "unsaid attack." That was the only ones they had found so far. Frank knew that.

Unfortunately one was the chief medical examiner. So there was no hope of a decent autopsy until the one from Houston could arrive, and there was no assurance of that. Franks' eyes drifted back to the television screen.

A rather sharp dressed fella from the CDC, a Felix Cherry, said we didn't' have anything to worry about. That the government had everything under control. They would pawn it off on swine flu or mad cow, which ever seemed convenient at the moment.

Frank knew bull shit when he saw it, and Felix oozed it. Today had a real bad vibe to it; same vibe he used to get every time first sergeant screamed "Gas masks!" He clicked the television off and went to find Henry before the briefing.

Part 6

Henry Myers stood silently staring at the photo taped to the inside of his locker. He stopped tightening his tie and ran a finger over his wife's face. He missed his wife. Faced with the facts this morning he needed her strength right now. It always shone through at times like this. He facilitated a lot of that was due to her temper. It had been a source or perseverance in trying times.

Henry pulled his tie tight and closed the locker door. Frank didn't have a whole lot of details at this point. When Frank had

called earlier he had stated that it was bad and it was world wide. Henry assumed it was a terrorist act. Yet the pattern didn't match any weapon he had ever heard of.

" Hey Bear." Frank sounded off behind him. " Just the man I was looking for."

Henry turned around to face the man. Frank had took Henry's position as captain of Jacob's Ladder police department. He didn't hold it against Frank. He had trained the man and knew that Frank was more than capable of leading. Henry knew the boy had been reluctant to take the job. Harry had been insistent saying that Henry had become too unstable. Henry admitted that his temper had got the best of him on more than one occasion. He was getting too burnt out to do this job anymore.

"Good morning Frank." Henry greeted his friend.

Frank reached out to shake Henry's hand. Henry took the man's smaller hand in his own and gave it a hearty shake.

"I wanted to catch you before the briefing." Frank started off. " Whatever is going on Henry, I want you to promise me no hero stuff. Whatever this is already got the medical examiner. Calls have been pouring in all morning by people saying their husband, wife, ect. were dropping like flies. The EMS people done washed out once they realized it could be contagious. Harry has a plan. We do this how he wants so we all get to go home."

Henry nodded his agreement. He took his department issued forty caliber handgun from his holster. Henry made sure it was loaded. Frank was eyeing him cautiously as Henry placed the weapon back in its holster. He secured it with a snap of the button. He managed to smile at his friend. Henry knew Frank worried about him. Henry wasn't sure if it should be him that the man was worrying about at this point.

"Lets go and see what the chief has planned," Henry said as he slapped his friend on the back.

Part 7

Jessica Teach sat in the back of the Jacob's Ladder police department. Chief Harry Raines went over the briefing. She had felt sick to her stomach ever since this morning. The night shift dispatcher had called and told her the news. There were many calls coming in from all over the Ladder about the recently deceased.

Those that had family members were found, but this was a retirement community. The majority of the citizens here were old and widowed. A lot of them didn't have close family members living with them. No one came to check on them daily.

At this point there had only been 50 confirmed cases. Whatever this was had people running scared. Jacob's Ladder had 5 full time police officers. Only three of them had bothered to come in besides the chief.

" Judging by how fast word travels in a small town I suppose y'all know what's going on." Harry started in a big booming voice. "Nobody is coming to help us as far as I know. At least no time soon."

Jessica looked around the room. This was to be a meeting of all the branches of the emergency services for Jacob's Ladder. There were no Fire fighters or Medics present. They were missing two of the other polices officers. The only lower ranking officer was Lester Fields. The boy wasn't even twenty yet. Frank and Henry were here. You could always count on those two to help out in a pinch.

"Frankly people this ain't looking good. We have no idea if this is contagious, but you can bet your boots it's fatal. So right now before we go any further., there's the door if you ain't got the stones. I ain't gonna judge ya. Nobody here will. If you gonna chicken out once this starts to get tough then be on your way now." Harry stated without emotion.

Jessica looked from one officer to the next. After a moment of silence Lester stood up. Jessica felt a pain in her head. This was a small town. 3,126 at the last census. Yet it was plenty of ground to cover. They were gonna need every hand on deck.

"I'm sorry guys......I have a daughter...." Lester got out with a stutter.

Jessica watched Harry nod his head at Lester as the man left. She couldn't judge him. Everything in her brain screamed leave.

"Alright now that we're past that let's get down to brass tacks." Harry started. " I want to go around and start checking the residences.

Especially the ones that you know only has one person that lives there. You find something. Put a black X on the door and radio it in. Jessica here will keep up with it on the map. Don't touch them and don't go near them. Let the CDC and the military deal with it. This is recon boys. Ain't nobody playing hero today. You got your orders ladies and gentlemen. Dismissed."

Jessica watched as Frank and Henry made their way out of the conference room. She eased herself up from her chair and started towards the door herself. Harry motioned for her to come over to him. She weaved between her chairs and stood in front of the podium.

"I just wanted to thank you for coming in girl. " Harry said with his big Texas smile. "You do your job justice. People take notice to that. I know you're gonna have it rough today. So when you had enough you tell ole Harry and you can scoot. No questions asked. Okay?"

Jessica nodded her head and Harry motioned for her to carry on. She made her way back to the dispatch office and set down at the computer console. The phone lines were already flashing as she picked up the headset. Jessica said a small prayer and pushed the call button.

"911 what is your emergency?" Jessica stated in her usual helpful sounding voice.

Part 8

Pastor Jimmy Clark sat at his desk reading over his Bible. The dreams had been constant the last couple of days. The black wraiths with the red eyes. The woman with the red eyed toddler that was consuming her face. Jimmy wondered if this was how the visions came to Peter. Did they take him for a mad man?

He knew that if he was to tell people what he saw and thought, he would be hospitalized. They would label him with some moniker. Paranoid schizophrenic or mental psychosis. It would surely be one of those. If he hadn't had the dreams he would think the same way. Yet Jimmy couldn't get over the sense of dread he felt right now. He knew that he wasn't crazy. Something was coming. He could feel it hanging in the air.

The phone was ringing on his desk. The sudden realization snapped him from his thoughts. He scrambled for the receiver. He picked up the phone and placed it to his ear.

"Hello" Jimmy spoke into the receiver.

Jimmy listened for someone to speak. All he could hear was someone breathing. He waited patiently. He was about to hang up.

It wouldn't be the first time someone had prank called him while he was here. He pulled the phone away from his ear.

"Jimmy it's Cecil." a voice spoke.

Jimmy placed the phone back to his ear. It was odd that he was calling him this early in the morning. Cecil had been a deacon at the church for years. He had preached sermons in his absence on several occasions. Jimmy thought the man was quite in touch with the word of God. "Brother Cecil it's good to hear your voice." Jimmy stated as he tried to fight the fear out of his voice. "How are you this fine morning?"

Jimmy listened as the silence seemed to drag on again. He heard what he thought was a sob and then silence again.

"Cecil my friend….what seems to be troubling you?" Jimmy asked.

It was like his words had broken the dam that had been holding Cecil together. He heard the man begin to cry and sob. The first thing that popped into his head was Cecil's wife Jamie. Had something happened to her? Was it his son Steven? As far as Jimmy knew Jamie was in good health. His son Steven had a stroke at a very early age. Cecil and his wife took care of their son at home. Slowly the crying died down on the other end of line.

27

"Jamie and Steven have gone to be with the Lord." Cecil got out between sniffles.

Jimmy felt the weight of it plop down on him like a heavy blanket. How could they have both died on the same day? It must have been a fire or some freak accident. Jimmy's mind was going with all the possibilities and how to best approach the already upset man.

"I am so sorry Cecil my friend." Jimmy stated with true concern in his voice. "How did this happen?"

There was another silent spell. He was concerned that his friend had been overcome with grief.

"I don't know...."Cecil started."It doesn't matter now I don't guess. I simply wanted to let you know that I wouldn't be there today."

Jimmy had noticed how the man had went from near hysterics to a almost scary cold. The man was filtering through the stages of grief a little too quick.

"Let me come and help you with the preparations brother." Jimmy proposed to his friend.

"I will be fine. Thank you for listening. I must be going." Cecil stated and then the line went dead.

Jimmy placed the receiver back on the hook. He felt cold at this point. It was like the room had taken on a great chill all the sudden. Jimmy reached down and rubbed his arms with their new goose flesh. Jimmy felt the fear start gnawing on the corners of his thoughts.

Part 9

Cecil Phillips placed the phone down on the receiver and looked back towards his den. His son's lifeless eyes staring back at him made a pain shoot through his chest. How could this be happening to him? Had he not been a good enough person? Had he not been a charitable enough person?

His son's lifeless gaze felt like it was burning a hole through him. Cecil glanced down to his wife Jamie. The broken bowl that had contained his son's oatmeal still clutched in one of her hands. The oatmeal was all over her green Sunday dress. Her gaze was the same as his son's. Heavy and weighted to drive him down. Cecil felt the tears and they began streaking down his cheeks.

"WHAT DID I DO?!?!?" Cecil screamed to the empty house.

Cecil had called 911 for the paramedics. The operator stated that all their units were on calls. They had instructed him on how to check for a pulse. He had felt for one and found none. It hadn't been ten minutes and they were already ice cold. The operator told him that a unit would come as soon as possible.

It had already been over an hour when he had called the funeral home. Nobody had answered there. Nobody was coming to help him. He should cover them at least he told himself as he rose from his easy chair. Their eyes seemed to follow him as he started down the hallway to the linen closet. He reached for the door knob. His hands felt like they were lead weights as he turned the knob.

Cecil stood there staring into the linen closet. He reached up and pulled the pull rope. With a click the closet flooded with light. Cecil looked at the shelves full of fresh clean linens. He looked from one shelf to the next. He wasn't sure if he could do this.

Cecil's gaze finally drifted to the twelve gauge shotgun that sat propped in the corner. He smiled as he remember how him and his son had went duck hunting with it. Since his son's accident it had sat in that closet untouched. Cecil ran his fingers over the black matte finish of the barrel. Cecil grabbed the shotgun and two fresh sheets and made his way back towards the den.

Cecil propped the shotgun up on the end of his son's hospital bed. Steven and himself had an estranged life for the longest time. When Steven was a small boy he wanted to go everywhere his father went. They went hunting and fishing. Played football in the back yard after church every Sunday. Once the boy grew up and went to college they stopped talking.

The night the state police called to tell them of his son's accident had been a blow to his wife Jamie. They had rushed to the hospital. The officer told them his son had run off the road. Steven's blood alcohol limit had been two times the legal limit. It had been a while before someone noticed his car in the ravine. The doctors had managed to drain the blood off his brain, but the damage was done.

"God will see him through," Cecil had told his wife.

Cecil reached down and closed his son's eyes. The pain shot through his chest again. He knew he should take a nitroglycerin table before his angina got too much. Cecil covered his son with one of the sheets. He lowered himself down and gave his son a kiss on his covered forehead. His eyes drifted to his wife laying in the floor. He felt the tears well up again. He hastily wiped them from his eyes as he stooped down and closed his wife eyes.

The whole ordeal had broken his wife. There was nothing like watching your son deteriorate before your eyes. The pain of never being able to hear them say 'I love you' again. The medicine cabinet full of depression medicine she took on a daily basis proof of that. Cecil covered her with the last blanket and tucked it underneath her.

" I love you darlin." Cecil said as he placed a kiss on his wife's covered forehead.

Cecil looked down at the two covered forms and began to sob once more. He grabbed the shotgun from the end of the bed and made his way back to his easy chair. The pain in his chest was getting worse. Cecil sat down in his recliner. He had the barrel of the shotgun gripped in his hand so tight his knuckles had turned white. He placed the barrel of the gun in his mouth and reached for the trigger. He couldn't do this by himself.

The sound of the shotgun was loud on Sunset Drive. People were outside on their lawns. Those fetching their Sunday papers or watering their flowers looked. From one face to the other. The sound was startling but none cared to investigate its source.

Part 10

Sam Roberts had watched the emergency broadcast feed in a daze. He was still in shock when his phone vibrated again. Mike Miller, it had said; he ignored the call and turned off the TV. Something in Sam's gut had told him to do it. This had to be an elaborate hoax. They had explained on the news a few days ago that swine flu was close to pandemic. He shook his head to himself and it hurt; he had too much bourbon the night before. His dreams were starting to get worse. He pushed the power button to the television on again. The headlines kept scrolling across the bottom of the screen. He swallowed the hard lump in his throat and called Abby.

Part 11

"Put the weapon on the ground!" Frank Pearson screamed at the man holding the bat.

Frank Stared at the man who had a two handed grip on the wooden bat. The car he was standing beside of had dents running the whole length of the car. It had been called in as a traffic collision. Now it looked like it was spinning straight into an assault attempt. The thin blonde male cowering inside the dented car let out a scream as the man raised the bat again.

"I said put it down or I put you down!" Frank yelled as he sighted down his pistol at the man.

Frank could tell this was a rough customer. Not only did he have a bat and the intent to use it; the man was a walking mountain. Frank considered the man's hands as lethal as the bat at this point. He could tell there would be no arresting this one without someone getting hurt. Yet, if he could get the man to calm down and go on his way it would work out for everyone. Henry was on the other side of town. It was a one cowboy rodeo at this point.

"What choo gonna do about it pig?" the large man asked as he turned towards him.

Frank sighted down the pistol and fired a round. It connected with the brick wall behind the man and showered him in bits of debris. It was a warning shot. He could kill the man. It wouldn't bother him to do so. Yet Frank hoped to deescalate the situation before it came to that. The man didn't even bother to acknowledge the shot. He reached up with one of those big hands and dusted the brick chips off his shoulder.

"The next one goes through your head hoss." Frank stated bluntly.

The large man stared into Frank's eyes. He could see the intent to kill there. Frank hadn't bothered to hide it from the man. He hoped the man would see it and realize that one of them would die if this didn't go how Frank wanted it to. The big man tossed the bat into the bed of the pickup truck to his let his hands rest down to his sides.

"Alright officer. Alright." the large man said with a chuckle. "Ain't no need to get bent outta shape."

Frank let his eyes leave the man for a second to glance back at the male driver in the car. He could hear the man crying in the car. Frank could almost bet the man had peed his pants by this point. Frank glanced back to the large man who was standing there staring at him. A big "awe shucks" grin spread across his face.

"He ran inta me and called me an S.O.B officer. I don't take kindly to pee pa talkin about ma momma like that." The large man said as he raise his hands in a shrug.

Frank glanced back at the man in the car who was now looking at him. He could bet that was the likely truth. Little guy didn't realize what mountain was in the truck when he said it.

"Well I'm pretty sure he is sorry for what he said." Frank stated in his calmest police officer voice. "Aren't you fella?"

The thin male nodded his head yes rapidly. The big man looked from Frank to the thin man and laughed a big booming laugh.

"You two let by gones be by gones and be on your way." Frank said and motioned for the man to get in his truck.

The man continued to laugh as he started for his truck door. Frank didn't take his eyes off the man as he opened the door and got inside.

"What eva you say officer." the large man said as he started the truck and drove off.

Frank motioned for the thin man to move on as well. The man mouthed thank you as he started his car. Frank holstered his weapon and made his way back to his patrol car. Normally he would have arrested the man. Yet it would have been more trouble than it was worth. They already had more trouble in their hands than they could hold.

Frank pulled a cigarette from the pack and placed it between his lips. He figured things would get worse before it got better. He lit the cigarette and took a long drag as he watched the people scurry to and fro on the streets. A lot worse he thought and he climbed into the squad car and closed the door.

Part 12

Jimmy Clark had planned to be more fire and brimstone this Sunday's sermon. He knew that with the horror in their eyes it would save their souls. The collection would be teeming with retribution, but he knew it would be at a loss. He continued to read over his notes as he always did every Sunday. For the first time in a long while during his reign over the pulpit, he aimed to change people. Jimmy could see it all play out in his head.

Billie Carmack would eye the Peterson girls in his usual sick demeanor. Everyone would pretend and pray with him. Jimmy's heart sunk knowing they would return to their devils as normal. Some would confess to him and he would try and save them. Not a one of them would listen to him though.

Jimmy felt a chill go up his spine and he swore he heard the beating of wings; those red eyes staring out of the shadows. He felt an eerie dread sink into his heart as he organized the song books in meticulous order among the pews. Sam had said he would visit today.

Jimmy knew he had been too harsh on the boy, but only in hope he would become greater. He had never understood it all until after Betty had passed. He placed the last book in line with the rest and made his way towards the door. He would have his usual Sunday breakfast and be ready for his battle. The light switch clicked off and in the darkness his doubt grew.

"This Sabbath has been lost", Jimmy whispered to himself.

He fiddled with his keys until he found the right one. He had locked these doors a thousand times, but as the lock closed, he felt ill. Something was wrong today; something was bad wrong.

Part 13

Nick Birdwell sat quietly staring at his computer screen. He had read through most of the blogs his group had posted today. The mainstream media had been quiet for the most part about the "Event." Reports on the main media outlets only stated the government had it in hand. That everything was gonna be fine. Yet the underground reporters and bloggers had been putting the truth out there. Several of the videos posted on the private server were disturbing. Military and emergency service packing people out of buildings. The streets lined with black body bags. Reporters and prying eyes kept behind barricades. Nick wasn't sure what this was. Yet as he clicked through the videos posted on **The Blind Eye** message board; it brought concern.

Nick was surprised when the blue chat bubble popped up on the screen. He knew alot of these bloggers. Not as in personally but had many correspondences with them on weekly basis. Nick looked at the name. **Phoenix2843**. This guy was upstate New York if he remembered correctly. He was a journalist for one of the daily news blogs. They usually had readable material. Maybe he had news on whatever this was. Nick clicked on the icon.

Phoenix2843: How is Texas?

Spartan2295: Not too bad in Jacobs Ladder. Only fifty confirmed so far. What about New York?

Phoenix2843: Not so great. The military is here. They won't answer any questions. My sources say its not any weapon they know of in existence.

Spartan2295: Maybe it's something some terrorist cooked up in a lab somewhere. I don't think it's a disease.

Phoenix2843: The pathophysiology is too wide spread. I have seen videos where it kills everybody in one building. I have seen where it only gets a hand full of people. Whatever this is. Man made or not. Its lethal to who has it. My neighbor said his wife was in the middle of ironing his shirt when she dropped dead.

Spartan2295: Holy shit.

Phoenix2843: Yeah man this stuff doesn't play. I gotta jet. Gonna try and make it to my parents to check on them. The phone lines here are buggy. Let me know if you hear anything.

Spartan2295: I'll keep you in the loop brother. Let me know if you hear anything else.

Phoenix2843: Will do.

Nick closed the chat bubble. If he wasn't scared before he was now. He watched the screen as new videos uploaded every couple of seconds. Nick reached for the remote and turned the television on. There was a man on the screen. Sharp dressed fellow by the look of him. The director of the Center of Disease Control the tab on the screen read. Nick knew that if the Center for Disease Control knew about this they weren't gonna tell anyone. Yet the puppet for the government sat there and smiled. Nick watched as he continued on about staying indoors and letting the military do its job. Nick couldn't help but roll his eyes. They were already dead and they didn't want to panic the public.

Part 14

"Reverend Clark may I have a word with you?" the voice called out behind him.

Jimmy placed the keys in his pocket as he turned around. The stranger behind him was elegantly dressed. His black hair stretched down to his collar, but that was the only thing out of place. The rest of him was all business. The man's suit was custom tailored by the way it fit him. His gait towards him oozed stature. Jimmy could only smile as his eyes met his. They were of the purest blue he had ever seen. He extended his hand toward the stranger.

"It's not reverend. It's pastor, Jimmy Clark. What can I do for ya?"

The nicely dressed mans smiled and gave a curtly bow, much out of date.

"A moment of your time, pastor Clark."

Jimmy Clark nodded to the man and motioned for the man to follow him. The man followed him towards his vehicle. Jimmy needed to eat. All the things going on this morning had his nerves on end. He was going to get nauseous if he didn't eat soon.

Jimmy opened the door to his late model sedan and motioned for the man to get in. With a fluid grace the man sat down in the seat. Jimmy looked at the man and smiled as he turned the key over and the car came to life. The man seemed harmless enough but something bothered Jimmy. What did the man want?

"What did you say your name was again?" Jimmy asked the stranger.

"Sebastian Mourning." the stranger stated. "Please call me Sebastian."

"Alright Sebastian. Let's get something to eat."

The man smiled and Jimmy felt a chill go down his spine.

Chapter 3: Wormwood

Part 1

Sam Roberts felt ill as he closed his cell phone. Abigale Myers had seemed almost robotic to him as he had talked to her. She had no idea what was going on, he could tell by the distance in her voice. Sam had tried to get her to come over, but she had declined. Abigale said her father had told her to stay in until he returned.

Sam Roberts and Henry Myers had never seen eye to eye on anything. Sam knew the man loathed his existence. Henry wanted a big man like himself to marry his daughter. To have mini-cave man grandchildren so he would have someone to relate to.

Sam gritted his teeth as he turned the television set off. It was eleven o'clock and still no answer to what was going on. The CDC couldn't find any trace of disease or toxin but they said "now results are inconclusive." If they were trying to keep from creating mass hysteria, they were doing a piss poor job. Sam clicked open his phone and tried to reach his father again.

The continuing ring of the phone made his heart sink into his chest. Was his father one of the recently deceased? Sam's stomach churned hard and he felt dizzy. He shook his head slightly and grabbed his keys off the table. His worries only grew as he closed the apartment door behind him. The shock of the day's events weighed heavy on his chest as he made his way to his car.

Part 2

Abigale Myers sat staring at her anatomy and physiology text book. She had been trying to study for her final but had been unable to keep attention focused on the text. Her father had left abruptly for work and told her not to leave the house. He hadn't said another word to her.

When she had turned on the news she knew why. That is when she found out what was going on. All those deaths and the people in the body bags. It had only taken a few minutes before she turned the TV back off. She respected her father and what he had done. It had been the only thing to keep him together when her mother had passed.

With an exhausted sigh she closed the text book and pushed herself back from the table. She needed some water. That was what she needed. She grabbed a glass and turned on the tap. What she saw out the kitchen window made her gasp.

"Oh my god." She squeezed out in a squeak.

Every car in the neighborhood was being loaded down by their owners. She couldn't believe what she was seeing. Was everyone going to pack up and leave? Where did they plan on going? She felt something cold on her hand and realized the glass was over flowing and spilling out on to her hand. Abigale turned off the tap and took a drink of the water. Old lady Miller was sitting on her front porch. I guess she had a front row seat to the exodus from Jacob's ladder.

Abigale took the water and sat back down at the table. She opened the book back up and began to read once more. Her phone began to play its familiar chime. She picked it up and looked at the screen. She smiled when she saw Sam's name on the screen. She hadn't talked to him yet this morning. She couldn't believe she hadn't bothered to call and check on him. Her mind seemed so out of focus. She clicked answer and put the phone up to her ear.

"Hello love." She spoke into the phone.

Part 3

"I have a proposition," the stranger said as he stirred his coffee.

Pastor Clark had been studying the stranger. He had been ever since they had reached Still Water diner. Quiet and gathered the stranger had seemed to him. Now as he stared at the bacon he longed to eat he felt sick.

"Is your food not up to your liking?" the stranger asked.

Jimmy had touched it several times with his fork but dared not eat it. Dr. Rhodes had warned him about his salt intake every time he had a checkup, but he loved bacon.

"Just not that hungry'" he said to the stranger.

The stranger continued to ravish his meal. He had already ordered twice and he could still see the hunger in his eyes. They were of the palest blue he had ever seen. He pushed his plate forward in disgust and reached for his glass of water. The stranger watched his hands and pushed his own plate forward.

"What is your proposition?" pastor Clark asked with sure disdain.

"I want you to make a choice'" the stranger said quietly.

The emergency broadcast cut like a knife through the silence.

The stranger's eyes locked with Jimmy Clark's eyes, and he was awestruck. He was lost until the stranger looked at the television behind the counter. Jimmy turned in his seat and looked for himself. The stranger's voice seemed distant as the chaos played across the screen.

"Do you believe in hell Pastor Clark?" the stranger asked.

Jimmy was no longer paying attention to the screen.

Part 4

The vibration of his cell phone on the wooden desk snapped Nick from his thoughts. He picked up his phone and opened the message.

Mike Miller: Dude please tell me you know something

Mike was a great many things. Nick wouldn't say bright was one of those. He had tried to get the boy on the right path in high school. Mike had been too interested in smoking weed and playing video games. Nick wouldn't knock the video games. He did like to partake from time to time. Yet Mike's need to be high had destroyed too many of his brain cells. Nick's phone vibrated again in his hands.

Mike Miller: Come on dude tell me something.

Nick shook his head. Mike was more than likely sitting in his Mom's basement looking at the same news feeds he was.

Me: Not much on the net besides dead bodies everywhere Mike.

Nick stood up and made his way over to the window. He hadn't even bothered to look outside yet. Nick usually stayed away from people for the most part. He found that most of them lacked even base level intellect.

Nick pushed the curtain to the side and looked out his apartment window to the ground below. The vehicles were still traveling up and down the streets. People still moving around outside. Maybe it was a biological attack and the little town of Jacob's Ladder was safe. That was why he still lived here. Most of the people he was friends with had moved to Dallas a long time ago. Nick knew that if terrorist ever attacked it wouldn't be here. The world didn't care about Jacob's Ladder.

The phone vibrated again. He looked down at the screen. He

needed to get out there and see the damage. He needed to investigate if he could. See if there were streets lined in body bags or if this was going to blow over.

Mike Miller: Dude I know you know something. Spill it.

Me: I don't know anything besides there are millions of people dead.

Mike Miller: Man this shit is killing my buzz. I can't even get high.

Me: I'm going out to check things out for myself. You want to go?

Mike Miller: Yeah let me put some clothes on. I can see if Sam wants to come.

Me: Sam can come if he wants. He doesn't like me though.

Nick placed his phone down on the desk. Quickly he pulled the hooded sweat shirt with the reflective skull on it over his head. Mike wasn't exactly his best choice for recon. Sam was usually a douche bag. Too much angst and for what? Yet the more the merrier he guessed. Nick grabbed his cell phone and digital camera off the desk. If there was anything out there to report he wanted to get in on something. He needed to help add to the intelligence online.

Someone had to report the truth.

Me: Meet me at the park in about 20 minutes. You and whoever else you want to bring.

Mike Miller: Alright dude I'm gonna blaze this and be on my way.

Me: Make sure and spray some cologne. Don't come out with me smelling like weed.

Mike Miller: Don't break my balls Nick. It's the end of the world.

Me: End of the world or not there will be cops everywhere.

Mike Miller: Sam's not answering his phone. Guess its you and me.

Me: See you at the park.

Mike Miller: Alright see you there.

Nick lifted the strap of the camera over his head and let it fall to his chest. He hoped that if he went outside everything would be the normal day to day stuff. Nick hoped for the best. Some part of him knew it wasn't going to be the case.

Part 5

Sam Roberts sat in the parking lot of the Elysian fields Baptist church. His father's car parked in its usual spot. He didn't know why but seeing it there had lifted a heavy weight from his chest.

Sam had thought about going in and catching his father's sermon. He was not one for the religious part but his father was gifted at moving people. Yet there was something that made him unable to stomach theology. The idea of a benign father figure with supreme power and righteousness, blatantly ignoring his children struck too close to home.

Sam reached for the shifter and put the car in reverse. He was about to back out when he saw the stranger. All dressed in black making his way up the concrete walkway towards the door. Sam could tell by the time the stranger was running late for the sermon. Yet the man seemed to stand out. He looked rich, that being the first thing. He watched as the stranger turned and looked right at him. It was almost like the man was reading his mind. Sam swallowed hard and backed out of the parking spot. He would go and see his father later. If there was a later.

Part 6

Pastor Jimmy Clark Stood behind the podium of the Elysian Fields Baptist Church and looked at the pews. They held a few of his parishioners. The events that had taken place in their town today had been a harrowing ordeal. Most had been too scared to leave their homes or had left all together.

Most that sat before him today were the grieving and the lost. All were there seeking answers and for once Jimmy didn't have any. He felt that he was lost himself.

The sermon he had typed out sat on the podium. He looked down at it and wondered if he should use it. Preaching about hell fire and demons seemed to much. He wasn't sure if it would help guide his flock at all right now. It would be necessary to get them to where they needed to be. If this was indeed the end of the world then they need to get right with God.

"Brothers and sisters…"Jimmy started and stopped.

Jimmy looked out again at the tear stained faces. The blood shot eyes that now stared up at him. Eager for him to take away their pain. To make all this go away. Jimmy lifted his black Bible up for all to see. He coughed to clear his throat and began again.

"Brothers and sisters this book you see in my hand is full of trials like the one we face today. The tribulations wrote down and given to you. People that faced great perils and darkness and through the light of God overcame. David overcame the giant. Noah saved the righteous from the flood. Moses lead the Israelites to freedom. It is all there to read. You may or may not have read it but it is there. Story after story of odds stacked against them and God saw them through. God will see you through this dark time if you look to him."

Jimmy watched as the doors opened. The black haired stranger from before stepped through into the church. Everyone turned at once to look at the stranger. The man motioned as if to apologize and seated himself on the back row.

In unison the people inside forgot the stranger and looked back to Jimmy. He swallowed hard and took a sip of his glass of water. Jimmy would be the first to admit that the stranger scared him. Yet he had a task to do. He would be afraid later, but not here. Not in his house.

"Romans 12:12 tells us ' Be joyful in hope, patient in affliction, faithful in prayer.' This tells us that there is a light in the dark people. We may not find it today. We may not find it a week from now. Yet if you are patient that hope will be there. Pray for the answers and they will come. We can not fall into despair and think all is lost. God will see us through this darkness. Jesus the light will guide the way.

Be there for your brothers and sisters. In this time your deeds will pave the streets in gold. You can be assured of that my friends. James 1:12 tells us 'Blessed is the one who perseveres under trial because, having stood the test, that person will receive the crown of life that the Lord has promised to those that love him'."

"Amen!" A voice called out in the crowd.

Jimmy looked to the dark haired strange sitting in the back pew. The man's piecing blue eyes seemed fixed on Jimmy. Jimmy felt a chill on his spine.

"Brother and sisters I can sit here and quote verses after verses all day long. It is all there for you to read. God's word will show you the path. His intentions shown in all things in life. If you repent for your sins and put your faith in him the light will shine. The darkness of this time and all times in your life may be a weary road. It has been traveled by many before you. There is a light in the end if you open up your heart and accept the gift that is given to you. You accept his grace and that light will fill you and no darkness will touch it. If you are lost come forward. I will show you the way. You must only step forward and ask for the gift. "

"Amen!" the stranger called out from the back.

Jimmy felt the weight of the man's gaze as his eyes drifted from one person to the next. All the bloodshot eyes staring at him. No one made an attempt to move. He understood their fear. He had the same fear in his heart.

"If no one wishes to come forward…..Sister Claiborne will you start us with a song. Please turn your books to page 12" Jimmy stated.

Jimmy watched as they all opened their song books. His heart felt heavy and burdened. He folded his sermon on Revelations and tucked it in his bible. Mariette Claiborne stood up slowly. The elderly lady had been going to his church as long as he had been a pastor here. The woman's sweet voice had gave him clarity when he needed it.

"Amazing grace…..How sweet the sound….that saved a wretch like meeeeee!" The elderly lady sang.

Jimmy watched as the rest joined in. Their voice low and almost inaudible. One voice sounded out louder than the rest. The melody of it almost soothing. Jimmy looked from one face to the rest trying to narrow down the voice. Then he realized it was coming from the back row. The voice of the man in black.

Part 7

Nick Birdwell sat on the park bench and watched the world come apart. On his side of town things had been rather quiet. He lived in an apartment off of Maxwell street. It was apartment buildings with a single gas station. The gas station was the only actual business on that side of town.

Nick was now watching people flood the **Shop and Save** for resources and realized it was gonna be bad. He had already seen one fender bender, between a large muscular man and and elderly gentleman, almost come to blows. It had been twenty minutes since the collision and no police officers had showed up. The two men went their separate ways. Neither seemed happy about it. Nick looked down at his cell phone. Mike was already ten minutes late. Nick wondered if Jessica was working today. She was a dispatcher for the local police/fire departments. Maybe she knew something about whats going on.

Me: Hey beautiful what's up?

It was a long shot and Nick knew it. Jessica had been his off again on again girlfriend for the last year. They would fight constantly. She was always at work and never had any time to hang out. That had been the focal part of many of the arguments. He still cared for her. Nick wasn't sure how he could tell her that. She was way too pretty to be with the likes of him. He knew that but she didn't seem to.

One of the local firefighters had been after her a long time. Jeremy Biskin was a jock if you ever met one. All muscle and balls but no brains. Yet no matter how hard Jeremy tried she always found her way back to Nick.

Jessica: I can't tell you anything more than you already know Nick.

Me: I just wanted to make sure you were okay.

Jessica: I'm fine just stressed to the max.

Me: Is it that bad?

Jessica: It's worse than bad Nick. I'm scared.

Nick knew how she felt. He was scared to death himself. You couldn't tell it. Nick was about 6'3" and covered in tattoos. The tattoos scared off most trouble makers. It had scared away Jeremy so far. Yet as dark and intimidating as he appeared he still got afraid. Like right now hearing the same fear mirrored by what should have been the love of his life

Me: Screw the heroics babe. Leave and we can get out of here.

Jessica: I can't leave Nick. Even if I wanted to. I'm the only one who hasn't left already.

Me: What do you mean?

Jessica: I mean its bad Nick. Almost everyone has left. The firefighters. The medics. Hell I only have two officers answering the radio anymore.

Me: I know doing this means the world to you.

Jessica: It does Nick.

Me: You can't do it by yourself.

Jessica: I know. I don't know what to tell anyone. How do you tell someone that helps not coming?

Nick felt the weight of those words like a ton of bricks. He thought it might be bad out. He couldn't say that he blamed them. He wouldn't want to be the only law left when the lawlessness started. Nick could tell that by the fist fight that had broken out over the new fender bender at the **Shop and Save**.

Two women were going at it at the back of a minivan like a pair of boxers after a title shot. Nick could see the blonde haired boy beating on the glass. He knew their were tears in the boys eyes. Why was this woman hurting mommy?

Mike Miller: Hey dude where are you?

Me: Over by the fountain watching a title bout at the **Shop and Save.**

Mike Miller: Man there are wrecks everywhere but no cops.

Me: I don't think there are any cops left Mike.

Mike Miller: Well I'm almost there.

Me: See you in a few.

Nick watched as the woman in the car won the fight. She left the mother of the boy laying on the ground beside her van. He could see the little boy staring down at his mother. The tears still streaming down those chubby cheeks. Nick felt that need to act stir up inside him. Heroes only get medals posthumously.

Nick rose from his seat on the park bench. He shouldn't get involved and he wouldn't if the little boy hadn't been in the van. He made two steps forward when the woman began to stir on the ground. Nick was glad to see the woman was okay. He returned to his seat on the park bench as the woman got up and began to comfort her crying child.

Me: You don't answer the phone.

Jessica: You can't be serious Nick.

Me: I'm dead serious babe.

Part 8

Jessica Teach sat at the Dispatch terminal and stared at the blinking call light. She couldn't count how many calls she had answered since she had been here. The call light was flashing on the terminal again. She was running out of excuses to tell people. She didn't have anyone to send. Frank and Henry had been going non stop since 9 this morning. The calls hadn't stopped either. Jessica moved the cursor over to the answer tab. She said another small prayer and clicked answer.

"911 what is your emergency." she stated.

Jessica listened as the caller poured over the details. Another call about not being able to reach their parents. There had literally been dozens of call like that since this morning.

"Yes sir. We will send and officer as soon as one becomes available. Yes sir. I will call you back as soon as we know something."

Jessica marked a note on the dispatch record with the man's phone number. Harry had been handling the calls so far. She didn't know if she could call all those people back and tell them that their family member was deceased. It was heartbreaking enough to place the X's on the map. Her cell phone beeped loudly in the quiet of the dispatch room.

Nick: Hey beautiful what's up

Jessica felt a smile spread on her face as she read it. She had been so busy today that she hadn't even bothered to check on him today. The call light was flashing on the computer terminal again.

"911 what's your emergency. Yes ma'am. All our officers are currently busy. I'll send one as soon as one comes available. Yes ma'am. You too ma'am."

Jessica preyed on the momentary silence and quickly text Nick back.

Me: I can't tell you anything more than you already know Nick.

Nick: I just wanted to make sure you were okay.

Me: I'm fine just stressed to the max.

Nick: Is it that bad?

Me: It's worse than bad Nick. I'm scared.

Jessica felt the gravity of the situation. She knew that the world was crumbling around them. She wasn't sure when help was going to arrive. IF it was.

Nick: Screw the heroics babe. Leave and we can get out of here.

Me: I can't leave Nick. Even if I wanted to. I'm the only one who hasn't left already.

Nick: What do you mean?

Me: I mean its bad Nick. Almost everyone has left. The firefighters. The medics. Hell I only have two officers answering the radio anymore.

Nick: I know doing this means the world to you.

Me: It does Nick.

Nick: You can't do it by yourself.

Me: I know. I don't know what to tell anyone. How do you tell someone that helps not coming?

Jessica stared at the call light as it flashed again on the screen. Into the fire again. She moved the clicked call on the screen. She didn't know how much longer she could keep this up. She had to pee so bad.

"911 what's your emergency. Yes sir. We will send an officer as soon as one becomes available. I'm sorry sir. If nobody is seriously hurt take down each others information. Yes sir. I know sir. I'm sorry you feel that way sir. You too sir."

Nick: You don't answer the phone.

Me: You can't be serious Nick.

Nick: I'm dead serious babe.

Jessica wished she could not pick up. Something in her just wouldn't let her leave.

Part 9

Henry stared at the burned out car sitting in the middle of the highway leaving Jacob's Ladder. It sat like a rock in the middle of a busy stream as the cars parted to the left and right to get around it. People were evacuating the town like it was a nuclear fallout zone. He couldn't count how many of these he had seen. Vehicles getting overheated in the traffic and being abandoned. Where did these people think they were running to? This shit from what he heard was everywhere.

The government had been quiet so far. The only thing he had heard was an address from one of the leading epidemiologists with the Center of Disease control. It had been the typical smoke and mirrors tactic they always used when they were clueless.

" Get out of the way!" a voice cried out followed by repeated honks of a blaring car horn.

Henry cut his eyes to where the voice had come from. The middle age bald man was still honking his horn. The freeway was on the other side of the tunnel. But traffic on this two lane highway was bumper to bumper. The man honked the horn again.

Henry reached over and turned on his blue lights. The man looked over at Henry and gave him the bird. Normally this would have got him a pretty good thrashing and a trip to jail. Henry didn't think it was worth it now. He rolled up the window and turned the radio on. The emergency broadcast siren blared over the radio with its usual bells and whistles.

"Stay tuned for the union address by the President of the United States. " a robotic voice stated followed by more Morse code style beeps.

Henry reached over and turned up the radio and he rolled up the rest of the windows on his cruiser. He wanted to hear what this had to say. He guaranteed he wasn't going to like it though.

Part 10

Jessica Teach sat there listening to Ms. Burns carry on about her mail box. Apparently one of her neighbors had backed over it when they had left. The elderly lady was upset that they didn't even offer to help fix it. Her late husband had put that mail box up and those ruffians had ran it over and left like cowards. This was about the most basic call she had heard all day.

"Ms. Burns I am sorry about your mail box. As soon as an officer is free we will send him over to do a report. Unfortunately its a long list and can be awhile. Yes ma'am. You're welcome ma'am. You too ma'am." Jessica stated while still managing to keep her composure.

Jessica looked up to see Harry standing behind her drinking a cup of coffee. The sight of him made her jump. She watched as he tipped the end of his cowboy hat up so she could see his face. Harry always had that big grin on his face no matter what seemed to be going on. She was glad one of them could keep their cool in all this.

"How are things going?" Harry asked as he took a drink of his coffee. "You still holding up in here?"

Jessica shrugged her shoulders. It had been crazy so far but with the lack of resources at their disposal it wasn't like there was a whole lot she could do.

"I'm making it Harry." Jessica stated in her most chipper voice as possible.

"The president is about to address the union. Thought you might want to watch it. "Harry said as he motioned for her to follow him.

Jessica watched Harry disappear down the hallway. She looked back at the console. The call light was flashing again on the screen. She took her headset off and placed it on the desk and started after the man.

Part 11

All the cameras trained on the black haired male standing behind a podium. The seal of the President stood defiant on front of it. The male continued to flip through papers before looking at the camera.

"Ladies and gentleman of the press. I would like you to save your questions until after the president finishes . I will answer what questions that can be answered afterwards. Ladies and gentleman I present to you the 47th President of the United States of America. Jordan J. Alexander."

The black haired man exited stage right as a elderly male entered on stage left. Many cameras flashed as the man made his way towards the podium. Most of the people had risen from their seats and were clapping. The man took up position behind the podium and smiled. The room continued to clap as the man raised his hands to motion for the crowd to quiet down.

"My fellow Americans. Its with a sad heart that I have come to you today. Today we have been faced with a global event. Most of you have read the stories in the news or have experienced this first hand. They were found in their beds or in the middle of their morning routines. If you have been apart of this or experienced it first hand you have my deepest condolences. I pray for you and your families and hope that your grief is outweighed by the fact that we will find out what did this. If it was caused by someone we will find them and they will answer for what they have done. There will be answers for the American people."

"I have been in contact with other world leaders in hopes that an exchange of information can be made. So far no nation has answers at this point. Several of the world leaders have fallen to whatever this is. Their succession is still being determined. The vice president is one of the few along with the speaker of the house in our government body. I would ask for you to pray for their families. "

"I have already called back our armed forces that have been deployed abroad. Until we learn what this it is in the best interest of the American people that our borders be protected. You may have seen military vehicles in your community. I have deployed the National Guard to help maintain the peace. "

"There has been a steady up rise of violence and tension. The larger cities showing the larger scales of unrest. So now I would like to announce that I have declared a state of martial law until we the American people have answers. Local military commanders will supersede law enforcement and local laws in the purpose of ensuring the peace. The constitution of the United States of America, and all the rights bestowed upon you by it, will be void until those answers are achieved."

"Do not be afraid. This is not a permanent change. This is to keep this country from unrest through panic. If you do not need to leave your homes, please stay indoors. Please allow the soldiers to do their job. To the rural communities do not despair. Help is on the way. Do not attempt to deal with these bodies yourself. A country wide curfew of dark will be initiated to keep looting at a minimum. Any person caught out after curfew will be shot without warning. A list of laws will be posted for the public to view at all government and public buildings. Please pray for those that have lost loved ones. Thank you."

The crowd erupted into a mass of shouting questions as the president made his way off stage. The black haired male made his way back to the podium. Multiple questions were being shouted at one time. The man continued to answer questions for a few minutes before he left the stage himself. Without many questions being answered at all.

Part 12

Nick Birdwell and Mike Miller sat quietly inside the food court of the Jacob's Ladder mall. It was eerie how quiet this place was on a weekend. Usually there would be dozens and dozens of shoppers browsing the stores and killing time. Now as Nick looked around to the few brave souls that were trying to pretend like it was all okay and this was another day. It only drove home the severity of the situation. Nick pushed forward his half eaten burger in its paper wrapper. Something told him to eat but he wasn't that hungry.

"You not gonna eat that?" Mike asked while trying to chew his own burger.

Nick looked back down at the half-eaten meal he had ordered from **Big Al's Texas Burgers**. It was a nice investment on his part. Yet somehow he hadn't been able to stomach chewing it. Jessica was still on his mind. Trying to fight the good fight. He was sitting in the mall at the burger joint hiding from the truth.

"Just not very hungry I guess." Nick stated in a matter of fact way.

Nick made eye contact with the security guard making his way towards them. Nick knew they guy from school. He had been nothing extraordinary there. Now he was working a 9 to fiver like the rest of the world.

Nick tapped on the table to get Mike's attention. The man too busy enjoying his burger to notice the rest of the world. The guard came to a rest beside their table. He struck that usual authoritative pose most guards like to strike. To install fear in the masses. It wasn't working today though. Nick had bigger fear fish to fry. Mike finally realized someone was standing beside them and drew away from his burger indulgence.

"Sorry fellas but I'm gonna have to ask you to leave." the guard stated with distinction. "The mall is closing early today."

Nick almost laughed out loud. Mike almost looked offended. It was the first bit of humor he had seen all day. It was not a loss in all the death and fear. It was a warm light. Nick watched this man. Who by all rights was stoned off his rocker. Looking as if you had slapped him. The face that there was ketchup and mustard oozing out of his mouth like some cheap horror movie effects. It was almost too much for him.

"What if I'm not done eating yet?" Mike asked the guard.

Nick looked from the burger zombie to guard. Now the guard had that look on his face that you had rained on his parade. Nick knew the guy's job wasn't easy. Several of the things he was forced to do for a pay check could be considered humiliating. He never understood how people could be rude to someone for trying to do their job. Yet as a society we were rude and callous.

"We were just leaving sir."Nick stated nonchalantly. " Come on Mike,"

Nick watched as Mike's horrified face turned to him. The world was ending around Mike Miller. Yet the man's only concern was his double bacon cheeseburger. It was possible Mike had destroyed the necessary brains cells for self preservation. He wasn't entirely sure. Nick stood up from the table and grabbed his tray. The utter disgust on the Mike's face would have been a priceless online video. If there was any care for those right now.

"Look fellas its nothing personal. My boss just told me the President is declaring a state of Martial Law. Which means the shit has got real. I'm going home to my family. I suggest you do the same." the guard offered as he turned to walk away.

Nick Shook his head in agreement as he took his tray to the return station. He could hear Mike cussing under his breath as he followed with his tray. Nick had seen the state of escalating tension here in Jacob's Ladder in the last couple of hours. If the president had declared martial law he bet the bigger cities were already in chaos. The unfortunate circumstance here was the law was already gone. The military wasn't going to come to a small town and police.

Not when they had the big cities like Houston and Dallas to worry about. Nick pulled his phone out of his pocket as he headed for the mall entrance.

Me: I'm coming to get you.

Jessica: Nick I'm not going anywhere.

Me: One of the security guards at the mall told me the President declared martial law.

Jessica: Yeah I watched it on the TV.

Me: So when will the National Guard be here?

Me: They are not coming are they?

Jessica: I don't think so.

Me: I'll be there shortly

Jessica: Nick don't.

Me: I'll see you soon.

Jessica: I love you.

Nick looked up from his phone. There were maybe four people leaving the mall not counting him and Mike. Nick made eye contact with the guard as he went out the door. Jesse his name plate read. I hope you make it home to your family Jesse. Nick put his phone in his pocket and stepped out into the sun.

Part 13

Jimmy Clark closed the door on his late model sedan and walked up the cobble stones towards his porch. The shock of the stranger's presence had almost brought hysterical laughter. The man asked to watch him preach. Yet when the man had sat there and watched it had terrified him.

The man seemed nice and rich enough. Sebastian was his name. How the man had tracked him down from a convention was a little unnerving. The man had seemed harmless enough. Sebastian had this spooky elegance to him that had Jimmy on edge.

Jimmy glanced at his gold plated wrist watch, 12:30 it said with its shiny gold hands. Sam had given him that watch last father's day. He thought it a cheap knock-off at first. Betty had told him that he had spent the larger part of his last commission on it. How trivial some things seemed at time of their inception.

He slowly touched the watch with a fondness he had never shown the boy. Hot tears raced down his face and he felt alone. The images that flashed behind his eyes were a wash of mistakes. Sam's first recital he had been at a convention in Kansas. His first gallery opening he had refused to go, because he felt it too wicked.

Now as the sand's began to trickle thin, Jimmy Clark wanted more time. He sobbed silently on his front stoop as the whole world fell into oblivion. he knew he would never have what he wanted most.

Jimmy drifted back to the call with Cecil. How the man had lost everything in an instant. He didn't want that for himself. He wanted to repair what had been broken. So that his son might know him for more than a preacher. That maybe he would know him as a father.

Part 14

Sam Roberts sat and listened to his agent rattle on. Sam had an art show he was supposed to attend tonight in Dallas. His agent was not enthused by the fact Sam was refusing to attend. He looked at the final piece sitting across from him. The field of buttercups and the speckles of red. The piece was a bit morbid but was still tastefully done by his standards.

"I understand what your saying Phil." Sam Started trying not to hide his annoyance. "I'm telling you after what the President said you're not getting me in Dallas. They can reschedule if they want."

Now it was Sam's agents turn to sound annoyed. He knew the man served to make a substantial cut off anything he managed to sell at the show. Sam would make a lot of money from it as well. Yet from the sounds of the news it was only going to get worse in the big city. If they were imposing a curfew then nobody would be there anyways. He didn't see the point in going. Sam heard a beeping coming from the phone and pulled his cellphone away from his ear. Abby was on the other line.

"Look Phil I got to take this. If they get huffy about the show let em get huffy. I'm not about to risk my life or my freedom for what I could make tonight. Yeah Phil you too. Later."

Sam ended the call but Abby was already gone. This day was starting to go to shit quicker than he wanted it to. He began hastily dialing Abby's number. The phone continued to ring and ring. Sam was starting to worry about if she was going to answer.

"You finally decide to answer?" Abby asked from the other end of the line.

Part 15

Abigale Myers watched as the bulletins kept scrolling across the bottom of the screen. The address she had watched with the President had made her sick to her stomach. The reality of the situation was starting to bear down on her.

Abigale reached over and picked up her cell phone. She scrolled through the text messages from her friends in Dallas. They had been out for break for the holiday. Now all her friends were asking her how she was doing. She scrolled through the group text. It would seem that Dallas was worse off than Jacob's Ladder. The military had already rolled in and taken over.

Abigale swallowed down the knot of fear that was swelling in her throat and dialed Sam's number. She listening as the phone continued to ring and ring. She hit the end key with mild disgust. She was going crazy in this house by herself. She wanted to go outside and breath the fresh air. Yet she dared not defy her father. If he came home and saw her outside she would never hear the end of it. Her phone began to vibrate in her hand. Abigale looked down at the screen. Sam it flashed in blue and pink. She hit the button and place the phone to her ear.

"You finally decide to answer?" She asked him.

Abigale listened as Sam explained his trouble with his agent. She knew that he was supposed to be showing his work off in a gallery in Dallas tonight. She waited for him to finish talking.

"Some of my friends from school were talking about the military setting up check points already." She told Sam. " You would have had a hard time getting there anyways."

Abigale tried to fain interest in Sam's grumblings about his agent sending him to his death. She began to flip through the channels as he talked. Every station had the same messages scrolling across the bottom of the screen. She wished her father would come back home. Abigale didn't like the idea of him being out around people. What if this stuff was contagious.

Abigale listened about Sam's newest painting. He had planned on revealing it at the show tonight. She agreed with him when he told her about it being grim. It reminded her of her dream she had last night. She dared not mention it to him because it spooked her a little bit and he already seemed rattled. Abigale turned the TV off with the remote and tossed it on the couch. Ms. Miller was still sitting on the porch. She thought about going over and saying hi. Abigale had been to the windows many times but had not seen her leave the porch yet.

"I'm gonna get off here in case dad tries to call alright babe." She told Sam. "I love you."

Sam agreed and hung up the phone. She stared out the window at the almost empty neighborhood. Only a few cars left now. She looked at the door. She knew her father had said to stay inside but she was getting cabin fever. Abigale gripped the door knob. What could happen? If it was in the air she was already dead.

Abigale turned the door knob and opened the door. The fresh air flooded her nostrils. She walked out on the front porch and looked left and right. These yards were usually teemed with screaming youth but it was eerily quiet.

Abigale looked at Ms. Miller sitting on her porch and waved. The woman didn't even bother to acknowledge her. Maybe she didn't notice her. Abigale sat down and began to swing back and forth. She thought the fresh air would make her feel better. It hadn't at all. The desolation of Silver Wood estates only seemed to hammer home the sense of dread that had been building in her stomach.

Chapter 4: Out of the pan

Part 1

Nick stood across from the Jacob's Ladder police station. He had been trying to think over the honking horns. Traffic was almost bumper to bumper on the main road out of town. Nick owned a motorcycle but rarely drove it. He preferred to walk unless he had to go out of town. Unfortunately today with all the traffic what was a 30 minute walk had turned into an hour and half. It looked like every family in Jacob's Ladder was going on vacation at the same time. Nick really needed to get to a computer. Someone knew something that wasn't being said.

Nick started across the street. He stopped between two parked cars long enough for one car to go by. The loud blaring horn almost made him jump out of his skin.

"Get da fuck outta the road asshole" the burly man in the car yelled at him.

Nick raised his arm in a " what do you want me to do" pose. You could cut the tension around here with a knife. Nick crossed the street between passing cars. Mike had agreed to meet back at Nick's place around five. He hoped he could convince Jessica to leave before then. He wasn't sure how that would go but he hoped she would see reason. Nick was sure that when the lights went out the more nefarious of Jacob's Ladder's citizens would come out to play. It would be best to not be outside when that happened.

Nick pushed open the door and found the receptionist's desk empty. Henrietta was as old as this police building herself. That white cropped hair without a hair out of place. Those black framed glasses that were straight out of the fifties. If she wasn't here something was wrong.

Nick walked past the reception desk towards the back. The huge security door to the back part of the building loomed ahead. Nick looked up at the security camera that aimed down towards the door. The door buzzed loudly and he stepped through.

Nick watched as Jessica's head popped out of one of the offices. He nodded his head and she disappeared back inside. Nick stepped inside the office to find her sitting at a desk staring at a computer screen. Those blonde curls bouncing as she moved around on the rolling chair from one computer to the next.

"911 what is your emergency." Jessica stated in her always chipper voice.

Nick watched as she began typing in information on the computer terminal. He was still amazed on how the system knew exactly where you were. It was almost creepy accurate.

"Ms. Burns I told you already that as soon as I can get an officer free I will send them to check on your mail box." Jessica stated still holding her helpful composure.

Nick smiled at her as she rolled her eyes. She was still listening as she typed away on the keyboard. Nick knew that she was better than he was. He wasn't happy about dealing with his own problems half the time. How she was able to deal with other's problems without pulling her hair out was beyond him.

"Ms. Burns an officer will be with you as soon as possible. Your name is on the list. Yes Ms. Burns I understand. The officers are working their way down the list. Yes Ms. Burns. You have a good day."

Nick watched as Jessica pulled the head set off her head and let out a loud sigh. He managed to smile at her again and she finally laughed. Nick wasn't sure if that was the first crack in her path to madness or if she needed that smile.

"You sound a little busy." Nick stated and tried to be coy at it.

Nick dodged as the pen went flying past him out in the hallway. Jessica was always a fiery one to not be a red head. He wiggled his eyebrows at her and smiled real big. He moved quickly to dodge pen number two.

"This has been chaos since roll call this morning." she stated as she put her head in her hands.

Nick could see the playful spirit drain out of her. The faint fray into humor had only been brief before the tide of stress came crashing back in. Nick reached over and began to massage her shoulders. He watched as her hand reached up and touched his. The small comforts are what mattered in the worst of times.

"26 to Dispatch. I have two D.O. A at the the 224 Bledsoe St. Marking the house and moving on to the next." Frank Pearson came across the radio loudly.

"That's 10-4 26. 2 D.O.A. Marking the map for pickup. Place an X on the door. Need you in route to 3462 Hasten Circle. Welfare check." Jessica spoke into the microphone.

Nick watched as Jessica stood up and marked an x on the map. As he started at the map and the huge amount of X's that were already on it Nick's heart sank. There were way more than fifty on that map. The original count was way off. There were hundred of X's on that map. Jacob's Ladder had not been excluded from whatever this was by a long shot.

"10-4 dispatch put me in route." Frank Pearson answered.

Nick could tell by the way Jessica put the cap back on the marker that she could tell the gravity of the situation. She knew better than most. She had been at the center of the "Event" since she came on shift this morning. Judging how things were slowly drifting towards chaos, he wasn't sure how they had left anyways.

"Come on babe lets go." Nick propositioned to her.

Nick watched as her shoulder shrank down low. He could hear the first sob come from her and he wrapped his arms around her. Nick knew the thought broke her heart. He wouldn't be one to take her away from that but this was a lost cause. Nick held her as the crying slowed to a stop. He felt her shoulders stiffen as she pulled away.

"You should go Nick." She stated with a strength in her voice now. "I'll be fine. Ill come see you when I get off."

Nick looked her in her blood shot eyes. He knew there was no fighting her on this. She was to proud of her job to give up even if it was a loss. He smiled and nodded his head. He felt like she was making a mistake but it was her decision. There was no changing that.

Part 2

Pastor Jimmy Clark stood outside of Cecil Phillips house. The man hadn't requested him to come by. Something had told him to go an check on the man. Cecil had a sound to his that Jimmy hadn't cared for. It was that coldness. It had been on his mind since he got off the phone with him that morning.

Jimmy gathered his courage and reached up and knocked on the door. He could hear nothing but silence. Jimmy reached down and tried the knob. The knob twisted and he pushed open the door. Jimmy almost gagged. The smell from inside was terrible. He could see the bodies of Jamie and Steven in the den.

"Cecil it's Jimmy." He squeezed out." I know you said you were fine but I thought you might want some help."

Jimmy pushed the door open farther and stepped inside. It took his eyes a minute to adjust to the low lighting. Cecil was sitting in the chair. The weapon he had used to end his life still in his hands. Jimmy felt the sudden urge to scream but no sound would come out. He was too late. If he would have only come earlier this might be avoided.

Jimmy closed his eyes and began to say a prayer. When he finished the prayer he locked the door and shut it behind him. There was nothing more he could do here. Jimmy hoped he could find peace in death, if there was any peace to be had.

Jimmy looked up the street. The man in black stood down the street watching him. Jimmy felt his heart raise up in his throat. Jimmy made a dash for his car, and he jumped inside and started the engine. The tires screeched their protest as he pulled away from the curb and darted down Sunset Drive.

Part 3

Henry Myers stood at the door of the Phillips home on 846 Sunset Drive. Cecil had been a deacon at his church for longer than his daughter had been alive. Henry felt a sense of unease as he looked at the door now. His wife had been there to help Jamie Phillips pick up the pieces after her son's accident had left him a vegetable.

Henry knew what was on the other side of the door. Dispatch said they had received a call earlier that morning about two possible D.O.A's here. Any other attempt to call back to the residence had been unable to reach anyone. Henry swallowed hard and knocked on the door.

"Cecil buddy its Henry open up." Henry stated in a loud voice.

Henry listened for any sounds coming from on the other side of the door. There wasn't a sound coming from inside. Henry looked from the left to the right at the neighboring houses. Not a soul was around as he knocked again louder.

Henry looked towards the bay window on the porch to see if he could see anything. He stopped cold when he saw the red splatter on the curtains. Henry turned and with one swift kick the door swung wide. The smell inside caught Henry in the face. Henry swallowed hard the bile that crept up his throat. The smell of urine and feces was strong. Henry drew his side arm from its holster. He gripped the weapon in a comfortable two handed grip. Henry readied himself for whatever was inside

"Cecil I'm coming in." Henry Stated in his authoritative tone.

The site inside grisly. Henry Spotted the two covered bodies in the den. One in the floor and one lying in the hospital bed. Cecil and his wife had taken care of the boy every since the day he stopped being able to take care of himself.

His wife and other ladies from the church had come to help out for a while. They would cook and clean. Help her with moving and cleaning the boy. His insurance had paid for a part time nurse that would come and check on him once a day. Usually one of them was beside Steven's side day and night. The only time that Henry had saw them together in town was at church.

Henry looked to the right and all his thoughts stopped. Cecil was sitting in the recliner. His head from the jaw up painted on the walls and ceiling.

Henry looked to the shotgun barrel still gripped in one on the Cecil's hands. He knew this was self inflicted. It wasn't the first time Henry had seen this same scene. He holstered his weapon and reached for his microphone on his chest.

"20 to dispatch. I have 3 D.O.A. at 846 Sunset Drive. 2 possible disease related one self-iflicted GSW." Henry stated as he wiped his brow with his free hand.

Henry was glad his wife wasn't here to see this. It would have broken her heart. No matter how strong she was. Henry backed up and closed the door. He picked up the black spray paint can and sprayed a black X on the door.

"Confirmed 20. 3 D.O.A at 846 Sunset Drive. Marking map. Harry wants you to go and check the store fronts out on Main. We have had reports of looters breaking into places already." Jessica stated in a tired voice.

Henry looked down at the now empty spray paint can in his hand. How many had he already went through today. Was it four or five cans now? Henry was glad to be going on something beside a welfare check. He was tired of counting the bodies and marking the doors. He had seen enough death in his life without this. Henry tossed the spray paint can in the trash can as he walked around his car. He grabbed the microphone again and pressed its little black button.

"10-4 dispatch. 20 is in route."

Part 4

Frank Pearson sat in his patrol car. He had finished another "Welfare check" for 3426 Hasten circle. He had found the woman face down in her oatmeal. No signs of trauma. No signs of forced entry. The Sunday paper was still clutched in her hand.

How many had he seen like that today? Some had still been in bed. The majority of them had been in the middle of their early morning routine and just fell dead. Like God had reached down and flipped the off switch. It would have been scary if Frank had anything left to be scared about. He reached over and picked up the microphone off his dash.

"26 to dispatch. 1 D.O.A at 3426 Hasten Circle. " Frank spoke into the microphone.

Frank looked down the street. It was barely four in the afternoon and the street looked empty. These yards were usually full of playing children and little old ladies gardening. Now it was like there was no one left. The eerie feel of desolation hung in the air.

"Confirmed 26. 1 D.O.A 3426 Hasten Circle. Need you in route to Still Water Diner. Have reports of a structure fire. Report called into dispatch, appears its arson" Jessica stated with a tired sound to her voice.

Frank hadn't seen a soul in hours. Most of the people in the Ladder had fled town. Frank wasn't sure where they were headed. He doubt they even knew where they were going. He reached over and flipped on the lights.

"10-4 Dispatch you can put me in route." he spoke into the microphone.

He looked down the street as the V-8 motor of his police cruiser sounded out in its vicious hum. . This was turning into a long day. Something told Frank it was far from over.

Part 5

Nick had only seen a few cars on his way back to his apartment. The town was practically a ghost town at this point. He wondered how many people had fled Jacob's Ladder. Nick wasn't sure where they thought they could run to. All the reports he had seen early said this was a pandemic. Which meant it was world wide. Now as he looked up the street his apartment was on he felt he should have left. He could count two abandoned cars. The only person he had seen in the last twenty minutes had ran away like a roach fleeing from light.

Mike Miller: You back at your place yet?

Nick read the text message from his friend. At least Mike was still alive. He had wondered how he had done with driving in the chaotic traffic earlier.

Nick looked over at the **Gas and Go** Service station. Old Phil had taken care of that place. The shattered remains of the front glass said it had seen better days. It almost broke his heart. Had people sunk so low that the first hint of adversity sent them down the primal path.

Me: Yeah I'm fixing to walk in the building.

Mike Miller: Dude I'm on my way. I can't reach my mom bro.

Me: Have you seen her today?

Mike Miller: No man I thought she went to church. She's still not home.

Me: Have you checked her room?

Mike Miller: No I'll go check.

Nick stopped at the door to his apartment building and looked down the street. The desolation of it was a new sight. Nick could only shake his head and start up the stairs to his apartment building. The eerie quiet of the building only added to the desolate feel of the street. The only sound he could hear was the creaking of the wooden stairs. His apartment building was old fashioned. It used to be a hotel back in the day. He liked the old feeling it had.

Nick fetched his keys out of his pocket once he cleared the step to his floor. He pulled open the door and looked down the hallway. "Nothing here either," he thought as he made his way to his door. The key slid into the heavy old lock with a loud clanking of tumblers. It was usually at this point that Ms. Ashwood would come out be nosy. The fact that she hadn't yet made Nick worry. Was she one of the ones that wasn't accounted for? She did live alone. He turned the key and opened the door quickly closing it behind him.

Nick tossed the keys on the bar and made his way to his computer. There were hundred of new videos posted on the blog now. His phone buzzed in the quiet of his apartment.

Mike Miller: She's dead dude.

Nick stared at the text message his friend had sent. He felt sorry for Mike. Nick knew the truth though. That even if Mike called for help it wouldn't come. People were afraid of the dead. It was with good reason he supposed.

Yet poor Mike was helpless without his mother. Mike Miller was an overweight stoner with no motivation or will to be on his own. Now the tragic truth that he was alone must be devastating for him.

Me: Did you touch her body?

Mike Miller: No I was too scared. I called her name from the bedroom door but she didn't move dude. God, what am I gonna do? Who do I call?

Me: Mike this not me being callous. I'm sorry dude. Nobody is coming for a while.

Mike Miller:Dude what am I going to do?

Me: You're going to close the door. Pack your things and come stay with me. Before you leave I need you to place an X on the doorway big enough for people to see.

Mike Miller: I can't leave her.

Me:Mike buddy you don't have a choice. Pack your things and come on. You can smoke all you want. You can't stay there.

Mike Miller: Okay dude. God. Okay.

Nick placed the cell phone on the desk and went back to his computer. Mike wasn't Nick's best friend but he was close enough. He picked the phone back up.

Me:You can place another X at 472 Hillcrest Circle.

Jessica: Isn't that Mike Miller's address.

Me: Yep. Its his mom.

Jessica: That's terrible.

Me: He's coming here. So hopefully we will see you in a bit.

Jessica: Ok

Nick placed the phone on the desk once more. He started reading though the titles on the screen. The videos were from all over the country. Videos of the freeway out of L.A. was crazy. People were abandoning their vehicles and walking. Where did these people think they were going?

Nick looked at his watch. 4:56 it read on the digital screen. It would be dark in less than an hour. Nick hoped Mike would hurry. He had every intent on locking down once it got dark. Nick watched as blue bubble popped up on his screen. He moved his cursor and clicked on the message.

Phoenix2843: What do you know about a code name **White Knight**?.

Part 6

Jessica teach sat there looking at the dispatch terminal. There hadn't been a call come in for over twenty minutes. She knew if there was a time to leave now was the time. Jessica sat the head set down on the console. It seemed like a she weighed a thousand pounds as she pushed back from the terminal.

She didn't feel right leaving in the middle of a disaster. Yet she wanted to get to NIck's before it got dark. He seemed to think something bad was gonna happen by then. She stood up from the chair. Her legs felt like rubber. Jessica wasn't sure she had stood up more than twice since she had sat down there this morning. She gave herself a second to steady herself and started out the door. She used her name badge to buzz herself out and started for the stairs. Harry's office was on the second floor.

Jessica cleared the steps before she realized it. Harry was sitting at this desk. The room was almost foggy from smoke from his cigar. It was a wonder the building sprinklers hadn't kicked on from it yet. She stopped outside his office.

Harry seemed to be intently reading something on his computer. She knocked on the door frame to get his attention. Harry looked up from his computer screen and motioned her in. Jessica stepped in swatting to get the smoke out of her face.

"Time for you to scoot ain't it?" Harry asked.

Jessica smiled and nodded her head yes. Harry gave his big old Texas grin and motioned her out the door. Harry had said she could leave whenever she wanted. She had hoped he was going to stick to that.

"I'll see you tomorrow boss." she stated trying to hide the tiredness in her voice.

Harry smiled and shooed her on out with both hand. The cigar tip burned cherry red between his lips. She smiled and made her way down the steps. She would get her stuff and be a Nick's in no time. Hopefully the traffic wasn't that bad.

Part 7

Nick stared at the message bubble on his computer screen. The ominous message in the blue chat bubble disturbed him. What was **White Knight**? Why was Phoenix asking him if he knew what it was. He stared intently at the message bubble trying to figure out his approach to the question.

Spartan2295: I haven't heard anything about it. What is it?

Phoenix2843: From what my sources tell me its a government contagion protocol.

Spartan2295: Government contagion protocol?

Phoenix2843: Yeah. Pretty much if they are met with a contagious threat inside the United States. They will execute a non-nuclear strike. In attempts to stop the spread of the pathogen through fire.

Spartan2295: How did you hear about this?

Phoenix2843: Hacker friends of mine. Don't ask the details. The less you know the better.

Spartan2295: Do you think they are gonna use this?

Phoenix2843: I have seen the maps. Strike points. Fall back points. Jacob's Ladder is far off the grid. You should be fine.

Spartan2295: That doesn't answer my question.

Phoenix2843: I'm just letting you know that if you see big fires in the cities to stay away.

Spartan2295: Did you make it to your parents?

Phoenix 2843: Yeah they both are dead.

Spartan2295: I'm sorry man.

Phoenix2843: I kind of knew when they didn't answer the phone this morning.

Spartan2295: It had to still be rough.

Phoenix2843: Keep and eye on the sky. Good luck and Godspeed.

Nick watched as the chat bubble vanished. It was gone as quickly as it had came. If the government had contagion protocols. Especially ones that dealt with missiles. It was more of a problem for the big cities. Now if it was nuclear, the fallout from Houston could reach here. If the winds were right. He didn't think the government would be stupid enough to use something like that.

Part 8

Henry Myers stared out of the car in a hollow gaze as the flames at the Still Water Diner grew higher and higher. The sun usually set early this time of year; around six. As it made its solemn trek towards the horizon, Henry returned his gaze to the city's ravaged streets.

It reminded him all to well of the horror movie Abby had made him watch last weekend. He had never cared for those kinds of films, but as always he couldn't say no when she gave him that face. He never cared for the over abundance of violence they used. Abby told him it was for "shock value" and that it made money.

Henry had seen enough violence in his life. Yet as he stared around the streets, he was beginning to believe that maybe he hadn't.

"What you got over there Henry?" his radio echoed through the silence around him.

Henry reached up and grabbed the microphone attached to his uniform. He wasn't sure what to tell Frank. There was nothing to see here. The only businesses that hadn't been looted had their security gates still intact. Most had been closed for the holiday or hadn't opened after the TV broadcasts.

Henry couldn't help but feel the disgust creep up into his thoughts. This had been his home town. He used to bring Abby and his wife for sundaes after church at Still Water Diner, and in a blink of an eye it was gone. He hadn't expected much else when the Center for Disease Control spokesman said don't panic. That was exactly what happened.

Emergency personnel had been spread too thin in the city. Most of the people reserved to protect and help the city had abandoned their posts. Either to protect their families or to get out of the city while they still could. Henry had levied the idea in his head a few times himself but couldn't stomach the thought. He couldn't imagine how many people were dead in Jacob's Ladder. He knew that he had placed more than 50 X's himself today. Henry let out a deep breath the he didn't realize he was holding as he pushed in the button on his mic.

"The businesses over on the row are still intact. I radioed it in but haven't got a reply back from dispatch. It can't be this bad can it?" he reported.

The silence dragged on in his car as Henry put it into park in front of the Henderson pharmacy. It had been the only non-gated building that hadn't been looted. Henry suspected old man Henderson had ran them off with that shotgun. Jack kept it under the counter. It wasn't the first time he had used it either.

It was just shy of two years that he had pulled it on Billy Peterson. The kid was stupid enough to try and rob him. That kid had always been trouble. You had never seen Billy so pale as when they placed him in the back of the squad car that night. Henry had to threaten Jack with jail himself if didn't put the shotgun away. He never thought Billy would get his act straight, but after that night he sure did. Henry had heard that he got a job at one of the factories outside of town.

Now, as he looked at the opaque glass with the black lettering losing its muster in the fading light. Henry hoped Jack Henderson had remembered to keep it loaded.

" Yeah, I'm not getting any answer either Henry. You might wanna check on Abby and meet me back at the station. I'm getting a bad feeling about this," Frank finally replied.

Henry could tell by the melancholy in his voice that Frank was seeing the same thing he was. Which must mean it was just as bad on Frank's side of town. A shadow moved behind the glass as he reached up to put the car in reverse. Henry knew it was probably Jack in there trying to make sure the place was locked up tight, or at least he hoped it was. He knew he should tell the old man that he needed to go home and not be out on the streets. That it was unsafe with the lack of law in town at the moment.

Henry grabbed his dash then hit the blue light and spewed off the car

Part 9

Abigale Myers rocked back and forth on her porch swing and watched the empty streets. Jack and Kelly Armstrong had left an hour ago with the station wagon loaded down. The Carmack's had followed suit not thirty minutes later. One by one the neighboring families ignored the warning to stay at home. Abigale bet the parkways out of Jacob's Ladder was bumper to bumper by now.

Everybody was scared and she couldn't blame them. She continued to rock in the swing as she saw Sam's coming up the street. She glanced up at old lady Miller sitting in her rocking chair two houses down. Abigale noticed she hadn't moved since she had been outside. A solemn tear slid down her cheek and she continued to swing.

Part 10

Sam Roberts felt ill to his stomach as he weaved in an out of the burning and forgotten vehicles in the Silver Wood Estates. He kept going over and over his thoughts in his head. Abigale and his father a ripple in the dynamics of the days current events.

Sam jammed hard on the brakes as a blue rubber ball rolled across the road. His thoughts derailing and shy of giving him a heart attack. He looked in the direction of where the ball had come but there was no owner to be found. There was just the eerie nothingness that was the same since he left the city.

Sam couldn't remember seeing anyone since he had left his apartment. Everyone was either dead or hiding in their homes from whatever this " biological attack" was. He didn't believe it was terrorists. Sam always thought that was a word the government used like an ill bogeyman to scare the good people. If you can keep them afraid then they were more likely to listen.

Sam put the car into park in front of Henry Myers house. He could see Abby sitting in the swing on the porch as he unbuttoned his seat belt. She had a stoic stillness to her that made him frantically try to get the release to work. Finally with a jerk he made it unlock and he opened the door.

" Abby babe, are you all right?" he asked as he made his way up the walkway.

Sam watched as she stared forward, swinging to a perfect slow pace. He could tell she was alive because she was moving, but it seemed she wasn't hearing what he was saying.

"Abigale Myers, is there anyone at home in there?" Sam asked her.

Finally she looked at him and instantly the tears streaked down her face. She launched at Sam and clung to him like a scared child. He did the best he

Her. After the first whimper and racking sobs she finally quieted down and regained some of her composure. She still had a look of shock or absence on her face.

Sam looked towards the horizon. It would be dark soon. Dark shadows began to creep across the lawns of the nice middle class subdivision. The neatly cut lawns and arranged shrubberies were a bit to uniform for his taste. It was still a nice neighborhood if you wanted to raise a family.

Sam lifted Abby's chin so he could look into her bloodshot eyes. The eyeliner she had been wearing had made long dark streaks down her face. He could see a sadness in her eyes that pained a certain part of him. The part everyone had that doesn't want to be left alone to die. Sam placed a small kiss on her lips and tried to wipe away some of her tears.

"Everything is going to be alright baby." He lied to her.

Sam didn't believe anything was going to be alright. But sometimes a little lie is good for the soul. He convinced Abby to sit down on the steps with him and after a few minutes she stopped crying. The silence began to drag on as the sun began to set. He watched the empty road and lawns and let her gather herself.

Sam knew how heavy the events weighed and didn't dare push her. He himself still hadn't come to grips with it. Hoping to deny it until everything went back to the way it was.

He tried to think about the art expo he was supposed to show some of his pieces off at. He made a fairly decent profit off at the last showing. Priate buyers always loved the odd pieces. Anything to get his mind off today.

Finally Sam reached into his pocket and checked his cell phone. His father hadn't called him yet. Considering the macabre dream his father had and its relation to him and current events. Sam figured he would have called. Sam replaced his phone back in his pocket and continued to watch as the shadows began to darken and spread.

"Mrs. Miller is dead." Abigale said, breaking the silence.

Sam looked up the street at the Miller house. It seemed quiet and somber like the rest of the houses on the street. The street lights began to buzz and they began to come on one by one. The whole neighborhood looked abandoned and desolate. Sam felt a chill go up his back. The whole place gave him a bad vibe.

"How do you know that?" he finally asked her.

Sam was afraid to hear how she had come to know the woman was dead. Maybe one of her neighbors had told her. There were people dead everywhere. He kept waiting for ambulances and police to show up and start checking the houses. Wasn't the military supposed to set up a quarantine for those that were sick?

"She hasn't moved since I came outside." She said with a trembling to her voice.

Sam looked back at the Miller house, squinting in the dying light of the sunset. Barbra Miller always sat on her porch every afternoon . She greeted all that came to Dory Lane in Silver Wood Estates with a smile and a wave. She had asked Abby on a many occasion to walk her dog, and since she loved animals they had done so on plenty of occasions. Yet today her porch was empty and blank, like the rest of the neighborhood.

Part 11

Felix Cherry watched as the technician continued the autopsy on their latest subject; former house speaker Ryan McMillan. His assistant had found him dead in his office sprawled out on the floor. A large part of his desk supplies strewn around him. He was only one of the many they had discovered so far. They had gotten lucky the main cabinet, except for the vice president, had survived the initial exposure to whatever this was. Felix had spent a countless hours in the lab studying the most dangerous things on the planet. He had never seen anything with a kill rate like this. He didn't believe you could have found a more flawless predator.

Felix reached up and pushed his glasses back up his nose and pulled the note pad from his pocket. He read his notes as he flipped page after page. The president was already initiating a state of martial law. The mobilization of the military to the major cities to keep the peace step two. It was already too late for that he had thought. The rioting was already out of control.

He closed the notepad and replaced it in his shirt pocket. Felix had insisted on doing the exam himself. Watching the young woman work he wished he would have. He hated not being able to do anything himself. He adjusted the cotton mask on his face and released the brakes on his wheel chair; wheeling himself over to the gurney.

"Is there anything new doctor?" Felix asked the technician.

The woman looked at him with a grim look and shook her head and she began to sew up the corpse. Felix wheeled himself around and made for the door. He began to fetch his phone out his pocket when he heard the scream. He spun around quickly to see what was the matter and dropped his phone.

The house speaker was setting up on the gurney as the technician made for the alarm. Felix was awash with horror at the sight. Ryan McMillian's organs were falling out of his chest cavity yet the dead man was sitting upright. Felix felt his heart stop when the man turned to him with those burning eyes.

Part 12

Jimmy Clark sat at his dining table drinking his coffee. He had to lift the cup with both hands because he was still shaking. The stranger's words still burned in his head. Making his dreams make all the more sense. If this is what he had been trying to prepare people for his whole life , to get them to repent for, he felt that he had failed.

The reports had only gotten worse on the TV. Several of the world's leaders had fallen. To whatever sickness or disease that had already taken most of the world. Jimmy's eyes looked over his steaming cup to the pale words emblazoned in black.

Like a dead weight it clawed at him and he felt like everything was out of control. He sat the cup back upon the table. The government was trying to say everything was going to be okay. Yet the reports kept leaning towards grim and dismay.

Jimmy ran his fingers across the gold cross on his Bible. Doing so had always proved to calm him in trying times. He was beginning to think that trying times were about to come, and he had not seen anything yet.

His eyes wearily drifted to the clock on the wall. The red trim and apple garnishment had been a favorite of his wife for decoration. Jimmy looked at the long black hands. It was almost six and Sam had still not arrived. He had hoped with all that was going on his son would have been here by now.

Jimmy knew that his son didn't believe as his father did. Hell he rarely called him father. He was not the boys original father, but he had treated him like a son none the less, or at least tried to. Jimmy still hoped that he could prepare his son for what might come to pass. Make him ready in the best way that he could. Though absent as he might have been at times he only wanted the best for Sam. He picked up the phone and began to dial his number. He waited patiently and his ring back tone played its melody.

"Dad are you alright?" Sam's voice came across the receiver .

A wash of relief spread through the pastor and he felt a weight lift from him.

"Sam where are you? I thought you were supposed to be here by now?" Jimmy replied.

" I had to come check on Abby dad. Have you not seen the new?. Everything has gone to hell." He answered.

Pastor Clark opened his Bible as his son continued to talk.

"I'm afraid you may be closer to it that you might think. I want you to come here as soon as possible. We need to talk." He said with a sigh.

" I can't leave her right now dad. She seems in real bad shape, and she won't leave here until her father gets back. Hang on a sec." Sam said.

Pastor Clark opened his Bible to the book of Revelations. He had hoped that he would never have to see this day himself. Being a man of faith, he was not supposed to be afraid of this. He was supposed to be a herald for this moment. So that the wicked might repent and be spared the judgment that follows the rapture. Yet there were so many he felt he had failed, and he had so little time to complete the task he had set out to do.

Jimmy lifted his eyes from the page and listened into the receiver. A faint murmur of voices talked in the back ground.

"What do you mean Abby?" he heard his son ask his girlfriend. "What about her eyes?"

A scream pierced through the receiver end and Jimmy jerked

the phone away from his ear for a second. With a speed he had not known in a while he put the phone back to his ear.

"Sam! What is it? Who is screaming?" Jimmy exclaimed to his son.

The pastor listened for an answer. Praying it was nothing but a mouse or a spider. He felt a dread weight descend on him as a pain spread in his chest. He reached in his pocket and pulled out his little brown bottle of pills. Quickly Jimmy fished out one and placed it under his tongue. He waited the long seconds for it to melt, until it was finally gone.

"Oh my God dad. It's the elderly neighbor lady. Her eyes, are as red as blood." Sam explained breathlessly

The horror of his dreams come flashing back to him. The darkness and those set of eyes in it, crimson red and soul less.

" Sam you need to hide!" he exclaimed into the phone to the sound of breaking glass.

Another high pitch scream and the line went dead. The good pastor was up and grabbing his keys before he knew what he was doing. He opened the door to his house. The Myers home was only fifteen minutes away if you took the highway.

Jimmy didn't even bother to lock the door or even look up until he was standing beside his sedan. He was too busy searching for the ignition key on the key ring. When he finally got the door open he looked across the lawn to the neighbors in a brief glance and stopped cold. Phil Jenkins was standing in his yard, dressed in his night robe, but that wasn't what stopped him. It was his face and those burning red eyes.

Chapter 5: The Reaping

Part 1

Henry Myers shined his flashlight through the glass window of the Henderson pharmacy. He was trying to catch a glimpse of anything. He was sure he saw something moving inside the building before the sun went down. He had knocked on the locked door several times to try and get Jack to open up but no one had came. Henry decided to make for the side alley and check the back door. If he didn't see Jack's green pickup and the door was secure he would head to see Abby.

The street light had finally come on but the alley was as black as pitch. Henry pulled his 40 caliber pistol from his holster in one fluid motion. He leveled the flash light underneath it as he stepped into the darkness. The funnel of light barely cut through the shadows as he made his way past the first dumpster.

Henry tried to keep his mind on the task at hand. Yet he was worried about his daughter. Was she okay? He stepped to the right and ran his light down the side of the dumpster. Only a few bags of trash and empty soda cans scattered across the ground. He returned the light in front of him and continued on down the alley. Henry heard a glass bottle rolling across the ground. Its vibrant clanking loud in the empty alley. He spun around to face the direction it came from. The light going from left to right. Finally he had found his culprit, a small armadillo scuttled into the darkness.

Henry breathed a deep sigh of relief as he continued around the back of the building. Henry was glad to see the street light was working in the back parking lot. He looked towards the back door of the pharmacy and found it open. Jack's green pickup sitting in its normal parking spot. Henry knew if Jack was inside he wouldn't have opened the door unless he was hurt. Henry pushed the door open wide and stepped through the entrance way. He swept the light from side to side, checking his corners like he was trained.

"Jack? You in here partner?" he asked into the darkness.

No sound came from the shadows as he shined his flashlight. A continued flash of blue brilliance radiated in a steady rhythm from the front part of the pharmacy. Henry shined his light around the store room; the bottles of medicine lined in an ocd type fashion on each shelf. It didn't seem to be rifled through to him. Henry finally found a light switch on the wall and turned the store room lights on. To him it appeared to be abandoned. Jack had forgot to pull the door shut and left with someone else, a possibility but not very likely he thought.

Henry moved towards the front keeping the flashlight trained in front of him. This was a useful tactic when approaching an unknown. Keep the light in their eyes and out of yours. That second of blindness and hesitation is all that keeps you alive sometimes.

Henry heard a loud crash and hurried his pace up the hallway to the front counter. He stepped out into the main area of the pharmacy shining his light around. The brightness of his squad cars blue lights beaming in through the front glass in a strobe was blinding to him. Henry stepped out of the path of the blue light and into darkness. Once more he searched around with his flash light for the source of the noise.

Another loud sound came from out in the darkness, beyond the row of shelves in front of him. Henry heard what he thought were boxes hitting the floor. He could feel the adrenaline start to pump through his system. He stepped sideways and shined his light down the aisle that had been beside him. He noticed a several bottles of aspirin scattered across the aisle floor. Henry stopped cold when he heard a gunshot. He couldn't approximate how far away it was. He definitely knew it was further down the street.

" Did you hear that shot?" squawked Frank across the radio

Henry almost fell backwards. The burst of sound in the silence had nearly given him a damn heart attack. He shook his head and reached for his mike. Another crash of things hitting the floor came from the next aisle. Henry lowered his hand and leveled his flashlight beneath his weapon once more. Making a quick sidestep and beamed his light down the next aisle. A figure in a white lab coat stood in the aisle facing the other direction. He could tell by the bald spot and the gray hair that it was Jack Henderson. A wash of relief flooded him as he began to holster his weapon.

"Jack, what the hell are you doing in here in the dark? Didn't you hear me call out you name?" He asked.

Jack raised its head like he was alert. Looking from side to side to search for the sound, finally turning towards Henry. Henry gasped as he saw Jack's face. The man's eyes were a burning red color, like in the nightmare Henry had this morning. Jack opened his mouth and began to tilt his head. A hiss sound like a coming from his lips.

. "Jack, partner, you feeling alright?" Henry asked.

Henry kept his hand on the butt of his weapon as he watched the man. Jack's head s began to turn upright. Something is bad wrong here. Henry could feel it in the pit of his stomach. A blood curdling scream erupted from Jack as he lurched forward towards him. The scream was so loud it hurt his ears and he felt his face cringe. That's when everything started to slow down. Henry could tell that Jack meant him immediate harm. He didn't know how he knew, but his instincts had saved him in the past. Henry had his weapon out and trained in the blink of an eye. The gun was loud in the enclosed room as the first bullet caught Jack in the right shoulder. It was like it never happened. The man never slowed his pace. The second round caught Jack in the right leg, still he moved forward his pace quickening.

"Stop Jack, Don't make me do this!" he shouted at the man.

Jack was only five feet away from him. Henry could tell he wasn't slowing down. He could see it in those red eyes that Jack was gone. Henry had been trained as a cold calculated killer. Had it drilled into his head for years, but it had never been to a friend. Not someone that he had grown up knowing since he was a child. It was only a half a seconds hesitation before the third bullet caught Jack in the head. Henry watched as his body crashed to the ground mere inches in front of him.

Henry took a few steps back and flashed his light around to make sure there wasn't anyone else around. Clear he thought to himself and holstered his weapon. It was like a stone had sunk in his stomach. This was wrong in every conceivable way, but he knew the enemy when he saw it. This wasn't the man that he used to buy candy and comic books from, it was something evil. Henry had seen a lot of evils in his life, but this was the first to scare him. He reached up and pressed the button on his mic, his hands shaking from the adrenaline rush.

"Jack Henderson tried to kill me in the pharmacy. It was like he was possessed. His eyes were glowing red like some monster." He spoke into the microphone.

Henry's words didn't even make sense to himself. He still couldn't believe what had transpired. Was this some side effect from the biological attack? Henry's mind raced with questions as he made his way back towards the rear entrance. He stopped only for a second to check and see if the shotgun was still under the counter, and it was. Henry grabbed it and made his way out the door. Three gunshots sounded off in the distance. The eerie quiet rushed back in like the tide.

"Are you serious? I just had a run in with Ms. Cunningham that used to own that bakery on South Street. The one that had those amazing fried apple pies. She acted like a maniac. She had a huge kitchen knife. I didn't know what else to do. Her eyes were glowing red." Frank finally answered

.   A sense of dread spread through Henry like a fire through dry timber. Maybe it had something to do with all those deaths. Either it made you crazy or killed you. A single thought passed through his mind. Abigale is home by herself. He had taught the girl how to defend herself. Showed her some self defense take downs. Yet she never would go to the range with him. They had hunted several times when she was younger, but she had always appalled guns.

Henry was in a full run by the time he had made it back to his squad car. He looked up the street, and a few hundred yards up he could see two glowing coals in the dark. Henry slammed the car door. He put the car in reverse and jammed on the accelerator hard with his foot. The car lunged backed and he jerked the shifter down into drive. The only thing he could thing about was getting to his daughter.

"I'm going to get Abby and we'll meet you down at the station," he told Frank as he sped down the road. Henry only hoped he wasn't too late.

Part 2

Nick watched as the crack of light slowly faded between his curtains. He still hadn't heard from Mike or Jessica. This was starting to worry him. Nick figured the night would draw out the rougher crowd in Jacob's Ladder. The cover of darkness would bring anarchy to the streets. Nick had hoped his companions would have made it here by now.

Nick looked down at his phone. He should call them or at least message them to make sure they were okay. He would give them a few more minutes. Nick watched as more videos kept uploading to the **Blind Truth** website. One video title drew his attention. **The dead come back to life**. Nick moved his cursor to the video and clicked. What he saw took his breath away.

Nick watched as a young Brown haired male stood on the street. The street lights were on and the sun was setting in the background. He was dressed in the usual reporter attire. The young fellow looked all business. Behind him you could see men in army fatigues and gas masks. The soldiers were carrying black body bags and tossing them on the back of a huge flat bed truck.

"We are coming to you live from Queens, New York. As you can see the streets are lined with black body bags. The National Guard is here packing these bodies out of the buildings on this street. . This has been going on since early this morning. They have been hauling the recently deceased away by the truck load. Refusing to let family member's even say goodbye. Sir could you answer a few questions?"

Nick watched as the young male turned towards the soldiers carrying a body to the truck. He extended the microphone over the barricade towards them. The soldiers ignored the reported and kept on walking.

"Sir could you answer a few questions? Does the government know what caused the deaths? What is going to happen to the bodies? Sir! Sir!" The reporter inquired from the soldiers.

Nick watched as the men continued at their task. Another soldier came up to the reporter who was attempting to cross the barricade.

"Stop right there!" The new soldier directed. "This is a military quarantine zone!"

Nick watched as the reporter stopped in his tracks. The huge soldier came over to the barricade. The reporter froze with one leg hanging over the barricade. The weapon sitting on the soldier's chest a big enough deterrent for most. The camera focused on the soldiers face. It could only be partially seen through the glass of his mask. His stern eyes focused on the reporter as he pulled his leg back over the barricade.

"I will only remind you this one time pal. I catch you trying to cross this barricade again I will shoot you without another warning. Do I make myself clear?" the soldier asked as his right hand went to rest on the handle of the rifle.

Nick watched as the camera focused on both men together. The reported looked pale at this point. Nick was sure the reporter understood the soldier. You could tell by the reporter's face as he tried to compose himself.

"Could you answer some questions for the American people sir?" The reporter asked with a shake to his voice.

"You people need to go home. Do I need to remind you that a curfew is in effect right now? Directions will be given to you by the emergency broadcast system. " The large soldier stated.

The camera panned from the soldier back to the reporter who had gained most of his composure back now.

"As you can see the military is offering no explanation at this...."

"Holy shit!" a voice cried out behind the reporter.

Nick watched as the camera man side stepped and panned down the street to the soldiers carrying another black body bag. The black bag was shaking violently as the soldiers dropped it to the ground.

"Hey sarge! This one is still alive!" one of the cried out as he began to unzip the bag.

"Are you getting this?" The reporter asked the camera man.

The camera zoomed in on the two soldiers as they tried to get the bag unzipped.

"Wait!" the the large soldier yelled as automatic gunfire sounded off in the distance.

The camera turned violently towards the building on the right. Bright flashes could be seen in one of windows. A high pitch scream made the camera pan back to the two soldiers again. One of the soldiers was now gripping his throat. Blood could be seen pouring out between his fingers. The other soldier tried to pull a fighting body away from his friend.

"Oh my God." the reporter said.

The camera turned to the flat bed truck as all the bags were moving now. More gunfire sounded out in the distance. Breaking glass could be heard and the camera panned right to where the flashes had been in the windows. One of the windows was now broken.

Nick inhaled sharply as the camera panned to the body now lying on the street. The shards of glass sticking out of the body of the young female. Slowly the body began to move. The crunching of glass and bone as the woman turned to look at camera man. Her eyes were glowing blood red. The woman let out a high pitched scream and lunged at the camera man. The camera spun and a loud crash could be heard.

"Fire at will!" The large soldier shouted.

The video ended and Nick already had his phone in his hand and was typing numbers.

"They're zombies....they're zombies....they're zombies.." Nick kept repeating to himself as he tried to get his thumbs to work.

Nick listened to his phone ring.

"Come on Jessica pick up…pick up…pick up.." Nick said out loud. The fear now present in his own voice.

Nick thought his heart was gonna explode in his chest. He never in a million years thought this would happen. All those X's on the map. His stomach turned and he felt his head spin.

"What's up babe?" Jessica's voice came from his phone.

Nick felt his heart jump into his throat. She was okay. She was still at the police station behind that solid steel door. They had guns in that building. She would be safe. Please let her still be there.

"Where are you?" He asked.

Nick felt like the silence between them was infinite. Those mere seconds dragging on for a lifetime. Nick realized his hands were shaking.

"I'm on your street silly. About to pass the gas station. Why do you sound like your about to cry?" Jessica asked in an amused voice.

Nick felt his heart sink a little bit. He hoped she was still at the police station behind that door. She would have been safe there at least.

"The bodies….they're zombies baby….you have to…" Nick got out before she cut him off.

"What are you talking about? Have you been drinking? Wait……. What is that?" Jessica said sounding confused.

Nick stood up from his desk and opened the curtains. He should be able to see her by now. Nick looked down the street and saw the headlights of her car. He trailed the beams to the shadowed form hobbling towards the car.

"Jessica do not get out of the car!" He cried in a high pitched shriek.

Nick watched in horror as the driver side door opened. Those blonde curls bouncing as she stood up and looked towards the form.

"Don't be an ass Nick….the person looks hurt." Jessica stated in a concerned voice.

"Jessica they are fucking zombies…..they will kill you!" Nick screamed into the receiver.

Nick watched as she tossed the phone in the driver seat and started around the car door. He hit the glass twice in desperation as she started forward towards the creature. Another shadowy form stumbled into the beams of the head lights. A loud crash came from the apartment above him. Nick didn't dare take his eyes off her.

"Jessica get back in the car!" Nick yelled into the phone as another crash came from above him.

Jessica had stopped but the two creatures were now making their way towards her. Nick watched as she backed towards the car. Another shadowed form joined the other two in the head light beams now. Jessica turned to run but it was too late. He watched in horror as they pounced on her like cats on a mouse. He could hear the muffled screams coming from his phone as he sank to his knees.

Part 3

Frank Pearson stared out the windshield at the sight before him. He wasn't sure exactly what he was seeing. He had went to see if he could see anything at Still Water Diner and found nothing. The flames were too hot to get close enough to investigate. Frank surmised they would have to wait for the fire marshal to investigate it. He had climbed in his cruiser and started to make his way over to

Henry when he found what stood before him.

Frank glanced in his review mirror. The sun had set and was a red glow on the horizon. He reached up and pulled the switch for the head lights. Patricia Cunningham stood in the middle of the road way. Frank wouldn't have thought anything about if if she wasn't in her night gown holding a huge butcher knife. Frank put the car in park and hit the blue lights. He opened the driver door and stood behind it. Always have a safety net.

"Ms. Cunningham…..Is everything alright?" Frank asked as his hand went to the handle of his side arm.

Frank watched as the woman's head shot up and searched. As if she couldn't tell which way the voice was coming from. Frank eased the snap open on his holster. He watched as the woman swayed on an imaginary wind. Her eyes were closed. It was almost like she was sleep walking. Was she was a diabetic? He could believe it by how sweet she made those pies. Her bakery had been a lucrative business before she sold it. He still remembered the article they wrote about it in the paper. The **Sweet Tooth** bakery was owned by some out of town chain now. Frank knew the pies hadn't been the same.

"Ms. Cunningham…..can you hear my voice?" Frank asked.

Frank watched as her head snapped in his direction like a blood hound on the scent now. He watched as she slowly stumbled forward towards him. He thought about assisting her. Was having a diabetic emergency? It would explain the altered mental status. He knew if she was in her right mind she wouldn't be strolling around in her night clothes. Frank was having that gut feeling. Frank drew his weapon and aimed down the sight at the woman.

"Mam I'm gonna need you to place the knife on the ground." Frank instructed the elderly woman.

Frank watched as the woman stopped in her tracks. A smile spread across Patricia's face but she didn't drop the knife. Frank felt his finger go to the trigger on instinct. He didn't believe this was diabetes anymore. Frank had helped the EMTs wrestle several of those. None of them smiled.

"There nothing to fear dearie…..granny needs to please her sweet tooth."*the* woman said in a voice that sounded not her own.

Well the creepy factor just went up, Frank thought as he kept the weapon trained on the woman. Something wasn't right here. The old lady in her night gown aside. . Frank's eyes traveled down to the butcher knife still gripped in those feeble looking hands.

Frank watched as Patricia opened her eyes. For a second he was actually afraid. Hey eyes weren't human anymore. They were fire red coals in her skull. A shot rang out in the distance. Something sounded like a scream followed it. Frank reached up to his microphone and squeezed the talk button.

"Did you hear that shot?" He asked Henry.

Patricia took a step forward. Those creepy eyes staring right at Frank. The part where she was smiling almost unnerved him. She took another step. Frank let go of the microphone and put both hands on the weapon again.

"Stop right there ma'am and place the blade on the ground." Frank instructed again.

The woman continued to walk forward. One shaking step after another she closed the distance between them. Frank's finger touched the trigger. You better be sure about this Frank he told himself. You better be damn sure.

"Won't you help granny....Frankie?" Patricia said in a slow hiss.

Frank aimed down the sights at the woman's chest. Frank wasn't sure if this was some psychosis or if she had been one of the recently deceased. He knew those eyes weren't hers. The way she spoke wasn't hers. Frank also knew she was closing the distance and still had a dangerous weapon in her right hand.

"Last chance…blade on the ground…not another step."
Frank ordered in a emotionless voice.

Frank watched as the woman let out a feral scream and lurched forward. The blade raised over her head now. The first shot caught her in the heart and she jerked backwards. Patricia had her balance and was moving forward again. The second shot caught her in the chest again. This one spun her around. Blood was soaking through her gown now. Frank watched as she turned to face him again. Those red eyes only spelling murder. Patricia started forward again and the third shot caught her between the eyes. Frank watched as she fell backward. Blood and brain matter splattered the pavement as she hit the ground.

"Jack Henderson tried to kill me in the pharmacy. It was like he was possessed. His eyes were glowing red like some monster." Henry voice came from the radio.

Frank stepped out from behind the car door and made his way towards the body. The weapon was still trained on Patricia as he made his way to her. Frank kicked the weapon away from her as he reached for his mic again.

"Are you serious? I had a run in with Ms. Cunningham that used to own that bakery on South Street. The one that had those amazing fried apple pies. She acted like a maniac. She had a huge kitchen knife. I didn't know what else to do. Her eyes were glowing red." Frank answered.

Frank looked down at Patricia Cunningham. Frank was pretty sure she was down for the count this time.

What could have caused her to be like this. Was she one of the bodies they hadn't found yet? It fit the profile now that he thought about it. She was a widow with no children. No one would have asked about her. How many of those were like that in Jacob's Ladder. How many X's were on that board. Hundreds if he had to guess about it.

"I'm going to get Abby and we'll meet you down at the station," Henry told Frank.

Frank could hear Henry's cruiser motor through the radio. He guess that Henry had about the same realization he had. Frank made his way back towards his own police cruiser. His eyes searched the darkness as the street lights started to hum to life. If this was what Frank thought then they were in a lot more trouble.

Part 4

Sam Roberts had been sitting on those wooden steps with Abby for a while when his father called. Abby had tried to convince Him that Ms. Miller had been sitting on the porch all afternoon. He was sure she was imagining things. Ms. Miller had gotten up and went inside when she wasn't looking he told her. A more logical view point than Ms. Miller the zombie. Sam Flipped open the phone on the third ring.

"Dad, are you alright?" he asked before his father had a chance to say anything.

Sam had a bad vibe about everything that had transpired so far. Abigale had finally started to calm down, but she still had that horror to her eyes. He didn't know if she was going to be alright or not. He wished her father would show up so she would come around. Henry and Sam had never been close to the same level but they both cared about Abby, which was a start at least.

" Sam where are you? I thought you were supposed to be here by now?" his father's voice asked him through the phone.

Sam knew he had told his father that he would come see him

today, but that was before he had seen Abby's state of mind. She had been in state of pure hysterics by the time he had gotten here. Yeah she seemed better but he didn't think she should be left alone right now, and he wasn't about to leave.

"I had to come and check on Abby dad. Have you not seen the news? Everything has gone to hell." Sam explained to his father.

Sam knew his father had to be aware of what was going on in the world. There was no way anyone could not know. Unless they were out in the wilderness without any communication line. He had tried to get Abby to go inside so he could see if there was any new information on the television but she wouldn't go in. She had told him that she didn't wanna see anything more about it. Sam tried to explain to her there might be more information, but she didn't care. He had never seen her act in such a way.

"I'm afraid you may be closer to it than you think. I need you to come here as soon as possible. We need to talk. " his father replied

Sam knew his father was all about the fire and brimstone. That his father believed it was his mission to save every soul on the planet. Leave it to him to think this was the end. Well as far as Sam knew he hadn't seen any angels today. It angered him sometimes when his father went down this path with him, but right now he would let it slide. Everyone was under enough stress right now. There was no need to get into another shouting match over nothing.

"I can't leave her right now dad. She seems in real bad shape, and she won't leave here until her father gets back. Hang on a sec. " Sam finally replied.

Sam could have swore he seen something move in the distance. His eyes were playing ticks on him too now. He tried to dismiss the thought when Abigale touched his arm he looked at her. She had a scared look on her face.

Sam watched her hand as she pointed to a shadowy figure standing on Ms. Millers porch. He couldn't make out who it was with only the street light to go on. Was it a prowler trying to break into her house? Either way it would be safer if they moved indoors. Sam took her by the hand and pulled her up the steps and through the door.

Part 5

Abigale Myers had been trying to wrap her head around the whole day and got lost. She had been in a state of shock when Sam had arrived. She remembered that much. Now she was worried about her father. She hadn't heard from him since he left in a rush early that morning. She knew that she had seen Ms. Miller on her front porch. Abigale knew that she had. Sam was convinced she had hallucinated the whole thing. Was he was right? Did she did get up and go inside? She wished her father would call or come home. She looked down as Sam's phone started to ring. She knew it was his father calling to check up on him.

Her tired eyes looked out across the lawn, watching as the street lights tried to chase the shadows away. Usually the yards were porch lights and tiki torches this time of year. The children running and playing. Trying to enjoy the last of summer before fall took over everything and cold set in.

Now everything was so dark and desolate. A huge mass of emptiness was all she could see. There were no porch lights on. Hell there weren't any lights on at all and that made everything see so much worse. She could hear Sam tell his father she was in bad shape. Abigale didn't see herself in that bad a shape. How can one describe a person being in a good state of mind considering the world seemed like it was ending. The only person she knew that could make her feel any better about this was gone from this world. Her father had always been there if she wanted to talk, but no one could make you feel better like you mother.

Abigale glanced back up to wards the Miller home. She knew that she wasn't crazy. Ms. Miller had been sitting out there, and that's when she saw it. There was someone standing on the porch now. She couldn't make out who or what it was but it scared her.

Abigale reached over and touched Sam's arm. He looked over at her and she lifted her arm, pointing to the wraith like creature. His eyes follow her finger until he saw it too. She could tell by the look in his eyes it startled him as well. Abigale followed as he took her hand and made their way up the steps and into through the front door. She watched as he shut and looked the front door.

"What was that?" She whispered to Sam.

He only waved her off as if he meant for her to be quiet. Abigale watched as he looked out the front picture window in both directions; as if to see if they had been followed. He still had the phone in his hand. She made her way into the kitchen. The window over the sink gave a better view of the Miller house.

Abigale saw the person making its way across the Armstrong's front lawn. It moved in a jagged almost forceful way. Terror began to crawl up from her stomach and lodge in her throat like it was trying to claw its way out of her body. Abigale couldn't even breathe as the creature stopped and looked directly at her. In the dull light of the street lamp she could make out that it was Ms. Miller. Those burning coal eyes cut deep into Abigale's soul.

Abigale felt the first hot streaks of tears as she tried to speak. She wanted to speak so bad but she couldn't. Abigale was too terrified to utter a word. Finally she drew on every ounce of courage her father had tried to instill in her, since Brittney Carmack bullied her as a child.

"Ms. Miller is standing outside. Sam her eyes are red, burning red" she finally got to come out of her lips.

Abigale heard Sam's footsteps coming into the kitchen in a hurried pace.

"What do you mean Abby? What about her eyes?" Sam asked her.

She could hear his words, but they sounded so far away to her. She could fell the horror welling up in her as Sam looked out the window. A blood curdling scream erupted through the air. Abigale didn't realize it had come from her own lips until she felt Sam shaking her. She saw his lips moving but she couldn't make out the words. That's when she heard the glass breaking in the living room.

Part 6

Nick sat in his floor with tears burning his face. This all seemed unreal to him. How could this have happened? There were no such things as zombies. He was a fan of horror movies. Now that he was trapped in one his stomach wouldn't stop rolling.

Knock. How was he gonna survive this. If Jessica would have listened to him. **Crash**. She would have been able to get here. They could have left for the country. Made it far enough away these things would leave them alone.

Knock Knock. This was the end of the world. Where could they run to?**CRASH**. All those X's on that board. Jesus there must have been hundreds of them.**KNOCK KNOCK KNOCK.**

"Come on man let me in." Mike Miller's voice sounded almost faint.

Nick looked at the door. No it couldn't be Mike Miller. He was dead like Jessica. Like all the rest of Jacob's Ladder. What if he was the last person alive? How long could he possibly survive? One person versus all the zombies. He didn't even own a gun.

KNOCK KNOCK KNOCK KNOCK.

Nick looked at the door again. His thoughts slowly fading to the background. **CRAASH** .His gaze drifted to the ceiling. There was one in the apartment above his. Would in claw through the floor to get to him.

"Man I'm really starting to freak out." Mike Millers voice called again.

Nick snapped from his daze and started towards the door. Was Mike was on the other side of the door? Was he going crazy? Nick stared out the peep hole into the hallway.

Mike was standing there. His auburn curls looking unkempt and greasy. Mike pushed his glasses up on his nose. His eyes. The were the same brown that they always were. It was Mike! Nick heard a crash come from some where on the other side of the door. Mike turned in the direction the sound came from.

The horror set in for Nick when he noticed his neighbors door was standing open. Those glowing red coals burning in the darkness of the doorway. He watched as Agatha sprung from the shadows and grabbed Mike. He twisted the lock and opened the door but it was too late. She was dragging his friend screaming into the darkness of her apartment. Blood covered Nick as he listening to his friends screams die into gurgling sounds.

Nick stood there and stared into his neighbors dark apartment. Blood rolled out onto the wood floor of the hallway and began to pool at Nick's feet.

"Hello baby." A voice hissed to his left.

Nick turned and what he saw made him freeze in his tracks. Jessica stood at the top of the stairs. Her uniform shirt was ripped and bloody. Those beautiful blonde curls matted to her face her with her own blood. Nick tried desperately to breathe. He wanted to run but none of his muscles were responding.

"Did you miss me lover?" Jessica stated with shrill laugh.

Run you bastard. You need to run. The thoughts hammered his mind but his body wasn't responding. The cold chill that ran through his body made him shiver.

"Come and give me some sugar baby." Jessica stated with a giggle as she started towards him.

Nick screamed as he started to turn for his apartment door, but it was too little too late. Jessica hit him from the side with such force it took his breath away. Nick's head hit the floor hard and he felt himself go limp. The whole room was spinning as the pretty face smeared with blood came spinning into view. Those burning red eyes blazing into his soul.

Nick opened his mouth to say something but no air was coming out. He couldn't breathe. Why couldn't he breathe? He reached up and felt those dainty fingers around his throat. The pressure was intense. Nick tried to fight the fog spreading through his skull. He tried to reach up and fight her but his arms weren't responding. They were so heavy.

"What's that lover? I can't hear you." Jessica hissed.

It wasn't Jessica's voice. Nor was it her red eyes staring into his eyes as she and everything else slowly faded to black.

Part 7

Frank Peterson exited his squad car at the Jacob's Ladder police station. It had once been the town's courthouse before they built the new fancy one on the other side of town. After the move the mayor had decided that the old police station was too small. So they voted to move it into the old courthouse.

Frank noticed that the lights were on inside but almost all the parking spaces were empty. He saw that the police chief's white SUV was still sitting in its spot. Yet the place looked abandoned to him. He opened the main door and found the reception desk was empty. There had been 3 of the original 5 officers to show up for duty today. Yet he hadn't gotten anyone but Henry to answer him on the radio since four.

Frank used his electronic key card to get into the back part of the station. They had installed the security lock to up security after the police station massacre that happened over in Montgomery. He continued down the hall, checking all the offices as he made his way back towards were they kept the S.R.T equipment.

Frank didn't know what was going on but he thought at this point he needed a better weapon. Something besides his standard issue forty caliber. Frank checked the dispatch room. Jessica wasn't there. Frank guessed she might have called it quits. She was a strong willed girl if he ever met one. If he thought he could he would have cut a trail too. He was already too far in to turn around now.

Frank gave the lockup door a tug. It was locked. I guess considering today's circumstance Harry decided to lock it. It was a wise idea to keep their good equipment from walking off. Frank turned around and headed back out the security door and up the steps.

As he entered the squad room he was amazed at all the empty desks. He thought some of the officers might show up once they realized it was bad. It seems they had left with the rest of the town. He could see Harry through the glass in his office, sitting at his desk, puffing on one of his big cigars.

Frank felt a sense of pride at seeing at least one person that hadn't abandoned their post. He weaved through the desks and chairs until he came to the office. He knocked two times on the open door and Harry looked up at him. A look of wonderment seemed to spring to life on the man's face as he dropped his ashes in a coffee cup.

" I thought you said you were giving those things up boss?" Frank asked.

Now Harry was a big guy. A bit overweight but the man carried it well. He had his usual white cowboy hat on and that gold badge all shined up. He had been one of the best bosses Frank had ever had. He was a compassionate man but don't let it fool you about his temper. He was a mean cuss if you managed to ruffle his feathers.

Frank had only been on the police force for about six years. He had came back after surviving the Iraqi war by some grace of God. Frank had stepped off the bus and Harry was there waiting on him. The funny thing was Harry never asked him if he wanted a job. He told Frank when and where to show. Harry had been the chief for so long nobody even bothered to run against him anymore.

"Hell I only quit because I thought the damn things were going to kill me. Seeing as I'm not going to live that long. I might as well enjoy what I can. "

Frank let out a chuckle as he opened his shirt pocket and pulled out a cigarette of his own and lit it, taking a long drag . You weren't even supposed to smoke in the building. If one of the council men were to walk in they would have his job. The democrats and hippies wouldn't stop until they took away everything. Harry was right, fuck it.

"So where the hell is everyone? " Frank finally asked.

He took another drag off his cigarette and dumped his ashes in the cup. He glanced at the computer screen harry was looking at. News Articles from around the world. **The dead come back to life** read the first article. **The end has come** read the one below that. Guess it wasn't only Jacob's Ladder this shit was happening to.

"You're the only one that has come back so far."Harry stated with a huff.. "Jessica left a little while ago.. This is some bad shit were dealing with. One news article I just read said if you die by one of these things you come back as one soon after; like a fucking zombie. I can't believe I said that out loud."

Harry took another drag off his cigar and dropped it into the coffee cup. He moved the mouse to another article and clicked on it. Frank glanced at it and began to read.

Sunday Sept. 22

Lafayette Parish, Louisiana Police are baffled by a shoot out that happened a short while ago. Local police responded to an assault in progress off State Route 39. What they found when they arrived was something out of a horror movie. Proprietor of the Miller and Sons Funeral home was trapped inside a back room. The bodies of three of the recently deceased clawing at the door to get in. Officers opened fire after non-lethal means were exhausted. One of the officers was gravely injured in the altercation. Leaving his fellow officers no choice but to use

lethal force. Officers refused to comment on the situation. Josh Miller was taken to a local hospital by emergency service. Police chief Hernandez denied to comment on the actions taken by his officers. He only offered that it was a sad time for the Lafayette Parish Police department. More news as this story breaks.

Frank took a last drag off his cigarette and dropped the butt in the coffee cup on the desk. Deep down he had known this day was going to be bad when Harry had called and told him the news. Now reading it was getting worse made a sense of dread come over him. They had always been warned about chemical warfare when he was in the army but he had never seen it. Deep down Frank didn't believe this was a "biological attack." If it was he had never heard of any nerve gas that could do this.

"Henry said that the old Jack Henderson tried to kill him over at the pharmacy. I personally had a run in with that Cunningham lady that used to own the bakery. I have never seen a zombie use a knife before though. I heard several gun shots while I was out but I only seen the one. "

Harry gave him a curious look as he reached into his desk and pulled out his sidearm; placing it in his holster.

"I suspect it's going to be a long night son, but my Momma always told me if you wanna win the fight, carry a huge stick." Harry said as he stood up and gave him a pat on the shoulder.

Frank believed there was no truer a statement he had ever heard as he followed the chief out of the office.

Part 8

Sam Roberts couldn't believe what he saw out the window. He only caught a glimpse before Abigale's piercing scream. He grabbed her by the shoulder and gave her a good shake. All the color had completely left her face when he heard the glass break in the living room.

Sam instinctively looked for a weapon to defend them with. Abigale sank to her knees and became unresponsive. The frying pan sitting on the stove was the first thing he saw. He grabbed it and turned to face the living room.

*"**Come now tasty flesh, let us it let us in."*** A voice called from the doorway.

Sam ran into the living room; leveling the cast iron skillet for a good swing. He looked down at the glass shards scattered by the front door. Whatever it was had busted out one of the stained glass panes that went up in rows on both sides of the front door. He looked up to where the pane was broken out and saw the dainty arm reaching through the hole for the door handle.

Sam looked to the frail arm sticking through the how. Blood stained the flowery patterned dress covering it. Small shards of glass stuck out of the arm in odd angles. With an animosity he didn't know he struck the arm hard with skillet. A feral scream erupted from beyond the door but still it tried for the lock.

Sam put all his strength into it and hit the arm again. He heard the crunching of bone this time and the arm disappeared back through the hole.

"Come now come now. Let us in let us in. we won't ...hurt you." the creature cooed.

Sam looked at the hole where the arm had went, and saw part of Ms. Miller's face; her burning eyes staring back at him.

"Won't you let us in......Samuel?" the creature said with a little giggle.

Sam felt all the hairs on his arms stand up as he looked into her eyes. If there was a devil then this was him. He didn't believe what he saw but he knew evil when he saw it.

"Saaaammmuueeellll....please let us in. We want to play. We never get ...to play." the creature begged him.

Sam didn't know what to do. As long as it stayed outside they were safe but what if there were more of them. He glanced over to see if Abigale was fine. She was still sitting there on her knees, staring off in the distance. Sam returned his gaze to the hole and the eyes were gone. "Where did it get off to?" he wondered to himself. He had this entrance guarded but what about the rest of the doors. "Were they all locked?" he asked himself.

"Tick tock time on the clock next time we won't knock" the creature said followed with a hunting laugh.

"Abby baby I need you to go check the rest of the doors for me, or watch this one while I do. Abby baby are you with me? I need your help."

Sam looked back at his girlfriend. She was still sitting there. He didn't believe she could even hear him. He assumed she was in shock but he couldn't comfort her right now. He needed her help.

"ABBY damn it I need you to check the other doors, or WATCH this one while I check them!"

Sam looked back and she was finally looking at him. She had that lost look still on her face but at least she was looking at him. He watched and she climbed to her feet; her motions slow and robotic as she made her way over to him.

"I'm okay. " she said as he handed her the skillet.

Sam could see headlights shining in the kitchen window as he started for the back door. Maybe it was Henry coming to check on them. Sam raced to the back to check the door. Luckily it was already locked.

Sam moved through the lower level checking the windows. He couldn't find any sign of the old lady outside anywhere. Sam was checking the last window when he heard the gunshots coming from the front lawn. He raced back to the front of the house to find Abby standing like a statue.

Sam took the skillet back from her and waited. He could feel his heartbeat in his head at this point. Like a drum it beat on and on at a hard pace. He tightened the grip he had on the skillets handle. "Please God let this be help," he prayed. He never prayed, and the thought came funny to him. It's so funny how one turns to help on high, but not any other time; such a fickle way of life.

"Sam are you in there?" a voice asked from the other side of the door.

Sam felt his heart skip a beat at the sound of his father's voice. He hadn't expected his father coming to his rescue. He hadn't expected that at all.

Part 9

Henry Myers was driving way faster than he should have been, but he was worried. The V-8 motor under the hood of his police cruiser hummed as he sped towards his home. He had seen several more of those red-eyed bastards on his way through town. He was hoping beyond hope that Abigale hadn't ventured outside after dark. She was a strong willed person, but he didn't know what her breaking point would be.

Henry watched as the city limits sign went past in a blur. He noticed he was coming up on another car. The first one he had seen since dark. The car began to ease off the road, like today he was in the mood for a traffic stop. He swerved to the left as he went by the car.

It appeared to be the preacher whose step-son was currently dating his daughter. He should turn around and tell him to get back in doors; that it wasn't safe to be out. Yet at this moment in time his first concern was his daughter. Henry reached up and cut off the blue lights. No need to cause any unneeded attention if he didn't have to.

Henry jerked the wheel to the left and jammed hard on the breaks; sliding on to Dory Lane. Henry had to weave around an abandoned car and pulled up diagonally behind what appeared to be Sam's car. Well at least he hadn't left her alone during all this.

The lights shinned across the yard and on to what appeared to be Ms. Miller. Henry opened the car door and stepped out. He grabbed his flashlight off his belt and drew his weapon. He did the the hand over hand carry like he had been taught in the academy. Henry leveled the weapon and made his way towards the woman.

"Ms. Miller, Is everything okay?" Henry asked cautiously.

She looked at him with those burning eyes. A twisting smile crept across that once friendly face that he had known for years. Her left arm looked almost mangle below the elbow. He could see the pieces of bone protruding from the skin. She should be in so much pain that it would be unbearable. Henry felt a pain in his heart as he sighted in the weapon.

"Well aren't you a sweet little snack. Come let granny give you a kiss....Henry."

The creature said to him.

This wasn't the first time he had to do this. He thought this kind of life was behind him. The first shot caught her in the heart. Henry felt the emotion well up in him and he closed it off. Trapped it in the steel box he called survival, because sometimes that was all you could do. The second shot caught her in the head as she fell backwards.

Survival always felt so hollow to him. That's what it made you feel afterwards, empty inside. Henry heard movement and turned around quickly. Pastor Clark was coming across the lawn towards him. He had come here to check on his son like Henry was his daughter. A stranger that he hadn't seen was climbing out of the passenger side. Henry directed his attention back towards the house. He motioned with his hand for the pastor to stay behind him as he approached the steps.

"Sam, are you in there?" Jimmy called out into the darkness.

Henry noticed the broken glass pane and readied his weapon. He watched as the door opened. He could see the life and relief spread across Abigale's face as she rushed to him. He wrapped her up in a big hug. Henry could tell she was crying but he hoped it was tears of joy. Sam gave him a nod as he walked out. Henry saw that he carried one of his cast iron skillets in his right hand. That would explain all the damage to the old lady's arm.

Henry holstered his weapon as the strange man that had arrived with the preacher, stood back and watched. Henry bet that the man in black had a story to tell. After today, he bet they all did.

Part 10

Pastor Jimmy Clark stood in horror as he watched his neighbor slowly lurch towards him. Phil Jenkins had at first only stared at him in a daze of wonderment. Similar a new born babe seeing people for the first time. The blankness to his face was astonishing to behold.

Jimmy watched as it fell away, like water thrown on fresh paint, to a face of rage and animosity. Phil Jenkins Let out a roaring scream as he began to run towards him. Jimmy let out a startled yelp himself as he started to get into the car.

In his haste, Jimmy made a fatal mistake, his keys skidding underneath his car. He felt around underneath his car in a desperate haste to find them. His hand searched left then right then back left again. "Oh please God let me find them," he thought as he heard Phil's erratic breathing get closer and closer. The shuffling of the man's house slippers through the grass was terrifyingly loud to him. "Find the keys damnit!" he told himself. His fingers finally brushed the ring and he snatched them with deliberate intent.

When he looked up he saw Phil Jenkins, his mouth drooling as if he was looking at some glorious feast. Jimmy felt his heart jump up into his throat as he watched his neighbors arm extend towards him. He watched as the bulbous man, his eyes glowing with a feverish hunger, almost grinned as if he had won some prize.

Jimmy kicked out, slamming the car door into the monster. He staggered Phil and the man fell backwards and into the side shrubbery. The ones that separated his yard and his other neighbor Clyde Green. Jimmy quickly shut the car door and locked it.

He watched as Phil began to scramble to his feet, all the while he was trying to get his key into the ignition. Jimmy felt his hands were shaking so that he was having a hard time getting it lined up to fit.

Jimmy gave an exasperated yell of his own and struck the steering wheel a few times with his free hand. Nobody has that much bad luck he thought as the key finally slid into place. Jimmy started the car and put it in reverse. With a stomping on the accelerator the car lurched backwards down his driveway. He jerked the wheel to the left and spun the car around, Phil chasing him down the driveway as he went.

Jimmy put the car in drive and sped down Lincoln Street. He had to make it to his son. That was his top priority. Then together they could figure out what was going on. It had taken him a second to realize he didn't have his headlights on, and when he pulled the switch; he gave a scream.

Pastor Jimmy Clark stomped down hard on his breaks. The tires screamed in protest as the stopped a mere feet from the figure standing in the road. He looked into those pale blue eyes once more, and it scared him. More horrifying than the red ones could ever be.

The figure walked around to the passenger side and opened the door. In one fluid movement he sat down and closed the door. Jimmy watched as the man reached into his inner coat and removed a silver cigarette case. The man looked over at him as he placed one of the cigarettes from it in his mouth.

"You don't mind do you Pastor?" the man asked as he removed a matching silver lighter from his coat.

Jimmy shook his head no and the man lit his cigarette. A huge plume of smoked curled up from his lips like it would a dragon's mouth. The man gave a nod and off they went.

The streets were quiet for the most part. Every once in a while they would pass one of the red eyed beasts, but they never followed. They would only stop and stare. The man did not speak, and Jimmy didn't care to let the silence drag on.

Jimmy noticed something in his rear view mirror. It was a police car coming up behind him. Jimmy didn't believe he had broken any laws but he began to slow down and ease over the white line. The car never slowed as it flew by with its blue lights twirling out in the darkness.

Jimmy eased back out on the road and continued on. He hoped that that wasn't Henry and his son was safe. Henry was a like able fellow who used to come to his church quite often before his wife had passed. Jimmy had gone out to see if he needed some council after her passing, but the man had refused. Some people ask for help and others don't want it. Henry hadn't been back but a few times in the last two years.

Jimmy turned on to Dory Lane, the road that led through Silver Wood Estates. He was wrong, that had been Henry. His patrol car was parked in front of the house. The blue lights had stopped but the head lights were still pointed towards the house.

Jimmy saw a flash of light and then another as he pulled in behind the car. Jimmy quickly exited the vehicle and made his way towards the man. Henry turned with the gun but noticed who it was. He watched the man lowered the weapon, but he never put it away.

"Sam, are you in there?" he called out as he started for the door.

Henry raised up his hand and motioned for him to stay behind him. Jimmy glanced back at the stranger. The man in black was calmly crushing his cigarette out on the sidewalk with his boot. He looked back around towards the door to find his son standing there. Henry was hugging his daughter. Jimmy smiled for the first time all day. Everything was going to be alright.

Part 11

Felix Cherry watched in horror as the house speaker lunged on the back of Coroner who had been performing his autopsy. The arterial spray jettisoned across the few feet to wall. It covered the proper hand washing technique instruction sheet attached to the wall. Like a lion taking down his prey the man latched on to her neck and began to shake like a dog.

Felix began to wheel himself backwards, trying hard not to attract any attention. He could hear the banging of the other corpses in their refrigerated tombs, trying to break free. He watched as the doctor went limp. That serious of a wound it would have been quick. There would be more of them any time now; if he didn't get out of here.

Security should be here any second he told himself as he tried to wheel himself in the direction of the door. In a loud crash one of the slab doors kicked open, the body inside hastily trying to escape. "Please get here," he wished as he eased backwards a little bit more. Felix knew the door couldn't be much farther. "I'm going to die," he thought in his head as another of the slab doors kicked open. "Please God don't let me die," he prayed.

Felix watched as the House speaker glanced at the two emerging from their frosty sleep. Their hungry gaze meeting Ryan's own gaze. This wasn't medically possible. The dead cannot come back to life. The third refrigerated slab kicked open. The dead cannot come back to life he told himself again.

Felix this is a bad dream and you're going to wake up any second. He heard the electronic doors "whoosh" open behind him. Two orderlies came running into the room. The fifth and the sixth slabs kicked open at the same time. The first orderly only had a second to grasp the situation before the house speaker was upon him in a wave of savagery.

Felix spun and made his way out the doors. He pushed every ounce of strength into his arms and sped down the hallway. A security guard rushed past him. Felix didn't look back. He heard two gunshots then a scream. He could still make it to the elevator he told himself. Another guard rushed past him. This time he only heard one shot and this one was close enough to make his ears ring. Felix prayed hard that he could make it. Even with the wind in his ears he could hear the footsteps padding behind him.

Felix could see the elevator now only twenty feet away. His arms were giving out but he had to try. He should have exercised more he thought. A strange thought to have but what could he do? He looked at the numbers above the elevator door that was only ten feet away. The number 3 lit up in a white light. There was not enough time to make it to the elevator. The smell of blood and death was so thick around him he could taste it. Felix slowed to a stop and wheeled around.

There must have been at least twenty sets of those haunting red eyes looking at him. Their faces all covered in blood and twisted smiles. Felix pushed the glasses back up his nose. He swallowed hard the knot that had grown in his throat. He knew he was a dead man. He couldn't out run this evil. He pushed the knot of terror back down and coughed. They all stood so still in their bloody multitude. Felix's curiosity was the only thing left he had to sate.

"What are you?" he managed to choke out in a raspy whisper.

They all stared at him curiously, each one with that same Ghastly smile.

"We…..are legion, for we are many." They all replied at the same time.

Felix heard the elevator doors open behind him as they all sprung towards him at once, but all he could do was scream.

Chapter 6: The calm before

Part 1

Sam Roberts had never been so happy to see his father. In fact, he usually loathed the thought of it. It wasn't that he didn't love his father; they didn't have a whole lot in common anymore. Sunday breakfast had been a weekly ritual while his mother was still alive. They would all gather round the table and she would bridge the gap between father and son.

Jimmy Clark loved God more than anything else in the world. That is how he believed was the way it should be. Sam didn't feel that was exactly the truth, and he avoided the topic usually. Betty Clark had been the glue that held them together. Sam knew his father loved him in his own way, and he always loved him. His original father left him and Sam's mother when he was still too young to remember. So Jimmy was, and always would, be his father.

"Are you alright son?" his father asked, snapping Sam from his thoughts.

Sam looked to the man who had accompanied his father. The man was tall in stature with shoulder length hair; very well dressed for this part of Texas. The man looked out of place here. Sam watched as the man met his gaze; an odd fellow for sure. The man made his way towards the group in a well defined walk. Like the man had an air of confidence about himself. Jimmy followed his son's gaze and turned to face the stranger as he finally joined the group.

"I'm fine dad. Who is your friend?" he inquired as everyone gathered around.

The stranger smiled and almost gave a curtly bow to the group. Sam thought he looked the part of a Machiavellian villain. Like one from some old Shakespearean play. He had that look of craftiness to him. Yet he seemed to act like a gentleman would in the early 1900s.

"My name is Sebastian Mourning. I was on holiday when I caught one of your father's lectures in Austin a few months back; quite by accident I assure you. I was in the country working on a contract for my father's company, and the conference was being held in my hotel. I myself am a Roman Catholic, but your father has a way with words when expressing his love of the gospel. I found myself in Texas once more and decided I simply had to look him up. Then this dastardly business presented its ugly face. I hadn't anywhere else to go and your father, the good Christian he is, offered me shelter from..... this storm." He replied before Jimmy ever had a chance to speak.

Sam looked over to his father. Sebastian's story seemed rather convincing. The old man was in a bit of a daze as if something else had caught his attention. Sam touched his father's arm and it was like a switch had turned on and his father was there again. The whole deal his father unloaded about angels and red eyed demons. It had seemed crazy when he had spilled it out to him not even 15 hours ago, but now not so much. He could tell this all must be a heavy burden on the old man, but they never spoke of things like that to each other.

"That's right, Sebastian is a rather nice fellow." Jimmy finally managed to get out.

Sam watched as Henry extended his hand. They all went about exchanging pleasantries with the stranger. Even at the end of the world it was still nice to be able to show a bit of civility. Sam extended his hand towards the stranger as he was the last in the circle to do so. He started to say his name when he was cut short.

"It's pleasant to meet you Samuel. Your father speaks highly of you. It seems you're quite the artist by his telling." The man replied as he squeezed his hand.

Sam shook Sebastian's hand, but his words seemed to single him out. He knew his father had never cared for his art, or the old man had never confided such things in him. Sometimes it was easier to disclose to strangers what one could not say to those they loved. Sam nodded and smiled at the man. Sam thought Sebastian seemed like a rather nice fellow indeed.

"It's a pleasure to meet you too. And I'm sure he over embellished that one ." he said as he released the man's hand.

Sam watched as he nodded back in a gentlemanly show of respect between the two. Henry motioned for them to all go inside, and they followed suit in a single file line. Sam knew that Henry had a plan. A man like him always had a plan.

Part 2

A lone man walked through the double doors of the District of Columbia Regional Hospital. The charge nurse was quick to dismiss him, even though he was rather well built and quite handsome. The hospital's alarm, in a loud racket of a noise, a good enough reason as people hurried in every direction. He dismissed the commotion and pushed the down button beside the elevator doors. The digital floor read-out counted its red numbers down. He casually looked right and left. With a ding the doors opened before him and he stepped inside.

The stranger pushed the basement level button and the doors whooshed closed with automatic precision. He felt the quick gravity shift as the elevator began to descend. The stranger dropped down to one knee, removing a piece of black charcoal from his blue shirt pocket. He began to draw strange emblems on the floor in a circle around him. The man worked quickly at his task. With each floor the stranger descended his pace quickened. His hands moved with a speed that most would consider a blur. The man finished and stood up and replaced the charcoal in his pocket.

He looked at the floor number, and it started with a crackle. A faint whine that started out almost inaudible to human ears. He glanced down to the writing at his feet. One by one the letters began to take on their own blue brilliance; racing in a domino effect from one emblem to the next. The elevator interior was bathed in a brilliant blue as the last symbol burned bright.

The elevator dinged its completion like all mechanical devices did. The door began to open wide and time started to slow. He beheld the red eyed monsters falling on their prey; a small man facing a large foe. The air around the stranger had an electrical current to it now. So strong one could feel the hair stand up to the static state of it. Large arc of electricity shot off the man to any grounded source.

With mirage equal distortion he began to change. The police uniform Raphael was wearing began to dissolve in the electricity around him. The sight it revealed was magnificent to behold. The elevator doors were almost completely open when he crouched down once more. The starch white ivory of his armor was adorned, in golden embellishment, with the same writing that glowed on the floor beneath him.

Raphael's eyes looked straight ahead as the doors finally slammed in the open position. Time seemed to be at a standstill around him as he rushed out of the elevator. The glowing red of the eyes he had seen before. In a time he had hoped was long forgotten.

Raphael had no fear as he took a hold of the small man's wheel chair and thrust him in the opposite direction. Felix rolling towards the still open elevator doors and safety. The doors began to close as the man rolled backward towards the elevator. He would be safely inside and be none the wiser of the whole thing. Raphael looked at the man's face; his eyes closed and his mouth agape. Felix, as he was known, was lost to the closing doors of the elevator. His ivory and gold clad savior standing in his place.

Raphael could tell in those soulless eyes they were aware of what was about to happen. The weak shells they inhabited unable to respond to avoid their fate.

Raphael spun to the right and grabbed the first lunging attacker by the ankle. With a force that could move mountains he swung him like a mace back towards the others. The attacker's body connected with a concussive force of crunching bones and bloody mist. His foes smashed into the concrete walls to his left and right like water upon stone. Blood held in the air like rain, dripping down the white and gold in several rivulets, as he engaged the enemy.

Raphael pushed on; with malice he waded into his foes. Like a hurricane of sheer force he grabbed one by its skull. He smashed it upon the wall in a smear of blood and brain matter. Raphael came around in a backwards spin only to drive his fist through the skull of the next.

He continued down the hall from one enemy to the next in this fashion. A symphony or horror he was to behold. Raphael twisted and turned leaving his enemy no foothold as their number dwindled to the last one.

The house speaker stood there smiling at him. All the bodies that lay behind him in broken uselessness. Raphael watched as the house speakers head tilt to the left, a bitter laugh escaping his lips. With blinding speed and strength Raphael struck the top of the house speaks head. The body crumpled in a loud crack of bone and bloody entrails.

Raphael, his pale blonde hair now stained and matted with blood, turned and looked back down the hallway. The twisted masses lay left and right before him. He turned and ran for the door that led to the garage. With blinding speed he made his way out into the night as sirens descended upon the hospital. Like he had arrived, Raphael was gone.

Part 3

Pastor Jimmy Clark sat with the others in the small quaint living room. The unfurling of events seemed so distant and lucid to him as Abigale handed him a warm cup of cocoa. Jimmy had been watching the news broadcast with the others in the Myer's home. The shock of everything was taking a toll on the man. Was this to be the fate of the world? Jimmy brought the steaming mug shakily to his face as the news continued on.

The death toll had tripled in urban areas. Those that had attempted to flee had only saved the undead a trip to find them. Over head helicopter footage was gruesome to look at. He had remembered hearing the news caster saying it wasn't suitable for children. Hell it wasn't suitable for anyone to watch.

"This can't be happening, can it?" Abigale asked the group as she placed a dish of cookies on the coffee table.

If you would have asked him a few days ago, Jimmy would have said no. Anyone would have said no. Now as the screen changed to footage of one of the dead attacking a cameraman on the scene. The man's distant scream could be heard as the camera tumbled to the ground. Jimmy watched as the lens cracked but the camera kept rolling as the man attempted to fight off the man to no avail. The cameraman's bloody corpse remained still for a few minutes after the zombie had moved on to the next victim. Then it twitched and jerked a few times. Finally sitting up under its own power.

Jimmy watched as the camera changed angles several times. As if it were being shook by a mad dog, until finally coming to a rest. It fixated on the reanimated man's face. It seemed slack jawed and inquisitive as it looked into the lens. Jimmy felt his face cringe at the sight of his eyes, empty and burning. Then the camera took a tumble and it was back to the newscaster.

"It has to be some kind of biological attack. Some virus cooked up by some crack pot for money and somehow a terrorist got a hold of it." Henry Myers replied from his large recliner.

Jimmy had looked back at the television but couldn't bare it anymore and decided to become fixated on his cocoa. He knew what kind of madness this was, but he didn't dare utter it aloud. This was the wrath of the Lord swooping down to exact his vengeance one last time.

They had bitten too deep into the fruit of knowledge and exalted their throne higher than his. There would be no running, or any hiding that would save them. They should only make themselves ready for the end. Jimmy felt his heart sink at the thought of it. He couldn't count all the souls he had failed to save. How that failure now weighed on him.

"Fallen, fallen is Babylon the great. It has become a dwelling place of demons," Sebastian said over the rim of his cup.

Jimmy looked up to see his eyes were affixed upon him. As if the man had read Jimmy's thoughts. Sebastian was sitting there staring at him. He could tell by that comment every set of eyes in the room were fixated on him.

"Isn't that what you were thinking too pastor?" Sebastian asked as he leaned forward and took a cookie from the pink serving dish.

Jimmy watched as Sebastian took a bite out of the sugar cookie; munching on it rather loudly. He was sure that every set of eyes was on him now. Jimmy looked to his son standing behind the sofa. He watched as the disdain poured into Sam's eyes and he let out a huff.

"We can't all believe this is the end of days." Sam said as crossed his arms over his chest.

Jimmy knew that pose all too well. He could see the rigidity in his body as he went into that unmovable object routine. He had been there for Sam's rebellious phase as a teenager. Sam had made it pretty clear his stance on the subject. So much so that they didn't even go near the topic anymore. Betty would always have to almost separate them on the subject. Sam was not mad at the idea of God. Jimmy knew it was angst directed more towards him. He knew he hadn't been there enough for his son. Jimmy had placed a higher value on his job than his family life. Now looking back it was disenchanting. He had failed all those he had loved in the end.

"We can't ignore the possibility either." Sebastian was quick to chime in.

Jimmy watched Sebastian pull that silver cigarette case out of his pocket and begin to open it.

"Do you mind?" Sebastian asked looking towards Henry.

Jimmy hated smoking. He thought it was one of the most terrible habits out there. Yet considering these may be the last hours they had he wouldn't object. He watched as Sebastian lit his cigarette, the end bursting to flame and smoldering to cherry red. Jimmy watched as the flames cast a haunting light in the man's pale blue eyes.

" I don't see how it could be that. There are plenty of logical explanations to what's going on. I see no angels raining fire on the television." Sam chimed back sounding quite exasperated.

Jimmy watched as Sebastian gave a nod of acceptance to the boy. He knew it was to keep his son from getting any more agitated. Sebastian took another puff of his cigarette as Henry got up from his recliner.

" I think we should save the speculation until we have more solid evidence to go on." Henry stated in a matter of fact way.

Jimmy felt a sick feeling coming into his stomach. A knock at the door made almost all of them jump. Henry had his gun out and trained at the door.

"Who is it!" Henry ask in a stern tone.

You could hear a pin drop in the room. Jimmy was sure they were all holding their breath in anticipation. Time seemed to slow to seconds. The grandfather clock against the wall chimed loudly and Abigale jumped again.

"It's me Henry. Chief sent me to check on you." A voice replied on the other side of the door.

Jimmy let out the breath he had been holding. He felt the tension ease out of his shoulders. He set the cup he had been holding on the coffee table. His arms felt so tired to him. Jimmy believed his nerves may be at their frayed end. He only hoped his sanity would hold up through this ordeal; divine in nature or not.

Jimmy closed his eyes and said a small prayer. His hands gripping the gold cross he wore around his neck. When he opened his eyes he could see Sebastian smiling at him through the plumes of smoke.

"Are you alright old boy? You look as if someone walked over your grave." Sebastian spoke to him.

Jimmy nodded his reply as he twirled the gold cross between his fingers, but he knew he was lying. Things were only going to get worse. He knew that deep down in his soul, and it terrified him.

Part 4

Felix Cherry was still in a daze as the police officer looked down at him. He watched as the man scribbled in his note pad the last words Felix had said. He could tell by the officer's eyes he thought him a crazy person, but Felix could still picture what he had saw in his head.

Felix remembered the red eyed dead speaking to him. He even remembered screaming as he closed his eyes. Felix thought he was dead until his wheel chair had slammed into the back of the elevator. The impact spilling him out into the floor. He had heard the commotion on the outside of the elevator as the doors closed shut.

It had taken Felix several minutes to get himself back into his chair. He had opened the doors to the elevator, and beheld the savage mess before him. The corpses of the dead had been ripped asunder and broken. It had been as if they had fallen upon each other and fought to the last man. Felix shook his head as he took his glasses off and cleaned them on his shirt.

"Can I get you anything?" the police officer asked as he put his notepad in his shirt pocket.

Felix only shook his head and replaced his glasses on his face.

Why had they elected to kill all those people and spare him? Maybe the one that lunged at him missed his mark and knocked him into the elevator. That was the only logical explanation he had. One of the head nurses had said she had seen a blonde officer going down in the elevator, but he was nowhere to be found.

Felix knew the Bible quote the mob had said in their hive like reply, but his logical mind didn't accept it. There had been many reports of the dead coming back to life. The majority of the hospitals had been lost. The one police officer had told him that he was lucky to have survived. The majority of the D.C. police force were engaged in firefights all over the city. The National Guard had been called in to guard the president. They had elected to evacuate him to air force one until they could resolve the situation.

"Does anyone here smoke?" he asked out loud.

One of the officers handed him a cigarette and he took it. Felix took the man's lighter and lit the cigarette. He took a big draw and held it in, coughing as he exhaled. A nurse gave him a look of disdain as he continued to smoke.

Felix couldn't wrap his head around this one as he watched his hand holding the cigarette shake. He could still hear their words in haunting unison. He felt a chill go up his spine and grip his heart. "God help us all," he thought to himself.

Part 5

Frank Peterson felt better about the situation once the chief had let him into the S.R.T's locker room. Jacob's Ladder was a small town compared to most. They had the big retail stores and several shops. They had four schools and several of the larger fast food chain stores. So taking that into effect, they had finally gotten the funding out of the city to get some of the officers advanced training.

Frank himself had gotten enough of that while he was in the army. He had been an army ranger, one of the army's three special forces branches. Frank had advanced training and was a sergeant when he had opted to be shuffled out. He enjoyed the life but he didn't enjoy the politics of it. There comes a point in your life when you get tired of being shot at.

Frank had smiled when he got his hands on the AR 15. The rifle had both and optical sight mounted up top for medium range shots. It also had side mounted reflex sight for close range shots. Frank grabbed the body armor out of one of the lockers and pulled it over his head. With trained ease he had secured it with its side velcro straps; making it snug across his chest. He took the rifle by the strap and put it over his neck; letting the weapon sit on his chest.

Frank popped a magazine into the rifle and grabbed two more. He put one in each of this back pockets and closed the locker door. Frank felt a lot better about the situation. Frank looked up at his boss as he pulled the door closed behind him. The door's electronic lock clicked shut and room was sealed.

"I suspect you should go check on Henry. Make sure he is doing alright." Harry said as Frank adjusted the strap on his newly acquired rifle.

Frank gave him a nod and started back towards the front of the building. The stone steps coming back up from the basement echoed his steps. He listened to the sound bounce around him; giving a person a false sense of direction. He opened the door back to the main building and made his way towards the door.

"Will you be alright by yourself?" he asked Harry over his shoulder.

Frank heard a grunt of a laugh and knew that was a yes. He pushed open the door to the reception area. The door gave its familiar buzz sound as the electronic lock released, letting Frank step through. He was still was having a hard time getting used to the abandoned feeling that seemed to be everywhere.

Jacob's Ladder had that small town charm. The everyone knows everyone, neighbor helping neighbor that you only read about in magazines. Now it was desolate and empty, and Frank hated that. He glanced around through the front door before he pushed it open. He could see a pair of red eyes cutting through the darkness in the parking lot across from the police station. He slipped his right hand around the rifle grip and put his finger on the trigger. Frank knew deep down whatever these red eyed things were they weren't the people they used to be.

Frank eased open the front door of the building and slipped out. He crouched down to be less visible to see and made his way towards his car. Frank watched as those crimson eyes looked left and right. With eagerness they searched for the direction the sound had came from.

Frank dropped to one knee in front of his car and brought the butt of the rifle up to his shoulder. His eye adjusted to the enhancement of the optical scope. He slowed his breathing and placed the black arrow in the scope to rest on the creatures face. Frank had a good view of Dakota Branisk's face in the parking lot across the street.

Frank could see the man had finally caught sight of him. The black arrow bobbed around Dakota's face as the man started into a run towards him. Frank squeezed the trigger and the rifle kicked into his shoulder. He followed the body to the ground using the optics and lowered the weapon.

A scream, that sounded human but more animal like, sounded off in the distance. Frank saw two more sets of red bobbing eyes as they made their way down the street towards him. "Better save the ammo," he thought to himself as he pulled the sling over his head.

He opened the door and started the car. Frank pressed down hard on the accelerator; jerking the car into a u-turn and head west down main street. Frank turned on his headlights and switched on the radio; cycling through the presets. Each one was an emergency broadcast telling people to stay inside and avoid the reanimated.

Frank had expected the national guard or the CDC to show up, but he knew they had their hands full in the cities. He slowed the car to a stop at the intersection of Main and Wilkins streets. The one caution light they had flashed red over and over again. Frank looked left and turned to look right and that's when he stopped.

"Holy shit" he whispered to himself in the empty car.

Three hundred yards down Wilkins Street. In the glare from what had been Still Water Diner was a large amassed group of those monsters. And they were now running in his direction. Frank jammed down hard on the gas and jerked the wheel to the left. The tires barked their protest as he shot down Wilkins out of the city.

The motor of the car hummed as he swerved around abandoned vehicles. Frank glanced into his rear view mirror. He could see the red little dots like demonic fireflies in the distance behind him. He wondered if Harry would be okay by himself. Those things would follow him out of the city. That way at least they wouldn't be any harm to anyone left there.

It only took him ten minutes to make it to Silver Wood Estates. He turned onto Dory Lane and made his way down. Frank drove around yet another abandoned car and eased to a stop in front of Henry's home. There were several cars parked in front of his house. Henry's house was also the only house with any lights on.

Frank grabbed the rifle as he opened his car door. Maybe those things were like dogs and lost interest after a bit. He eased the sling over his neck and made his way up the walk. Frank noticed a busted pane of glass to the left of the door knob as he walked up the steps. He knocked on the door. Frank eased his hand down to the rifle handle and placed his finger over the trigger guard.

"Who is it?" Henry's deep voice asked from the other side of the door.

Frank took his hand off his weapon and reached into his pocket for his cigarettes. He felt tired for the first time all day. He knew he wanted a beer, and he was pretty sure that luxury was long gone.

"It's me Henry. Chief sent me to check on you." Frank replied as he pulled a cigarette from the pack and placed it to his lips.

Frank heard someone unlock the door from the other side. Henry pulled his lighter out of his pocket and lit his cigarette. The door opened and he looked up at his big bear of a friend.

"It's good to see you're in one piece." Frank said as he stepped inside.

Frank looked around at all the familiar faces. Well all familiar except one.

Part 6

Henry Myers had been sipping his cocoa with the others since they had moved indoors. The news painted a grim picture that he didn't like. Sebastian had thrown more wood on the fire by quoting scripture. He had been a man of God for the better part of his life, but ever since his wife had passed on he couldn't muster it anymore.

Ashley had been a good Christian woman. She had even taught Sunday school. So you think, if anybody in their time of need, God would have helped her. Yet there had had been no help.   Ashley had fought with the cancer until the last. She was at church every Sunday; never missing a day even though she didn't have the energy to spend.

"I don't see how it can be that. There are plenty of logical explanations to what's going on. I see no angels raining fire on the television." Sam spat at the newest face in town.

Henry felt about the same way most days. Sebastian was right in the sense of argument. Yet on most days you could never win an argument with a true believer. It was pointless to try and even change their minds. Yet he could tell that even though Sebastian had given leave, that he could be wrong, the boy was still agitated. Henry suspected that living in that big shadow, like Sam did, was why he was so fiery.

Henry felt what he was sure was sleep begging him. The digital read out on his black sports watch read 9:45.

"I think we should save the speculation until we have more solid evidence to go on." Henry chimed in after standing up from his to comfy recliner.

Henry stretched out his arms and his legs. He hoped that would help him wake up. There would be no time to sleep tonight. Henry needed to head back down to the station. Maybe the chief would tell him the National Guard was on its way to town. Some sign of relief and it hadn't gone completely to hell.

Henry remembered that soulless look his neighbor from two

doors down had. That sweet old lady that wouldn't hurt a fly. How he had done the only kindness he could and put her to rest. Hell on earth was exactly what was happening. A loud knock at the door snapped him so quick out of his thoughts that he didn't realize the gun was already in his hands.

Henry felt the pace of his heart quicken. Was it another one of those monsters here for his daughter now? Hadn't they taken enough from him already?

"Who is it?" Henry asked.

Henry felt his grip tighten on his weapon as he aimed down his sights. He would not stand by and lose anymore. They would see what a monster they had trained and made him into. Henry had seen things in his years of service that should have broken him. Yet he remembered his wife with her bright red hair and green eyes. The smile she still had on her face every time he would have to leave. The little blonde baby girl she would hold in her arms and make wave bye-bye to daddy. A very terrible monster if let out of its box.

"It's me Henry. Chief sent me to check on you." Frank's normal 'I don't get excited about anything' voice called from the other side of the door.

Henry felt the tension ease up in his body as he holstered his weapon. He was glad he didn't let the panic get to him. He had to square himself away and get his game straight. He didn't need to end up shooting the wrong person. It wasn't normally like that but his thoughts had led him down a dark path. You can't let this get the better of you he told himself.

Henry reached for the deadbolt lock; twisting it and opening the door. Frank stood on the other side. In what he guessed was the department's ballistic vest and one of their nicer assault rifles.

"It's good to see you're in one piece." Frank chimed in as he stepped into the house with a trail of smoke following him.

Henry never cared for smoking. He had always been a smokeless tobacco man himself. Henry still was fond of it quite often when it didn't give him such terrible heartburn. Henry shook Frank's hand as he closed the door behind him; securing the lock once more.

"Those things will kill you ya know," Henry said as he slapped Frank on the back.

Henry watched as Frank looked around at all the faces. He knew like he did most of the faces. Not the long haired Aristocratic newcomer, but this was a small town.

"I'm sure you know most of my company tonight; except for Sebastian here. Abby baby, get Frank some cocoa," Henry said as he motioned for his friend to take a seat.

Sebastian rose from his seat at the calling of his name. Henry knew someone who came from money would always hear their cue, and he knew that he was from old money. Only people you heard talk in the way Sebastian did was from old money.

"My name is Sebastian Mourning. Officer?" Sebastian introduced as he extended his hand towards Frank.

Henry had to smile as Frank tried to wave some of the smoke out of his face as he extended his hand towards the newcomer.

"Name's Frank Pearson" He managed to get out as he shook the man's hand.

Henry Gave a little chuckle as he watched Abigale making her way from the kitchen. A fresh cup of cocoa for the guest. Henry knew he loved his daughter more than he loved life himself. It was about the only thing he had left in this world besides his job. If Frank hadn't pleaded his case; he wouldn't even have that right now. Henry was glad deep down to have the both of them in this "storm" as Sebastian had put it. He felt a surge of happiness. At least he still had someone. So his luck had held out, and he still had his two that he cared for. How many people could say that out loud and it still be true?

"Henry I need to talk to you in private." Frank said as he took the cup of cocoa from Abby.

Henry could see all the eyes upon the two of them. He didn't believe this was a time for holding things back. Whatever "this" was; they all had a stake in it now. So every shred of information belonged to the group as a whole. Then they all would decide the best course of action.

"Whatever it is you might as well tell us all. I like to think that we are still the law, but it seems we're all in this together now. "Henry stated.

Henry watched Frank mill it over in his head. He could see the little wheels turning. Frank had always trusted him. Henry used to give him orders and the man never faltered in following them. In his position he would have weighed the options too. He was trying to find a way to break the news to them easy.

"I ran into a pack of those things on the way out here. There had to be at least two dozen or more of them. They chased me for awhile out of the city. They eventually gave up though. It would be best if we all loaded up and headed to the station. That's my opinion"

Frank said in a no bull shit assessment.

"You mean they are coming this way?" Abigale asked with a hint of fear in her voice.

Henry turned and made his way up the set of stairs behind him. He had a gun safe in his room. He had two pistols, a shotgun, and three rifles in it. He thought it was more than enough to give them at least a chance if they managed to come this far out. He reached in his pocket and fetched his keychain out. Henry flipped through the keys until he reached the small silver key that fit his lock.

"Daddy what are you doing?" Abigale asked from down the stairs.

Henry slid the key into the lock turning left then right; jerking down on the handle and opened the door. One by one he took the guns out and laid them on the bed. Henry grabbed the small bag from the bottom of the safe. Quickly he began grabbing every box of ammo and extra magazine he had and stuffed them in it. Henry slung the strap over his shoulder and closed the safe; removing the key from the lock as he stood up. He took the two hand guns and placed them in his pockets and wrapped the rifles and shotgun up in the blanket. Henry took the blanket in the bends of his arms and headed back down the stairs.

"I don't know what's going on. If it's terrorist, demons, or damn zombies; but I don't think any of us should be unarmed from now on." Henry stated in a dull flat tone.

Henry made his way towards the coffee table. He could see the others glancing around at each other. Jimmy picked up his coffee cup and Sebastian grabbed the pink dish of cookies off of the table. Henry bent over and rolled out the blanket full of weapons for viewing.

"I don't have the finest selection. Just what I have accumulated over the years, but you're all welcome to one." Henry stated.

Henry could see Frank watching him through the steam rising from his cup of cocoa. He knew that Frank didn't think it was wise, but as far as Henry knew they were drastically outnumbered. Sometimes desperate times called for desperate measures. He pulled the two handguns from his pocket and laid them on the table with the rest of the rifles and shotgun.

"Now I don't know if any of you have any shooting experience, but I think Jimmy here should use the shotgun. I have ammo to fit all of them in this bag I have here. Pick your poison people." Henry said as he laid the bag of ammo on the floor.

They were all watching him with bewilderment except for Frank. Henry knew that look in his eyes. He had seen it in a many of his brother's faces before. That cold hard look when you know what has to be done and you're already comfortable with doing it. It was the look of a survivor; with all the emptiness that it came with. That look that said you can cry later and wake up screaming in your sleep, but at least you got to wake up. Henry was sure Frank saw the same look in his eyes. The sun would come up tomorrow and everything would go back to the way it was, but he didn't dare to hope.

Part 7

Sam Roberts stared down at the 9mm automatic pistol he had chosen. Its black matte finish seemed to almost absorb all light. Henry had handed him two magazines and a box of ammo. Sam had played a lot of first person shooter video games. He knew the basic dynamics of how to use it.

Most people's fathers took them on hunting trips and out to the gun ranges for male bonding. Not everyone's father did. Sam gripped the slide firmly and pulled it all the way back until it locked. He slid a magazine, filled with 9mm ammunition, into the bottom of the grip until it clicked into place. Sam reached up with his thumb at pushed down the little lever; the slide slid forward an chambered a round. He pushed up the safety lever and placed the weapon down the back of his pants. Sam thought it would be safer in the back than in the front in case of an accident.

Henry had gone back to his room to see if he could find a holster for Abby and himself. Frank had followed him up the stairs. Sam watched as Abby turned the weapon over and over in her hands. He knew she despised violence, but this was no time to get squeamish.

"Here let me show you." He told Abigale as he took the target 22 from her hands.

Sam loaded it the same way he had loaded his own. When he finally found the safety he handed it back to her. She set it in her lap and stared at it. He looked at his father and Sebastian; both of whom were inspecting their weapons. Sebastian had Chosen a 44 lever action rifle. He could tell that was one of Henry's favorites from how polished and flawless the wood stock was on it.

Sebastian had the look of a seasoned shooter on him. He went hunting all the time Sam thought.

" I used to shoot competitively , in my younger days of course. I even won a few trophies here and there. Ah, but the coming of age and the learning of a business trade. They rarely leave time for the niceties anymore." Sebastian explained as if Sam had given him some mental cue.

Sam still felt a bit hot under the collar. Things had been bad enough as it was. Without scaring them with doomsday theories predating any known science. A burning bush tells you the laws to govern man its providence. Tell a doctor the same thing they are going tell you you're a schizophrenic and lock you up. You get one started and you can never get them to shut up.

Sam still remembered the days when his father had drug him to church. The older gentleman on the front row shouting amen after every sentence Jimmy said. Sam didn't call it faith he called it the lying game. They would come to church every Sunday and lie to each other. Trying to prove they were some holy utopia of perfect people. Sam remembered in all the packed pews there were only about 20 that were truly good in nature.

"Here you go son. It attaches to your belt and around your leg. You might want to take one of those rifles too. " Henry Myers said as he handed him the holster.

Sam watched as he handed Abigale a long hip holster for the target pistol. Abigale had protested, saying she didn't have a belt on, but finally went off to find one. Sam stood up and eased his belt through the back of the holster. The holster was an army green color with snap clasp that held the gun in place and a snap clasp to hold it in place on your leg.

Once Sam had gotten the weapon in place he took the 9 mm pistol and secured it in place with the black quick release. Sam looked down at the two remaining rifles. One was your typical deer rifle, with a huge adorned scope. The other was what looked like a 22 rifle made into a assault weapon. The weapon was matte black with a red dot sight for quickly switching from one target to the next.

Sam picked up the compact model rifle. It was light and being of low caliber capable of making repetitive shots. Sam picked up the long banana clip from the table and secured it into the rifle. He gave a quick tug of the bolt, loading the weapon and securing the safety.

"Frank and I think it would be best if we headed into town and held up at the police station. It has security fences and the doors and windows are made of reinforced safety glass. Truth is we don't have the manpower to keep this place secure. So I'll leave it up to a vote. If you want to go to the police station raise your hand. "

Sam looked around and watched as the hands rose upward in a unanimous vote for exodus. Henry reached down and picked up the deer rifle and slung it over his shoulder.

"We leave out in ten minutes. I suggest we secure what food and drinks that won't spoil from the kitchen and be on our way. I don't like the sound of facing a pack of those feral bastards." Henry stated as he made his way into the kitchen.

Sam stood up and followed behind Abigale. She fetched some reusable shopping bags from under the sink. She was always so earth friendly. Sam didn't understand why she did it. Her efforts were a drop in the bucket compared to the gallons being poured out. Yet Sam loved her for that bit of defiance. The road less traveled should be a way of life.

Sam took the items Henry handed him from the pantry and placed them into the open bag Abigale held in her hands. It only took five minutes to load up Henry's cruiser with what food and water could be salvaged.

"Alright people, the lesser amount of vehicles we have the less chance of an accident. So Sebastian and Jimmy will ride with Frank, and Abby and Sam will ride with me. In a few days if this blows over we will bring you back to your own vehicles. Saddle up people. "Henry said as he made his way back to lock the front door.

Sam opened the back door of the Jacob's Ladder police cruiser. Henry Myers had disappeared back inside the house when he heard it. Sam looked behind him and saw what was making the noise. Off towards the city lightning was racing to the ground. It appeared to be striking over an over in the same area.

"My God what is that?" Sebastian asked the group.

Sam stared on in awe as the lightning continued to strike either in Jacob's Ladder or just beyond it. They all stood and watched as it carried on for two minutes straight. Sometimes there would be many strikes sometimes only once every thirty seconds.

"What are all you gawking at?" Henry asked as he came down the walk.

All Sam could do was point in its general direction as Henry tucked what looked like a photo album under his arm. The group watched this rare electrical storm until it ended. They all waited in silence for a bit after it stopped, but like a fireworks show on the fourth it was over.

"We should head on and get indoors in case something like that happens again." Frank called to them in a robotic tone from the other police cruiser.

They all nodded their agreement and they were off.

Chapter 7: House of Storms

Part 1

Chief Harry Raines stood on the front porch of his Victorian style home. The smoke from his expensive cigar curling around the brim of his white stetson hat. The busted remains of the front door made his hand tighten on the handle of his 44 magnum revolver.

Harry had lived in Jacob's Ladder for 22 years. He couldn't remember the last time a house had been broken into in this neighborhood. This zombie apocalypse, terror attack, or whatever it was had turned this town to shit. With a quick tug he pulled the revolver free from his shoulder holster and thumbed the hammer back. The metallic clinking of the cylinder turning was loud in the ebbing darkness.

"I'm gonna let you know right now." Harry said out in a booming voice. "My wife loved that door."

The glass crunched beneath his cowboy boot as he clicked on his flashlight. The light cut through the darkness like a white knife. Harry felt his heart sink as he saw the disheveled chaos that had been his treasured memories. His wife had took such good care of this house. He couldn't think of one person that ever walked into this home that didn't feel welcome.

Harry felt his anger start to rise and his grip only tightened on his revolver. Seeing their wedding photo smashed on the floor made his blood boil. Harry froze when he heard the crunching of glass in the next room.

"The stupid sum bitches are still here," Harry whispered as he started down the hallway towards the sound.

Harry was gonna show them some good ole fashioned Texas justice. The crunching of glass narrowed the room to his son's room. Harry clicked off the light so his eyes could adjust to the dark.

Harry reached for the door knob. The glass crackled again on the other side and Harry readied himself. He had always been for justice done right, but these looting bastards didn't deserve jail. Harry swung the door open wide with deliberate force. The intruder must have been on the other side because it connected with a thud. Harry leaned into the force and watched the shadow go sprawling into the floor.

"Jacob's Ladder police cock sucker!" Harry shouted into the dark room as he clicked on his flashlight .

Harry felt his heart jump into his throat as the light leveled on his would be robber. Clarice Roberts had been his wife's best friend up until the cancer had taken her from him. Now seeing her sitting there in his son's old room. The butcher knife protruding from her chest ; he felt panicky.

She was covered in what he assumed was blood from the collar of her night gown to her knees. Harry quickly put his revolver in his holster and stooped down to offer the woman aide. It wasn't until he was eye level that the woman opened her eyes. The glowing red made Harry freeze where he was.

" helllllloooo hhharry, " Clarice hissed out from those black lips as Harry screamed.

Harry fell backwards as the woman took a swipe at him. He only had a second to crawl backwards as the woman began to move forward towards him. Clarice took another swipe at him with those bloody fingers.

Instinctively Harry's hand went for his revolver. He was a little too late as the elderly lady lunged on him and sunk her teeth in to his shoulder. Harry let out a yelp as he grabbed the woman by the hair of her head. With all the strength he could muster Harry jerked the woman off him.

Clarice from two doors down went careening back into the darkness

"Haaarrrryyyy..........your.... ssuccchh aa sweeeettt bboyyyy

195

*harrryyyy...tasstesss so ssweet. "*Claire hissed and laughed from the darkness.

Harry felt a chill run down his spine and sink its icy fingers around his heart. He watched as those burning embers stared at him. He heard a low growl like an animal before the pounce. Harry drew his revolver as the woman lurched forward from the shadows.

The shot was way too loud in the small hallway. The glass case beside him that his wife had kept her prize china in exploded in a shower of glass. The force of the impact from the shot sent Clarice backwards. The woman let out a deafening shriek as Harry sighted down the long barrel. He took careful aim and the second loud boom echoed through the house.

Harry reached over with a shaky hand as he kept the barrel trained on the darkness. Everything in his left arm hurt as he shined the light in the darkness of the room. Clarice from two doors down was sprawled against his sons bed. The woman's head was split in two like a log on the chopping block.

" How did you like the taste of that?" Harry asked the now dead woman in front of him.

Harry felt his head begin to swim from the blood loss as he raised himself to his feet. He was gonna need stitches. He was pretty sure the damn woman had crushed his collarbone as he made his way into the kitchen.

He sat the revolver on the sink as he reached over to turn the tap on. Harry froze in his tracks as he looked out the back window of his home. Six sets of red eyes stared towards him from his backyard. Harry knew he only had four shots left. The way his left arm was going numb he would never be able to reload.

Harry thought about making a break for the truck. Somewhere deep inside Harry knew he wouldn't make it far. He reached into his shirt pocket and pulled out one of his fine cigars. He even managed to light it with his bad arm. His good hand reached out and took the grip of the 44 Magnum. The burning eyes were still staring at him as he stepped out the door on to his back porch.

" I'm gonna let you guys in on a little something" Harry said as he took a huge puff on his cigar. "I'm from Texas. So don't think this is gonna be easy."

Harry pulled the hammer back on his revolver as they all lunged for him at once.

Part 2

Dianna Wheat Crouched in the shadows of the highway 36 overpass.

She instinctively pushed her daughter behind her and made her way up the side of the white vehicle. Dianna didn't know how they had made it this far. There was a group of them traveling about 250 yards behind them. She was sure she had even seen her husband in their ranks.

Dianna had protested when her husband Billy had suggested they head for her mother's place in Kansas. Billy was hoping to get somewhere remote. He had explained to her the less people and more remote a place meant better chances of not getting sick.

"Look mommy, someone made a finger painting." Her daughter said behind her.

Diana turned to her daughter and put a finger over her lips. They had to be quiet. She didn't know how well those things could hear but if they did hear them they were done for. Dianna noticed the bloodied hand print her daughter had be referring to. Even in the dark She could see the red and black congealed blood smearing down the side of the truck bed. Dianna could see a body of a man In a slump in front of the vehicle.

"Remember, we are playing the quiet game baby. We don't want to wake all these sleeping people and lose the prize do we?" she explained to her daughter.

Nikki's face brightened with a smile. Dianna touched her

daughter's cheek thoughtfully and began to look in the truck for the keys. First she checked the ignition to no gain. "Come on they have to be here," she thought to herself.

Dianna climbed out of the truck and motioned for her daughter to remain. Dianna crouched and made her way to the dead body. The bulky man in the blue overalls, his name tag read Phil, was missing the back of his head. She almost gagged at the sight of the brain matter and bone clinging to the grill of the truck.

Dianna spotted the revolver in the man's right hand. She continued to search the man's pockets. Come on where are they? She had gotten her hopes up with the truck anyways. Those things couldn't be more than a couple hundred yards behind them. She spotted something shiny in the big man's other hand. She pried on the man's hand until she finally wrestled the keys free. Dianna grabbed the revolver with her left hand.

"Thank you Phil." She whispered to the dead man as she made her way back around to her daughter. Nikki was sitting down playing with her dolls in her lap; oblivious in her child-like world to this horror. She picked her daughter up and put her up in the truck seat. Dianna climbed in with her daughter and quietly shut the door. They had made it this far on sheer luck. Was it too much to hope for one more blessing?

Dianna remembered what had happened in the tunnel. The small station wagon ahead of them was pouring steam out from under its hood. A blown radiator hose her husband Billy had told her. Dianna watched as Billy kept honking the horn at yelling obscenities out the window. Nobody would let them over in the other lane to get out from behind the stalled vehicle.

The owner of the stalled wagon had tried to stop traffic to let them out, and was almost run over every time he tried. That's when Dianna heard what she thought was a gunshot from somewhere behind them. Then came a scream from the same direction. Dianna looked to her husband. Billy had the same confused and concerned look on his face. They both looked in unison through the back glass.

It had all came in a blur after that. All the blood and the screaming, people trying to flee with nowhere to go. Billy had told her to hide in the maintenance access beside the station wagon. Dianna grabbed Nikki and hid in the room as the screams carried on. She had locked the door and hid.

She remembered the beating on the door. The people begging to be let in but she sat there holding her daughter in the dark.

"I think the scary people are getting closer." Nikki said as she tugged on her sleeve.

Dianna glanced back at the reanimated. She could see her husband's head sticking up from the second row. Their faces were emotionless as they continued towards the truck. They were getting closer. Dianna had been lost in her thoughts and the dead had gained ground.

She slid the key into the ignition. Dianna turned the key forward and the motor chugged and chugged but didn't come to life. A feral scream came from behind them.

"Mommy?" Nikki asked.

Dianna tried the motor again; over and over it chugged. She slammed her hand into the steering wheel. She could hear the footsteps coming towards them like deafening thunder. She watched with each defiant chug as the dash lights dimmed more and more. They weren't going anywhere. She grabbed her daughter and pulled her into her lap. Tears began to burn red hot paths down her face.

"You know mommy loves you don't you baby?" She asked her daughter as she stroked her hair.

Dianna watched her daughter nod her head as she started crying too. She pulled her daughters head in to her chest. Dianna pulled the hammer back on the revolver and put the barrel to her daughters head.

Dianna began to sing her daughter's favorite song. She felt her heart break as she squeezed the trigger on the gun. **Click**. She squeezed the trigger again and another click. A feral scream came again from less than fifty yards behind them. Dianna Began to squeeze the trigger over and over again. Each chamber clicked empty and she let out a racking sob. She squeezed her daughter to her chest tight.

"Mommy is here baby. I love you." She said as she heard thunder. The ground shook and everything went blue.

Part 3

Raphael felt the wind on his face for the last time as he fell through the clouds. The sheer force that he fell, ripping through the air, created a clap of thunder. He centered himself. Raphael felt the air around him crackling and popping with friction. He reached out with his mind to the currents around him. Each one he touched with a thought and moved on to the next.

One by one the currents touched and mixed with each other. He played with them in his head. Like a child playing pirates with his friends. With each mental prod they pushed back and receded like water. They had formed a cocoon of pure energy around him now.

Raphael closed his fists and drew himself in as tight as he could. The air around him barked with anger and energy. He felt bathed in the light; the energy around Raphael a comfort to him in the dark. He could see the ground rushing towards him. He could see the horde before him and he was unafraid. Raphael braced as he slammed into the ground. The force of the collision caused the cement below him to crack and retreat into the ground; as if to run away from the power of such a blow. Raphael watched as the dust shot outwards in a rushing wave around him.

The damned cowered back from the large crater now carved into the ground before them. Raphael stood staring out at the masses with a haunting smile. The pure force with which he had crashed into the earth; along with the electrical charge displaced afterwards, had slaughtered all those that had been close.

Charred corpses lay scattered in remnant pieces of their former glory. Raphael reached to his back and removed his sword. The gold handle and black blade of the weapon glowed in his hands. His blue eyes looked from one to the next. He could see their wrath and plunder clinging to the bodies in black and red splotches. Raphael only smiled at them. He waited for them to come in the heaving masses.

"You do not belong here arch. They belong to us now." The red eyed mass chimed in unison.

Raphael pressed forward. With each step he took they took a step back. Cowards would always be cowards. They had shown no quarter and he would give none. In a lunging flash he sunk his blade into the flesh of the closest one to him. He watched it's pitiful scream escort the life from his eyes and he moved to the next.

They rushed him in a wave of madness. Raphael twisted and twirled. Limb and life leaving his foes as another bolt of lighting crashed into him. He drew on its power as they tried to pile on him like ants on a piece of meat. Time and again the bolts raced down from the Heavens. It gave him enough space as not to be overcome.

Raphael released a fierce cry as he cleaved one of his opponents head from where it used to rest. They laughed and they clawed and he called the light once more. Again and again it slammed into the ground around Raphael as he pressed forward. Their numbers were dwindling as he sank his blade through the chest of a slack jawed woman. Raphael wretched it free in time to sink into through the neck of a lunging foe.

He had no idea how long it had been going on. He sliced and dodged until there were but three left before him. Raphael crouched and awaited their attack. He was covered in blood. The air around him reaked with bile and death.

They all rushed him at once. They moved like fattened calves to him. The one on the right reached him first. Raphael grabbed the man's lunging arm and jerked him hard to the left. He heard the bones explode like a shotgun blast. The one on his right now crashed in to the one headed towards him on the left. Raphael had caught the end result out of the corner of his eyes. They both had collided with the burnt remnant of car. The metal had groaned and gave as they exploded in a shower of gore.

The last one only had a second to realize what was about to happen next. Raphael wrapped his fingers around the creature's throat before it had a chance to change course. He squeezed and watched as its red eyes almost bulged.

"Thus far shall ye come and no further, and here shall your proud waves stop.......grigori." Raphael said in merciless tone.

Lightning crashed one last time into the earth. Raphael watched as the skin on its face began to split and burn. He clawed and squirmed but Raphael only tightened his grip as it burst into blue flames and fell away to ashes.

Raphael turned and looked at the fallen corpses. He could see the woman and the child looking at him from the back glass of the pickup truck up the road from him. Raphael smiled as he crouched. There was a massive crackle as his wings unfurled. Bright blue beams of light erupted from his back., and with a huge arc of electricity he was gone.

Part 4

Pastor Jimmy Clark sat on the roof of the Jacob's Ladder police department and watched. It would have still been beautiful even if these weren't such trying times. The meteor shower had been going on for more than an hour. Jimmy hadn't noticed the lack of stars in the sky. In truth he hadn't even glanced up all night. There had been too much going on and he needed to clear his head.

They were having a council down below of the male warriors about what they should do. Jimmy knew what they should do but none of them would want to hear him out. He didn't even waste his breath. Jimmy heard the metal door groan behind him. He figured it was his son coming to tell him what they had decided.

" I always thought Ragnarok was a much more fitting title than the end of days. Has a more poetic emphasis. Don't you think?" Sebastian's voice called from behind him.

Jimmy didn't even turn to the man. He wasn't going to let him spoil the scenery for him. He watched as the little twinkling objects shot across the sky one by one.

Jimmy brought up his mug of coffee and took a sip. It was still warm. That kind of surprised him. Jimmy looked at the time on his gold watch; it read 7:04 in the am. The sun should have been up almost an hour ago. He took another sip of his coffee and felt that tension ease into his shoulders again.

"What are you after Sebastian?" he asked in a tired voice.

Jimmy knew he should get some rest but he didn't want to waste any more time. He looked over the edge; down at street level. The reanimated had been pretty calm since they got here. On occasion one would walk, or actually shamble, down the street. Some would be wearing bed clothes. You would even see one complete nude every so often. About an hour ago he had seen headlights coming towards town, and then they went out.

"I think it would be most rewarding it we helped each other out." Sebastian answered.

Jimmy thought he seen the headlights come on again and then they went back out. Jimmy strained his old eyes to see if could make out what it was in the distance but he couldn't make anything out. And then he saw it again. It was definitely headlights. Jimmy thought he should go tell one of the others. They needed to make sure it wasn't somebody needing help.

"I don't see how we can help each other Mr. Mourning. I think someone may be in trouble up the road. I need to go tell the others. "Jimmy stated in a matter of fact tone.

Jimmy started across the roof towards the entrance. His body was starting to feel its age in those wee hours of the morning. Jimmy was lucky that coffee had woke him up a bit. He reached up for the door knob to the door. Jimmy gave it a twist and started to pull open the door. That's when he saw Sebastian put his hand on the door.

Jimmy gave it a good tug but it didn't move an inch. It almost felt like all the weight of the world was on that door. Jimmy turned to face the man. He could see those pale blue eyes had a very serious look to them.

"There will come a time when you will want to hear my words pastor Clark. I hope it's not too late." Sebastian said with an icy tone.

Jimmy gave the handle another tug as Sebastian stepped away from the door. He hurried down the small steep steps to the second floor. Jimmy found Abigale asleep in a cot in the hallway. The poor thing had been so exhausted when they found her a cot she had passed straight out. Jimmy found the men in the conference room looking at a rather large map of the county.

" I think there is someone up the road in trouble. I saw headlights come from the highway into town then nothing for awhile. A few minutes ago I saw them flash on and off two times. It might be more survivors." Jimmy managed to get out between breaths.

The men all looked at each other at once. They all had the same look of caution on their faces. Jimmy knew they were wondering if it was a trap, or if it was people in need of help. Yet even if it was a trap they should still go and see if anyone was there. They didn't have to get out of the vehicle if it looked suspicious.

"I'll go check it out." Henry said as grabbed his rifle from the wall.

The rest watched him as he made his way towards the door. Jimmy walked over and grabbed the shotgun he had been given and followed Henry out the door. He continued behind Henry as they made their towards the steps to the first floor. When they made it to the stairs Henry turned around and placed a hand on his shoulder.

"You need to stay here with the rest Jimmy. In case it was to be a trap. There isn't any reason why we should put anyone else in danger." Henry said as he squeezed his shoulder.

Jimmy watched as the man made his way out into the darkness of the first floor and was gone. Jimmy made the solemn trek back up the stairs. Henry should have let him come along. There was safety in numbers. Jimmy placed the shotgun in his lap and leaned back against the concrete wall. His eyes felt so heavy. Sebastian's words still echoed in his mind, but he couldn't focus on them or their meaning because sleep took him.

Part 5

Henry Myers made his way through the dark recesses of the first floor. He knew this building so well that he could tell where everything was at from memory. Deep down he felt this was a trap.

Definitely a bad idea to come alone, but the way things were going it was better one dead than two.

He slung his hunting rifle over his shoulder and slid his pass key through the lock. The electronic lock buzzed and Henry stepped out into the reception area. He heard someone behind him. Henry thought it was the preacher trying again. It was Sebastian who emerged from the darkness. into the faint glow of light coming from the front door.

"Where do you think you're going?" Henry asked the well dressed man.

Sebastian gave him a smile and it made a chill go down Henry's spine. In the low light coming in the room he could swear he saw hunger in those eyes of his. He raised a hand and motioned for him to go back to the others but the tall dark haired man stood defiant.

"I used to shoot at marksmanship competitions, and I always was the winner old boy. I don't think it would be at all wise for you to go out alone. I know you didn't want the old chap coming along, but I am far from incompetent." Sebastian replied.

Henry shook his head but motioned for the man to follow him. He didn't like the idea; not at all. Yet he liked the idea of being surrounded by those things by himself even less. Henry glanced out the front door in both directions.

They had all been debating why the sun hadn't come up. The biblical answer was the only answer. If these thing were the damned coming back to life. It was checkmate already anyways. As he watched the meteor shower in the sky he felt scared.

Henry hadn't been scared since Somalia. He had been trained how to defeat scared so he took all those feelings and trapped them in a steel box in his head. Doubt is what got you killed. He needed that out of his head first thing. Then he would set to his task and let the training take over.

"First things first, only shoot when you have to. If we were to get cornered try to stay back to back. We don't want to lose our best advantage when it comes to line of fire. I'm calling the shots out there. I wanna do this and come back alive. Comprende?" Henry asked.

Sebastian nodded to him and Henry pushed open the door. He looked around again but didn't see any red dots in his line of sight. Henry crouched low and made to his squad car. He glanced back to make sure Sebastian was following. The man mirrored his movements exactly. Sticking to shadow and keeping an eye on his surroundings.

Henry opened the driver side door and Sebastian piled into the passenger side. So far off without a hitch. Henry slid his key into the ignition and started the car. He pulled away from the curb and drove a block before he turned on his lights. They saw a couple of the reanimated roaming the streets and the alleys but these seemed to ignore them.

The dead seemed quite content to roam around in circles and do nothing. The preacher had said coming into town so he must mean the highway going east. At the corner of Main and Wilkins Henry turned right and sped along the highway. The streets seemed quiet to him. A little too quiet he told himself.

"This seems, how do you say, a bit too easy. Wouldn't you agree?" Sebastian asked as if to reinforce Henry's own fears.

Henry scanned the shadows through the windows as if he could see much. It was black as pitch out. Henry wished the moon was out or something. That's when he saw it up ahead. Headlights from a vehicle flashed on and off twice as if to signal.

Henry slowed the car and began to watch right and left. If this was a trap then now would be the time to watch for signs. They wouldn't rush them still in the car. That would be stupid on their part. They would wait until they were far enough away from the car to be able to escape. If it was his trap that would be how he played it out anyways, and he had laid a lot of traps.

Finally the cars light fell on the white beat up pickup truck that had been signaling them. Inside the cab Henry could make out a woman and a small child. Well if this was a trap then now they had to at least try and save them.

"Maybe this isn't a trap and maybe it is. How we play this out is how we determine the outcome. That dark set of bushes at my ten o'clock and that dark alley to your five o'clock. That's where I would hide. So you watch the five and I'll watch the ten. Let's make this quick and clean." Henry stated in an 'I've been in this situation before' tone.

Sebastian gave him and nod of acceptance as Henry put the car in park. Henry looked towards the sky and noticed the meteor show had stopped. He didn't know if that was a bad sign or not. He left the engine running as he opened his door and stepped out.

Henry tried to see if he saw anything move but he couldn't see anything in this darkness. Henry heard the creak of the old truck's door opening and he raised a hand for her to stop. The woman looked at him and stopped.

Henry pulled his 40 caliber automatic from its holster with a routine quickness. He placed the flashlight he had retrieved from his belt underneath it. Henry made his way towards the truck keeping a vigilant eye on the bushes to his left. He didn't like it when he got halfway towards the truck and the headlights cut his ability to see the brush.

Henry turned and shone his flashlight in that direction. It was still so black that he couldn't see anything moving. He made his way quickly to the driver door.

As soon as Henry saw her he knew it was Diana Wheat. Her and her husband Billy owned one of the only realty firms in Jacob's Ladder. Their little daughter Nikki sat in the seat beside her playing with a pair of dolls. Henry looked back towards the bushes as she eased open the truck door.

"Thank God it's you Henry. I thought we were done for again." She said as tears roll down her cheeks.

Henry glanced back at the bushes again. He looked forward to check on Sebastian. The headlights were blinding if he looked towards him. Henry tried to fight away the little white dots that tried to cloud his vision.

"How are you Mrs. Wheat and little Ms. Wheat? It's good to see you folks are faring okay, considering the current state of things. It would be best for all of us if you came back to the station with us." Henry said in the most helpful tone he could imagine.

Henry could see the relief spread across Dianna's face. The little girl glanced up from her dolls and smiled at him. Henry could still remember Abby giving him the same smile. He had missed a lot of those younger years. Henry felt a pain of remorse pass through him.

"Come along baby. It's time for us to go collect that prize." Dianna told her daughter as she took her up into her arms.

Henry heard the first shot **boom** loudly in the night. It startled him as he once again tried to look towards Sebastian. He couldn't see the man but he saw the muzzle blast from the second shot.

"Make a break for the car!" Henry screamed as he looked back toward the brush on his right now.

Another **boom** sounded into the night as he saw three sets of eyes come to life in the brush. Henry leveled his weapon and sighted down the barrel at one of the sets. He squeezed the trigger. The muzzle flash from his gun was bright in this darkness.

Henry heard another loud **boom** from the 44 caliber rifle sound into the night. Dianna bolted for the police cruiser. Henry sighted in on the next set of burning coals. The pistol kicked in his big hands and the 44 sounded off again.

It was all a mix of flashes and a high pitched whine as he started to sight in on the third pair of eyes. That's when something slammed into his right side hard. Henry felt his head make good contact with the concrete. He didn't see so much as hear his gun skidding out of sight.

He only had a second to react when he saw Heidi Sexton from the flower shop climb on top of him. Henry would never forget those eyes. Black swirled his vision for a second and he did the only thing he knew to do as she lunged for his neck. Henry threw up his arm in defensive mode to protect himself.

He thought he had screamed when he felt those teeth sink into his right forearm. Pain shot down his arm all the way to his shoulder as he slammed his left fist into her face. He felt the eye socket of her face crack under the blow but she didn't let go. Blood was now flowing down his arm and falling into his mouth and eyes.

Henry hit her again as hard as he could and thought he heard her jaw crack at the blow. He thought it would daze her but she only clamped down harder. Henry cried out in pain as he went to hit her a third time. He knew his left hand was broken but struck her again as she began to shake his arm like a wild dog.

Henry couldn't see anymore. He had gotten too much blood in his eyes. Henry heard two more gun shots as he struck the woman in the face. Black began to swirl with the red as he tried to fight the shock off. He went to hit her again and his hand failed to connect. He felt those slender little fingers slide around his throat.

Henry knew this was the end. He thought about Abby. Would they protect her? Would Sam keep her safe? Henry didn't feel pain anymore. He felt a sense of peace ease over him that he hadn't felt in a long time. Then he heard what sounded like the snapping of bone, and that's when he felt the slap to his face that made him open his eyes. Henry saw Sebastian standing above him.

"Don't you die on me old boy. Now open those bloody eyes." Sebastian said as Henry felt another slap.

Everything swirled to him as he felt arms begun to lift him up. Henry could see the white truck bobbing before him. He watched black begin to swirl again as he heard the distinctive sound of a car door opening.

" Is he going to be okay?" he heard a female voice ask.

Henry thought back to what he had been doing. "Had the Wheats made it?" he asked himself. Surely they did or why would he be hearing their voices. Henry thought he heard cloth ripping. "What was that?" he asked himself. He thought for sure that he was dead. Then that searing pain shot through his body. Henry didn't realize he was screaming until he felt another slap to his face.

"What's wrong with him mommy? Is he hurt?" he heard a tiny voice ask.

Henry felt something thick and cold slip over his arm. He felt the cool feeling slide all the way to his bicep. A firm pressure made him open his eyes. He saw Sebastian standing half in the passenger seat. He had a belt wrapped around his arm. He could feel the man pull it tight and wrap it under his arm; then another slap to the face.

Henry opened his eyes and looked at the man. Those pale blue eyes burning concern and he looked down at him.

"I know you have been worse off. This is shock. I need you to keep pressure on this or you will die." Sebastian said in a matter of fact way.

Henry nodded and took the loose end of the belt in his left hand and pulled tight with all his strength. He fought to keep his eyes open. It all seemed like a blur of flashing blue. Henry heard crying from the back seat. A small soft voice tried to explain everything would be okay.

He looked over to the driver's seat and saw Sebastian looking back at him. Henry felt his eyelids flutter and that's when he felt a true pain. Like a ravaging dragon it drove away all the fluff and niceness to the situation. He felt a pain shoot up the side of his face all the way to the temple. He looked at Sebastian and could see the blood on his right knuckles.

"Sorry about that, I am, but you need to keep your eyes open."
He stated without remorse.

Henry felt the belt tighten again and he did the best to grip it. It
only took him three tries to grab it. Black began to cloud his vision
once more. He heard a few sounds but they sounded so far away.
He thought he heard doors opening. He could have sworn he heard
his wife say something.

"It's in his left right pocket. The card is red and black." He heard
a non-distinctive voice bark into the clouds.

Henry felt his grip loosen on the belt, and then came a scream.

Part 6

Felix Cherry sat gathering his thoughts. The smell of gun oil and
tobacco filled his nostrils with each new breath. His newly
acquired guards, military elite, sat motionless and without words.
The bewilderment of his experience in the hospital morgue hadn't
even begun to wear off. Then these soldiers had showed up at the
hospital to whisk him away. Orders had come straight down from
the top they said without much more explanation. He had
protested but it had been to no avail. They rolled him towards the
door. Straight to business these men were, but you could tell that

by looking at them.

"Charlie one actual to bravo two actual, containment has failed! I repeat containment has failed!" A voice shouted across the two way radio in the dash.

Felix watched as the men on either side of him gave each other a blank look. He knew deep down they had shared that look before. It had been a look of fear in a past life; when this world had been fresh and full of life, but that time had long passed. Everywhere you looked now there was death. Felix heard the V-8 motor come to life in a growling roar as one of the men pulled his safety belt tighter.

"What does containment failed mean?" He asked as the SUV lurched sideways; missing a flaming car.

The two men shared another empty glance. The man (Henders his name patch read) to Felix's right pulled back the slide on his weapon. The weapon made a distinct clicking sound. Felix knew that the message was a bad sign. The end was here Felix though as the man to his right followed suit with his own weapon.

A cold dread crept up between his shoulders. Felix began to twist his hands together into fists one over another. There was a knot forming in his gut as Felix finally realized what was happening. They were fixing to bomb this place.

"When containment fails they will execute a surgical air strike on the city's center. Code name **White knight** sir." the reserved youngest member of the group chimed in from the passenger seat.

"Charlie one repeat your last," the voice came across the two way again.

Felix felt the knot growing bigger in his stomach. He tried hard to swallow but couldn't get his throat to work. "What about the people still in the city" he thought to himself. They couldn't be serious. Yet as he watched all the floating red coals hanging in the air he knew deep down it was.

"Containment has failed!" The voice screamed out of the radio between loud bursts of automatic gunfire.

Felix watched as Henders' fists tighten so hard he heard his gloves crackle like kindling.

"Hunter if you can hear me. I love you brother." The voice said between gunfire and screams.

The radio finally went to static. Felix wondered if Hunter had heard the message from his brother. He knew things were bad in the city but he had no idea it had gotten to that extent already.

"God dammit!" Henders shouted and slammed his fist into the back of the seat in front of him.

The man struck the seat two more times before he settled down. Felix could see emotion began to break the still waters of the man's emotionless face.

"He'll be okay Henders. Hes a survivor. " the bearded man to his left chimed in a voice meant to be hopeful but felt flat and robotic.

Felix sensed the camaraderie from his fellow soldier was lost on Henders. He didn't think it was possible to ease his tension at this point. He wanted to try and comfort the man. Yet as the thought passed his mind he could watch the emotion sink back down into Henders face. It was almost like watching someone turn off the light and he was gone somewhere else.

"All call signs this is mission command. Excalibur. I repeat Excalibur."

Felix knew the accelerator pedal had been jammed to the floor. He could tell by the sheer force in which he was pushed back in his seat. Felix assumed they were still well within the blast radius. Judging by the way the driver was weaving in and around the stalled or abandoned cars. He never could see very well in the dark. But he saw the obstruction of cars ahead. Along with the line of dead in front of them.

"Mount the fucking curb!" The man to his left shouted at the driver.

The large SUV jerked to the right violently. The sick feeling was still rising in his stomach. Felix watched a body disappear underneath the vehicle. The rag doll sound of the body bouncing between the undercarriage and the road only made it worse.

Felix had to cover his mouth with his hand when the second body hit the brush guard and went flipping out of sight. He didn't believe the driver cared if they were human or zombie. His gaze fixated on what looked like gore and fragments of bone that had been splashed on the windshield.

"Delta Six this is command. Do you copy?" The voice chimed across the 2 way again.

Felix watched as the younger man in passenger seat picked up the c.b mike. He could see the boys hand shaking in the dim light from the headlights.

"Command this is Delta Six. Precious cargo is on board. We are still four mikes inside the kill box. Repeat precious cargo is still inside the kill zone." The boy spoke into the receiver.

Felix could hear the first tinge of fear crackle out in the younger man's voice. It matched his own at the realization that they weren't gonna make it out. If the order had been sent then the bombs were already on their way. They had way less than five minutes. Three if they were lucky.

Henders gloves crackled again. This time in the silence of the car it sounded more like snapping bones, or tree branches, than mere kindling.

"Command copies Delta Six. Bird are inbound and cleared hot. They will be on station in 3 mikes. This will be danger close Delta Six. Good luck and Godspeed." The voice said in a tired tone.

The younger boy sat the mike back on its stand slowly, as if it had the weight of the world on it. The SUV jerked back off the curb in time to miss a hot dog vendors cart. Its tattered red and white umbrella fluttered briefly at their passing.

Felix closed his eyes and tried to breathe. At this pace they would either make it or crash and die long before the dead could get them.

"Does anyone have a cigarette? Oh and hey fellas I didn't get your names. " Felix tried out his chipper salesman voice.

Felix got a huff out of bearded man. He wasn't sure if it was a laugh or a cough. It was better than listening to the sound of the motor until they all died in a baptism of fire. Felix took the cigarette offered to him by the man and let the man light it for him. He took a long drag off the cigarette and held the smoke in his lungs.

Felix coughed and shook his head.

"Names Jessup. But you can call me Scarecrow" the bearded man said as he replaced the lighter in one of his vests pockets." The younger one in the front is Grifter. Hades is on your right, and Sandman is your chauffeur this evening."

No one made any greetings. Felix hadn't felt that awkward since his first A.A meeting. They were like the four musketeers he thought. With Grifter being their very own Dartagnan. Swooping in to save the day, but there was no saving this day. There was only going to be one eventuality to this scenario.

"We've got sixty seconds. We need to find cover. " Grifter said in an almost more poised tone than earlier.

Felix guessed the boy fell back on his training. Dug down deep and hoped for the best. He spotted the broken parking sign in the faintest reach of the headlights. Felix was about to open his mouth when he heard the deafening boom that sounded off behind them. Felix felt the rumble and pressure down In his bones as the windows exploded out into the night.

"Everyone brace yourself this is gonna get bumpy!"Sandman tried to shout over the noise.

Felix's sight was lost to glowing white brightness. It swallowed every shadow around them. The screeching of tires seemed so far away. The sound of twisting metal and breaking glass a whisper. This was a terrible nightmare and any second he was gonna wake up.

Felix wanted to be whisked away. To open his eyes to his favorite pillow and enjoy the warmth of his expensive comforter. Anything but this was his thoughts as he felt weightless. An overbearing heat and pressure was all around him, and then everything went dark.

Part 7

Frank Pearson sat of the top step of the second floor and drank his coffee. He didn't mind that it was only by the security lighting. The dim yellow light actually was better than bright lights right now. The end of his cigarette burned bright as he took another draw from his cigarette. It lit his facial features in a haunting red glow.

Frank was worried about Henry. The boss had insisted he stay put. Give him more time he said. They had heard multiple gunshots about ten minutes ago. Frank knew Henry could take care of himself. He was a big guy, and not big as in had too many meals and not enough exercise.

They all called him bear when they were joking with him.

Frank remembered the first week he had started on the job at the station. They had gotten called out to incident outside the city limits. One of those motorcycle groups was at this little dive joint tearing up the place. That was the only time he had ever seen someone actually try and hit him.

Frank knew his partner had went far past excessive force. He knew that when Henry had smashed the guy head first into the patrol car door, but it was four on one. Henry had given him orders to stay out of it unless he needed help, and he didn't need any help.

The one stupid enough to pull a knife got the worst end of the stick. A broken arm and his jaws wired shut. Frank didn't think it was right that Henry got suspended a week without pay. It was to save face to avoid a lawsuit against the city. Henry and Frank had become fast friends and even went fishing every other weekend.

"To hell with it," he thought as he stood up and walked down the stairs. They had a rule about leaving men behind and Frank didn't like breaking the rules. He should have never been out alone to begin with.

Frank had just stepped off the last step when he heard a scream. He Drew his 40 caliber from his holster and started out the stairwell door. Through the diamond shaped pane of glass he could see flashing blue lights. Along with what appeared to be two shadows.

Frank was in a full sprint towards the door. He heard the buzz that sounded when the electronic lock released. A woman holding a child rushed inside. Next through was the out of town stranger practically carrying Henry by himself.

He went to the other arm and put it over his shoulder. Frank grabbed the belt that was being used as a tourniquet and pulled tight.

"What happened?" Frank asked.

The Englishman had looked nice before but he was covered in

blood. The majority of it was Henry's he bet. Frank didn't know anyone else had gone with Henry but he sure as hell should count his lucky stars. If there were any stars left to count. Henry gave a groan as Frank pulled the belt even tighter.

"The bloody bastards were waiting for us is what happened. Henry here had it fancied out rather smart. I was to watch one direction and he the other. When my end was all clear I turned to look for the old boy; he was already down you see. I got him up and got him home right away. If you have a first aid kit I do rather nice stitch work" Sebastian replied to the man.

Frank nodded okay to the man as they started up the steps. The first thing he thought was man Henry was heavy. He had no idea how the smaller guy was even going. Frank went to the gym quite often and he was already puffing by the time they made it to the second floor. The woman opened the door for them; quickly moving out of the way. Frank recognized her face from the newspaper ads. Her and her husband where in the real estate market; buying and selling most of the properties in the county.

"We could use a little help here." Frank barked at the others.

They started towards conference room when Sam met them at the door; lifting the man's legs. They all lifted him at once and set him in the middle of the table.

Frank made off as fast as he could to the first aid station. He grabbed the kit and the purified water and bolted back to the conference room. Now the preacher and the girl were up and the old man restrained Abby. She was screaming and crying and carrying on a good deal. Sebastian was removing his ruined suit jacket and rolling up his sleeves as Frank set the kit on the table.

"I'm going to need you to assist me. Think you are up to it? I need you to keep pressure on the arm until I can suture it. Its that or he's going to bleed to death," Sebastian said in a cold but determined tone.

Frank nodded and grabbed the belt and pulled it tight once more. He watched as Sebastian's nimble hands had the needle out and threaded will a skilled quickness. The bite looked rather deep and nasty. Sebastian doused the wound in purified water and went to work.

Frank prayed he knew what he was doing. He had seen field medics work before, and that's exactly how he worked. Sebastian had some medical training of some kind. Time seemed to drag on at a wretched slow pace, but after about forty five minutes he was done.

Sebastian had managed to have covered himself in blood. What hadn't been covered in blood already; but it was rather nice stitch work. Sebastian made off for the bathroom without a word and Frank pulled up a chair for Abby to sit in.

"Is he going to be okay?" Abby asked him.

"I think he is going to make it." Frank replied as he started out into the hallway.

At least Frank hoped he would. Henry was a good man and didn't deserve this. He didn't deserve it at all. Frank knew that Henry had been having a rough time but they needed him. "God please help us," he thought to himself, because they were in need of some help.

Part 8

Abigale Myers sat in the conference room with the others as her father slept on the conference table. She felt as though she had just closed her eyes when the yelling had started. She was groggy with sleep but she remembered the two men carrying her father in. She had thought it a dream for only a second. That is when she recognized the cold hard truth of it. Now she sat holding her father's hand as they all stared at the newly arrived Dianna Wheat.

"Now please tell them what you told us." Frank asked the woman politely.

The woman began her story in a car in one of the tunnels leading out of Jacob's Ladder. Then she explained how they had hid as the damned seemed to come out of nowhere. Dianna explained how she and her daughter had stayed in the room for several hours after it was quiet.

They then had made it almost completely out of the tunnel when they triggered a car alarm. Dianna and her daughter had made off into the woods and moved quietly as the damned came back. So Dianna and her daughter Nikki then moved through the woods until they came to the overpass. The one outside of town. There Dianna had spotted a white pickup truck that had been abandoned.

Dianna explained in detail her searching of the keys and finding a man name Phil dead. A death by self-inflicted gunshot; An apparent suicide. Dianna admitted to taking the man's keys and gun. Dianna hoped everybody understood. As a whole most people nodded. The woman paused a second as if to gather her thoughts.

" Please continue." Sebastian asked from behind her.

The woman begged them to listen and not to think she was crazy. Dianna said she had tried to start the pickup over and over again. The mob of the reanimated behind her heard the noise and proceeded to come for them. Abigale watched as the woman began to cry; sobbing several times.

Once Dianna had stopped crying she continued. She had tried

to do the only thing she could think of. Dianna tried to kill her own daughter. She thought it was the only way to keep her daughter from being ripped apart like the others. Yet she was unable to do so because there were no bullets left in the gun. Dianna looked at her daughters sleeping form out in the hallway. Abigale watched as Frank squeezed her shoulder. She reached up and touched his hand as if to say thank you.

"Then what happened?" Sam asked from the door.

Dianna assured them once again she wasn't crazy. She said she heard a clap of thunder and then the ground shook as if something had hit it with a great force. Dianna explained that there was a very bright blue light and for a while she couldn't see for the dust.

She said that she saw a man with short pale blonde hair of decent height and rather nice build. Dianna stated he was wearing white armor with gold trim. Dianna explained that the man had climbed out of a hole in the ground and carried a sword. She told them that she couldn't tell how many of those…things stood in front of him. Dianna guessed at seventy five or a hundred.

"You can't be serious." Sam stated from the door.

Frank raised a hand to silence him. Dianna continued her story. She explained a lot of it happened so fast she couldn't see. She said the man started attacking the red eyed people. Dianna explained they came at him in a waves. The man had moved so fast she could barely see him.

Dianna stated that every time she thought he was done for lightning crashed to the ground and saved him. She explained that there was so much lighting she had to cover her eyes for a bit. She said when she no longer saw blue light she had looked back at the man. Dianna said his armor was no longer white he was covered in so much blood. She even swore the man smiled at them. Dianna said he bent over and this white light expanded from his back in the shape of wing and he shot up into the sky.

Abby could see the fear on Dianna's face. It was the same look she had on her face in the mirror earlier, but Dianna looked like she believed what she said. Abby watched as the woman gently twisted a paper towel in her hands like she was wringing water out of it.

"Please continue Mrs. Wheat." Jimmy asked her.

Dianna explained that she had tried the truck one more time and it finally started. She had driven back to Jacob's Ladder and had just reached the city limit sign when they had ran out of gas. She stated that she had tried to start the vehicle two more times and then thought it best not to make any more noise.

Dianna said she had waited on daylight to come but it never did. Her and her daughter had sat and watched the meteor shower. Until it stopped and that's when she saw the headlights coming towards them. Dianna explained she turned the vehicle lights on to signal the person that she was there. That was when she realized it was a police officer. She had attempted to get out of the vehicle when Henry had motioned for her to stay inside the vehicle.

Dianna explained that Henry and she had been talking when the first shot sounded out. Henry had told her to run to his car when shooting started from both sides. Dianna explained she and her daughter hid in the back of the car until the shooting had stopped.

That was when she saw him, and she pointed to Sebastian, pull the woman off of Henry and twist her neck. Dianna went on to say that Sebastian had placed Henry in the car and bandaged his wounds. Dianna said that he had struck her father repeatedly in an attempt to keep the man awake. The next thing she knew she was at the police station.

"So you're saying an angel saved you?" Sam asked in a sarcastic tone.

Dianna continued to twist her towel as more tears went down her cheeks. Frank led the woman to a seat. They all looked around at each other not saying anything. Abby knew somewhere deep down what the woman said was true. They all had to stop and at least think it might be true.

In Jacob's ladder, this time a year at least, the sun was up by 6:30. It was now well past eight o'clock and it was still dark outside. The

235

key point of the story was she had seen the lighting with her own eyes. Most of them had been outside of her father's house and seen it with their own two eyes.

"I believe you Dianna. I think we all do." Abigale said out loud.

Abigale looked from face to face and watched them think it over in their heads. Considered all that had happened in the last twenty four hours what couldn't they believe? The dead had come back to life and had fallen on those that had been living. The sun hadn't come back up like it should. Abigale didn't want to believe it herself. But how hard was it to believe that Dianna Wheat and her young daughter had been saved from certain death by an angel? At this moment Abigale was beginning to believe that anything was possible now.

"Well the last time I read Revelations the only thing angels helped was our genocide. So why, would one single angel, try and save us from it?" Sam asked bluntly.

Abigale couldn't believe Sam was such a stubborn ass. She knew he hated religion, but he was right. Angels brought on the end of days not saved them from it. So why did this one angel help Dianna and her daughter? Why save two souls if this was the intended path set before them? Was it providence that had saved them?

"Maybe this angel doesn't believe what's happening is the right path." Sebastian suggested.

Abby looked at him; as did all the rest. The proper man standing there in his fancy silk shirt stained with blood. Sebastian looked at her with those blue eyes burning into her. Abigale was thankful he had been there with her father. He had saved him from those things. Yet as deep and piercing as those eyes were, she could sense tiredness in them.

They had all grown a bit older in having all this knowledge pushed upon them. Given the state of events anyone should feel old beyond their years to have lived to see this. Abigale squeezed her father's hand. Her hand was so small and tiny compared to his. As bad as things were she was glad she was alive. Abigale was glad they all were alive. She only hoped it would stay that way.

Chapter 8: Genesis

Part 1

Pastor Jimmy Clark pushed open the door to the roof and found Sebastian sitting on its edge. There had been a great deal of talk among the others. If this was the end of days what would they do? Where could they go? Jimmy had watched Sebastian leave quietly. He wanted some peace and quiet, and Jimmy could understand that. The warrior angel saving the helpless had made Jimmy's spirits turn around. Though everyone else seemed to the think the world at a loss, he didn't believe so anymore.

" Would you like some company?" Jimmy managed to say as politely as he could.

Sebastian never turned to look at him. He only motioned for him to sit. Jimmy walked over to the edge and took a seat beside him. He looked down at the roaming corpses. Jimmy noticed a few of the faces as some of his own parishioners. Their number had grown in the everlasting darkness.

Frank had said he only seen one here and there but he already counted ten and that was as far as he could see. Jimmy thought about what it was like in urban areas. If there were ten here he bet there was ten times that many. Jimmy did the math by how many streets where in New York City.

"What if I told you the book you have based your whole life on is only half of the story?" Sebastian posed to him.

Jimmy ran the thought over in his head. He was not a complete fool. He had been to seminary and he knew the difference between it and the truth. Yet it wasn't if the stories were true, it was the message. The message was what made it an ideal lifestyle to him. To do good and teach others to be good and help others. That was the message it relayed to him. Most people did it for the money, but he did it to help others.

"I would say that there are always two sides to every story." Jimmy replied.

Jimmy watched Sebastian shake his head yes to agree with him. He could see the man's face, though rather handsome, had a look of age to it now. Jimmy would say it looked like a face of mourning. He didn't look like he was grieving, but that stage afterwards. Where you have come to accept the loss, and are not happy with it. A mix between anger and sadness.

"What if I told you I have lived and seen things, things so tiny it's almost hard to fathom they happened at all? I have watched the rise of nations and the atrocities they claim sanctioned by heaven. That I have been here since the dawn of what you call time?" Sebastian stated with almost a bitter hiss.

Jimmy saw no lie on the man's face. Either he was crazy or he was telling the truth. The only crazy thing he had noticed was the red eyed demons claiming friend and becoming foe. The night sky being absent of both stars and moon but no clouds. That was crazy. Jimmy didn't believe Sebastian was crazy at all.

"I would say, after hearing Dianna's story it wouldn't be that hard to believe. The question for you is, who or what are you?" Jimmy asked.

Jimmy watched the man as he sat there on the roof. The man lifted his hand from the edge where it was resting and pulled the silver cigarette case from his pocket. He flipped it open quietly and placed one of the white sticks in his mouth. He lit the end of the cigarette with his lighter and Jimmy could see his eyes. They were black as coals. There was not one stretch of white in them. Jimmy gasped and stared with his mouth agape at the man.

"My name is not for you to know. In our language it is a word of power for the bearer, and forbidden knowledge to mortals. I will tell you part of my story, but only so that if you survive this, you may set the story straight. If you tell the others, by any means, there will be no place in this verse or any other that I can't find you. I am only bound by one rule, and your demise or that of all the rest is not part of it. To put it in terms you can relate; I am an angel in your tongue. Yet I am not allowed to go home. So ask your questions as you came to do. " Sebastian said as he took another puff off his cigarette.

Jimmy felt a chill through his bones. He suddenly felt very scared. He had thought that Sebastian knew more about what was going on that he had let on. The shock of hearing the angel story had played out on his face. Yet sitting there on the cusp of opening Pandora's box, Jimmy wasn't sure he was on the path that he thought he was going to head down.

Sebastian laughed out loud. A good hearty chuckle that seemed like it came from somewhere down deep. This being as it were did not help Jimmy's rising fear.

"I mean you no harm as long as you covet our agreement and keep what I tell you secret. If the weak is survived then you may tell anyone you want." Sebastian managed to get out between laughs.

Jimmy felt the tension release some in his shoulders and he slumped over. He was sitting next to one of the fallen. Those cast out of heaven for their war. He wasn't sure if he had any questions he wanted answered that bad. Yet considering the state of the world what did they have left to do but converse? It wasn't like they were going anywhere fast.

"Why can't you go home?" Jimmy got out barely above a whisper.

Jimmy watched as the smile grew on Sebastian's face. The man had struck a chord in him as he watched Sebastian take a long drag off his cigarette. Jimmy was glad to see that his eyes were normal looking again. That eased down the fear that had spread like a fire in his gut.

"That is a good question. It has been a question that had plagued me for a very long time. You see you and I are pretty much the same thing except I cannot die. Religion has painted us unable to disobey or having no free will. It's not so much as I don't have free will as it's that I already know all the answers. I can't choose to not believe in God because I have seen the streets of gold with my own eyes. I know that this is the end of days. That the trumpets have sounded in the void. I have heard their call. What you see before you is the same thing Peter saw when he wrote Revelations. You have the ability to not believe. If you so desire that is your "free will." I know it's true and I'm incapable of disbelief. Angels have the ability to use all the brain's potential. Humans barely use two percent. Your kind has always been filled with doubt and a desire to learn. Humans have always yearned for more." Sebastian said.

Jimmy listened to the man and didn't understand. That really wasn't an answer to his question. He tried to grasp what Sebastian had said.

"I am incapable of not caring for everything created by God. You choose to love or not to love. I have to love. The Creator made angels and I loved my brothers. He created you and I love you. I cannot go home but I still love my Father. I am incapable of hate. Does that help?" Sebastian stated.

Jimmy still didn't get what the man was getting at. He was on the point of rambling. Jimmy reached back and rubbed his neck. He thought he might upset the man if he asked the wrong question, and one does not poke a mean dog with a stick.

"I thought the reason why the angels couldn't go home was they aided Lucifer's attempt for the throne. " Jimmy said. "Causing them to be expelled from heaven and sent to the lake of fire."

Jimmy didn't want to anger the man but Sebastian was not making much sense. I mean it explained things but it didn't say why he couldn't go home. He knew that wasn't what happened but if he gave the man a starting point then Sebastian could better explain. Sebastian gave a scoff of a laugh as if insulted.

"He didn't want the throne. Does that answer even make sense Jimmy? It is part of the lie woven by the writers. If the devil was so powerful that he thought he could take the throne from a being that created everything, even Satan himself as you call him. Would he not been destroyed? What would you do to a spider in your home if you felt threatened?" Sebastian asked.

Jimmy thought on Sebastian's words as the man got up and stared at the black sky above him. If he was incapable of hate he sure sounded heated enough to him.

"Anger and hatred are two different things my friend." Sebastian replied while he lit another cigarette.

Jimmy felt his mouth open as if shocked. The man could read minds. Sebastian shook his head and began to pace on the rooftop. Jimmy pictured the man as a train on a child's toy track doing circles with that train of smoke following him.

"Then tell me Sebastian, why were you exiled?" Jimmy asked.

Jimmy watched the man pace some more as if gathering his thoughts to answer. The trail of smoke followed him in his train like circle for a few more paces. Jimmy could see the gears turning in the angel's head. Sebastian was forming a plan on how to relay it into words Jimmy could understand.

"The war in heaven was over man. Those of us that thought humans should be spared and let flourish were met with resistance. Humanity was a construct experiment. The father created us and bestowed within us the knowledge of creation. We could do nothing but love our father like you love your parents. We knew what creation was so we loved life. To understand creation is to know the true beauty of life. Yet God wanted to create something that loved him without all the knowledge. To make a creature that loved him because of the perfect God created it. To have that creature believe in him without a doubt, in short to have faith. So the garden was created as a environment. Adam was given a perfect existence. No cares of hunger or pain. No knowledge of fear or death. The experiment failed each time. Each Adam chose to pursue knowledge over faith. Each Adam ate the fruit and was destroyed until the father refused to go any further. I blame the brain's potential being limited in Adam. It left too much to be desired. God became disheartened. One final Adam was created and was given a mate to keep him company. Some of the the higher choirs believed that man was evil and should be destroyed. Instead God made man mortal. Others did not even think this was a fitting enough end, and so began the war. " Sebastian finished.

Jimmy sat and thought about what the man said. He could see where it was starting to make sense. Well it was making about as much sense as it could. Jimmy was wondering if Sebastian was listening to his thoughts and it was only met with a chuckle.

Jimmy looked at the man lit another cigarette and continued his "choo-choo train" path. Jimmy thought about what the man said about the evil part. Jimmy was starting to get what he was saying. Man was the only creature on this planet that was capable of evil. Some people were good because they loved and some people were evil because it was more fun not to care.

"Exactly what I was getting at. With animals its instinct and nature. Animals hunt for food but never for the joy of killing. Predators were created to keep the population of the herbivores down. It's the cycle of nature as we know it. Humans were created to see if you could give something with no control the ability to love and be happy. Yet humans are never happy. They can choose to never love him or be happy. I can never die but still I love him. The human majority is only godly on its deathbed, and still if asked they shall receive. Every sin they have a name for is some form of unhappiness. Gluttony for instance; the majority of those people eat because they are sad. Greed is from not wanting to worry about money. How many rich people worry about money? It's a never ending process. Humans are unhappy because they think there is something more around the corner. " Sebastian finally finished.

Jimmy went over the man's words in his head. He was starting to make more sense of it now. It made more sense why they went to war, but it didn't explain why they were exiled. If they had been on the right side; then why would they be forced to leave?

"The war was a gridlock for its entirety. Angels were made for creating and cultivating. There were only five made for war. Raphael absolved himself from taking a side. Uriel talked to no one anymore. Gabriel had fallen when light was brought to world. The morning star had been for preserving humanity but had never engaged in the debates. He had been as silent as the father. It was a stalemate for a stretch of time. Angel fought angel but there were no casualties," Sebastian explain. "It was only when the arch Michael stepped in that the weakest of our race were forced to join a side as well. Michael and the morning star were chosen as champions for each side, but did not engage in the battles. I still remember it to this day. When Michael finally did attack, the morning star stopped him. The battle between the two was a sight to behold. The realm of heaven shook that day. It was arch versus arch; a clash of Titans and in the end the morning star bested Michael. He did not slay Michael as he had intended the lesser ones, but he made him submit. The morning star refused to destroy him, and when he turned his back Michael tried to slay him. Michael would have succeeded had one of the lesser angels not pushed him aside. As Michael's sword pierced that angel's chest the heavens shook with the wrath of the maker. A voice that had been silent during the conflict since its inception. All in Heaven bowed before the anger of it. We had never known such a thing had existed before then. That was when the golden rule was implemented."

Jimmy watched as the man lit another cigarette. He would speculate Sebastian would die of cancer if he were not immortal. Jimmy knew the golden rule. Do unto others as you would want them to do unto you. In jimmy's eyes it meant do well by others and they would do well by you. He believed the angel was telling him the truth. Jimmy could tell by Sebastian's body language he had been waiting a long time to tell his story.

"The human interpretation of the rule is right by your knowledge of it. Yet it was not a rule for humans in its creation. The golden rule is much simpler for my race. Angels are forbidden from taking the life of another angel. If an angel kills an angel he is marked for death by both the fallen and the divine. Simply put, if an angel kills another angel means the murderer wants to die. That is the only way for us to kill one of our own; if they have broken the golden rule. There is no way for us to die any other way. We are immortal. To do so means you forfeit that power. " Sebastian explained.

Jimmy could only felt pity for the man. He knew the weight of a life of not days or years must be terrible to bear. The thought of being alone was to terrifying for Jimmy to think about. He knew his own death was not in the too distant future. Yet Jimmy could not grasp a feeling of not being able to go home. It was too much for him.

"So the death of an angel stopped the war? Then why were

you made to leave?" Jimmy asked.

Jimmy could see Sebastian's eyes were black again. Like a dark bottomless hole they seemed to go on forever. Jimmy felt unnerved by them but Sebastian felt able to be himself around him. He watched as Sebastian smoked his cigarette. Jimmy would say he was gathering his thoughts but you couldn't gather anything from those eyes.

"We weren't made to leave we chose to leave. After what one of our own did in selflessness we could no longer stay. There is no way to change the minds of the already decided. We sought exile here. If you leave on your own accord you cannot return until the sounding of the seventh trumpet. I have spent mankind's entire life span watching. Among the many atrocities I have seen, the countless deaths, I have also seen good deeds. I have seen so many acts of sacrifice like I saw that day. I still have faith in your kind if no one else still believes; I do. We shall continue some other time. Your son is coming up the steps." Sebastian said in a solemn tone.

Jimmy had but a second to think when the door opened and Sam stepped out. He looked from Jimmy to Sebastian and only frowned. Jimmy himself had taken a bite of the fruit that day. How many a scholar would have loved to hear the tale he just heard. Yet from the mouth of someone who had seen that day, he found no joy in its knowledge. Sebastian was right in his elaboration that unhappiness was the root of all sin.

"Henry is awake," Sam stated. "You two should come down stairs."

Jimmy watched as his son left without another word. Jimmy rose from his seat on the cold stones of the roof's edge and felt the age of his bones. He could only look at the man who had shared his tale of woe. Sebastian looked back at him with those cold blue eyes. Jimmy knew there was a lifetime of knowledge held behind them. He gave the man a nod of friendship and headed towards the stairwell door.

Part 2

Frank Peterson sat in the chair across from the conference table his friend was resting on. Frank smiled for the first time since all this had started. Abby's head rest on Henry's leg as Frank pulled a cigarette from his pack; lighting it somberly. Everyone else had trekked off to find a place to sleep but he wasn't sleepy. Considering the current situation, Frank guessed he would be sleeping for the last time soon enough and he would rather see it coming. Sam had taken first watch, but still Frank didn't trust the situation.

"Sure you don't want to get some rest officer?" Sam called from the doorway again.

Frank looked at the boy and shook his head no. He rested his hands on the handle of his rifle and continued to enjoy his cigarette.

There had been too many sleepless nights while he had been in the military. Frank had become all too accustomed to them. "You'll sleep enough when you're dead," his buddy Jake used to tell him. Frank stood up and strolled across the uniform tile floor and looked out the window into the dark. The damn things were multiplying. At first he had only seen one or two now he could count at least twenty sets of red eyes roaming in the blackness.

"Can you get me some water?" an all too familiar voice called from behind him.

Frank turned around to find Henry resting on his elbows in a somewhat upright position. Frank reached over to the bag in the chair beside him and pulled out a bottle of water. Frank could feel a weight of dread begin to leave his body as he quickly made it to the Henry's side.

Frank twisted the bottle's lid off and went to help the man take a drink, when Henry took the bottle from him. Henry had that look in his eye so Frank didn't object. Henry finished the bottle off and gave it back to Frank.

He watched as Henry reached up and felt of the knot on the back of his head. Henry's face winced as if he had felt a sharp pain and looked at the stitches in his arm. Frank turned around to get him another bottle when Henry raised his hands as if to say no.

"Bitch got me good didn't she? Who did the stitches? Where are Sebastian and the woman and child?" Henry asked in an irritated tone.

Frank walked out of the room and down the hall to the first aid station. He rummaged through the box until he found a couple packets that said pain reliever. He walked back into the conference room as he tore two packets open at once. Henry still had that look of irritation as Frank emptied the packets into his hand.

"They are fine bear. Sebastian managed to get all of you back. He also managed to sew you up while he was at it. Damn lucky he went with you brother. Damn lucky." Frank said as he retrieved another bottle of water from the bag.

Frank handed the new bottle to him as Henry took the pain medication. He knew it would never do much to ease Henry's pain but at least it would make it tolerable. Frank watched as Henry opened the bottle and took another long drink. He didn't see how the man was sitting up under his own power as much blood as he lost. Yet he knew "the bear" as they called him was tough as nails anyways.

"I should have been paying better attention. That blow to the head stunned me pretty good. I felt the bones breaking in her face but she was like a wolf latched on for the kill. How did he get her off of me?" Henry finished as he looked at his swollen left hand.

Frank started back to the first aid station but Henry's head shaking no stopped him. Henry's hand eased down and rubbed his daughter's sleeping head and looked around at the emptiness of the room. Frank could tell his friend was in a moderate amount of pain but he knew an old dog like that was hard to keep down.

"Mrs. Wheat said he snapped her neck like twig. Sebastian even managed to get you in the car and pack you into the building by himself; before I went to help him that is."Frank replied in an empty tone.

Frank watched as the same wheel began to turn in Henry's head that had been turning in his own earlier. Frank's paranoia had been running at full heels ever since the shit had hit the fan, but it didn't mean it wasn't right. How had a man that was not that bulky managed to have gotten Henry in the car and into the building as well?

Frank was stout himself but he wasn't sure he could pull it off. Where did he learn to stitch like that? It was hospital quality at the least. Which meant the man obviously had medical training. Frank's money was on ex-military. Quite possible Sebastian was British SAS or something of that equivalent.

"You think he is ex-military too don't you? How else would he know how to snap someone's neck like that?" Henry said out loud as the wheels still turned in the man's head.

Frank milled the thought over in his head for a second more. It was a likely chance the thought. He opened his pack of cigarettes once more and took one out. He left Henry to his thoughts as he fetched his lighter from his pocket once more. Frank listened to the crackle of the burning paper as the end of the cigarette burst to cherry red. He inhaled the smoke and held it for a second, and finally exhaled as he could see Henry was about to speak.

"I had a really bad dream Frank. I saw the preacher on a car surrounded by those red eyed creatures. Flaming meteors were shooting through the sky; crashing into buildings and homes. It was me, you, Sam, Abby, and Sebastian. We were completely surrounded. I can still hear the gunshots in my head. Then the circle around us got bigger and something crashed into the ground in front of us. A man in white armor and long white hair stepped forward through the dust. The red eyed people would not get close to him; as if they were afraid of the man. The white haired man looked me in the eye and said there is no escaping the reaping mortal." Henry explained to him.

Frank could see by how pale Henry's face was that the dream bothered him. Hell it bothered Frank too. Henry didn't know about Dianna's tale of the man descending from heaven in white armor. Unless somehow Henry heard the conversation. Then subconsciously incorporated into his dream. There was a possibility of it but Frank didn't dare to hope for possibilities. Frank looked up at Henry and could see the man's eyes were fixated on the door. He turned to see what the man was looking at. Sam stood in the doorway. Frank could see that same spooked expression on the younger man's face. The boy seemed pretty one sided when it came to religion. The fact that he may have been on the wrong side played all across Sam's face.

"Go get your father Sam. I think we should be having a talk with him about this." Frank said in a low voice as if not to wake anyone else.

Frank watched as it took the boy a second to even realize he was being talked to, and in an instant he was gone. Frank hadn't been a 'holier than thou' type either but he had managed to go to church every Sunday. Frank didn't believe in all of it but it helped ease his mind a little over some of the choices he had made. He had done a lot of bad things in the service of a noble cause. A lot of them he still hadn't been able to reconcile as noble, but it were too late to change any of it

. Frank hoped that if God had mercy he would save it for those that deserved it. He knew he wasn't on that list but he had made that choice. It was all for the greater good, or he had always hoped.

Part 3

Henry Myers looked at the puzzled look of Jimmy Clark's face as he reiterated his dream. Henry had been standing in what appeared to be a small town fair. He remembered the bright red banner that had been stretched across the front gate. County Fair stood out in huge block letters. They had been by the ferris wheel when the red eyed monsters had caught back up to them. Abby and Sam were in front of him as he turned and fired into the approaching mob. Each would scream and their eyes would go dark as they fell to the ground. Yet for every two he killed three more poured through the gate.

Henry turned to run towards the others as he saw Jimmy climbing up on the hood of a parked car. "Go with the others," he had said. Henry saw Frank in front of him; his rifle leveled as he took pop shots so Henry could escape. Yet as Henry looked over his shoulder, he noticed they seemed more interested in the preacher than him.

He remembered the first thundering crash. A flaming ball connected with the top of the ferris wheel in a fiery crash. The all too familiar sound of twisting metal and the pops of cables breaking was deafening in the air. Henry watched as another meteor went crashing into what looked like a livestock expo. There was a thunderous boom and the ground underneath his feet shook. Henry watched as Frank waved him on. The sounds of gunshots echoed again before being drowned in another boom of impact. Frank hoped they would make it out but doubted it. He soon realized that fear was right when he saw Abby and Sam standing hand in hand in front of a wave of bodies.

Henry could see them closing in around him. Henry glanced back one time at Jimmy as he saw the man holding a Bible high in the air. He could faintly make out the man's lips moving but his words were drowned out in another thunderous boom. Henry could see hope drain from Frank's face as he saw the legion before them.

They were completely surrounded. They had been running for so long. Henry looked up at the skies. The streaking balls of flames stood out but that wasn't the only thing. The complete blackness that had stood starless now had a faint sheen. A sparkle that looked a lot like the northern lights but very faint.

Henry looked from one face to the other. Each one had the same purple splotched face and burning hungry eyes. All their mouths hung open with cracked teeth sparkling yellow. Blood stained as they stared at the survivors in awe. Frank was standing beside him now, and with a quick deftness raised the rifle. Henry put his hand over the top of the barrel and motioned for the man to lower it. Frank gave him the 'I'm not going out without a fight look,' Henry had shaken his head no.

In one unison wave the dead took a step backwards from them. Then another and continued until there was a good twenty foot difference all around them. Another loud boom echoed as a meteor struck somewhere out of sight behind the house of horrors.

Henry thought he had remembered a whistle. Then something struck the ground about ten feet in front of them. Henry had raised his arm up to protect his face when the wave of dust exploded against his clothes. Henry could taste the dust in his mouth as he lowered his arm.

What he saw stepping out of the five foot crater in front of them was a man. He had long hair that was so blonde it was almost white. What his wife Ashley had called a "platinum" blonde. The man was handsome for what it was worth. He wore battle armor that was linen white with gold symbols and embellishments all over it. Henry still remembered the words the smiling man said before him.

"There is no escaping the reaping mortal" the angel had said.

Henry watched as the Pastor thought it over. Sebastian stood at the door watching Henry with curious eyes. Henry thought for awhile that the man could visualize exactly what he had told them. It had been even scarier when Frank had told him about the angel story Dianna had told while he was out. It was possible that his dream had come to be because he had heard them talking about it. His description of the armor had been more detailed that hers. Yet the way Dianna had said the man had fell to earth was the exact same way; almost word for word.

"Well if you're looking for a religious viewpoint, you may be having prophetic dreams. Yet, the overall truth is, you were having a dream and overheard the other lady's story. I'm sure we all will be having dreams like that. Scary times always means bad dreams old friend." Jimmy replied as he squeezed Henry's shoulder.

Henry knew that Jimmy was right. Ashley had done it on more than one occasion. She would fall asleep in his lap while he was watching TV. When he would wake her for bed she would tell him about the dream. Parts that she said were strange were almost straight out of the script of the show he had been watching. Henry knew he wasn't a prophet but he liked it better when someone agreed with him.

"It seemed so real. It was like one of those dreams you can't tell is a dream. That man looked more malevolent than holy. Like the angel got a kick out of all this death and destruction," he said with a sigh.

Henry reached down and lifted Abby's head from its still sleeping position on his leg and stood up. He felt his knees try and buckle and Jimmy took his arm to steady him. Henry waited a few seconds to see if he was going to be able to stand and took a step forward. He felt weak and the pain in his arm was terrible. Henry needed to get some rest and he would feel better. Yet the cot in the hallway seemed so far away.

"We should get all get some rest. Then we can figure out a plan. We will need to scrounge up some more food and water for sure. We should head over to the Shop and Save and get as many supplies as we can. So all of you that's not on watch get some shut eye." Henry said as Jimmy led him out of the conference room and to the nearest cot.

Henry eased down to a comfortable position. His mind was still playing through the nightmare, but he never finished it before sleep took him.

Part 4

Sam Roberts sat between two aisles of food in the Shop and Save when he heard a loud crash the next aisle over. He felt his already elevated heart beat speed up even more. Sam had turned his flashlight off when he realized they were not alone. He hoped this was a nightmare and he would wake up. Yet it never happened like that.

Sam looked further up the aisle where Frank was crouched. Sam was hoping the man had a plan. They had only seen one when they had entered the building and took her out first. They had almost finished filling the two duffle bags. They were loaded down with food when the second one had burst out of the stock room. Sam had remembered that feral growl as he stood beside the large end cap display of pickles.

Sam could see his face plain as day. It was Rodney Perkins standing there in his neat white shirt and red apron. As soon as the man lunged towards Sam he had grabbed one of the quart jars of pickles and threw it at the man's face. Sam watched as the jar connected with Rodney straight to the face. The man had never even lost speed. Rodney was almost on top of him when he heard the gunshot reverberate through the grocery store. Sam noticed the piece of glass sticking out of the man's right cheek, before his brains covered a sign that said 100% real beef.

Sam's left ear rang with a high pitched whine. Sam looked at Frank but the man said nothing as tried to get his ear to stop ringing.

"If you want I can let the next one eat you." Frank said in a flat tone.

Sam shook his head no to that idea as he heard the huge front glass explode behind him. He also heard the shopping cart collide with the tile floor as it landed. Sam assumed that was what those things had used to break the glass. He stood up on his tippy toes to glance over the shelf. He watched as they appeared to know they were in there. Each set of eyes burning like the beacon of a lighthouse in hell. Each one was searching in all direction for the person who had shot.

"We are so fucked." Sam whispered with and exasperated sigh.

Sam could see Frank was looking at him in a strange way; as if to say cowboy up. This was no apocalyptic western. There was going to be no happy ending to this story.

Sam jumped as glass jar in the next aisle crashed to the floor. The sudden burst of sound was like a shotgun going off next to his head. He didn't believe in all this stuff. He thought it was too far fetched to be true. Yet all the discussions of angels couldn't be a coincidence. Maybe he had been wrong, but this didn't seem to be a loving God to him. Sam didn't believe the extinction of all these people by zombies was the most painless of deaths.

"You stay here and be quiet. If we start shooting we may get overrun. I'll take care of this." Frank said as he set his duffle bag on the floor.

Sam watched as he moved down the aisle. Frank stopped for a second in front of what used to be eating utensils. He heard the almost inaudible sound of cardboard tearing in the darkness. Sam could now see what Frank was up to as he saw the silver sheen on the butcher's knife. Sam could see Frank for a few more seconds and then he was gone from sight. He wondered what they had done to deserve this. The world was actually rather peaceful for the first time in decades. Yet now as the race had advanced to a pinnacle of achievement they were to be snuffed out like pests in the pantry.

Sam heard a crash in the next aisle over. Sam listened to the silent struggle, the busting of more glass, and finally the silent gurgle. Frank had finally found one of them Sam hoped. He tightened the grip on the 9 mm pistol in his hand and looked from left to right. Sam caught a moving form in the peripheral vision in his left eye. He turned to his left to see the red set of eyes at the end of the aisle he was in.

"Oh Jesus," Sam whispered out loud to no one but himself.

This wasn't your normal red eyed freak. This one was a bodybuilder or a seasoned ranch hand. Sam looked at the man's wide shoulder stretching his t-shirt that said welcome to the gun show. You could barely make out what the shirt had said for all the blood caked on it.

Sam felt his heart crawl up into his throat. He didn't even move as the burly man stared down the aisle in his direction. He hoped that if he didn't move the large creature would assume him dead and move on. He wished on a bloody star that they didn't have the ability to sense life.

Sam eased his thumb up and pulled the hammer back on the pistol in his hand. The hammer clicked in the darkness as it locked in place. Sam's eyes darted to the safety to make sure it was off. He glanced back to the big man who was making his way down the aisle towards Sam.

"Frank?!?" Sam managed to get out in hurried tone.

The large man stopped and let out a large hiss. Sam turned and leveled the pistol as the man's head. Mr. gun show burst forward with not grace but power like a train. Sam imagined for his size he would be slow but the man was rather fast.

Sam looked down the sights of the pistol. He lined up the two rear dots with the one front dot on the big man's little head. Sam could see the gap was closing fast and he tried to scuttle backwards on the floor. He began to squeeze the trigger. Sam kept the three dots square in the middle of the man's face. Sam knew he was dead when the hammer clicked but the round never went off. He reached for the slide, ejecting the round in the chamber. Sam tried loading another one, but this one jammed and refused to feed right.

Sam looked at the big man just five feet away. Sam caught the movement to his right out of the corner of his eyes. Frank leaped from the top shelf of the aisle to his right and tackled the large man into the shelf wall. The momentum of the two toppled the shelf over on its side. The big burly guy froze for a second as if confused when Frank sank the blade in Mr. gun show's throat and jerked to the left. A jettison of black blood covered Frank's right arm as he crawled off the man. An animal like scream erupted from somewhere to the left of them. Frank dropped the knife and went for his sidearm.

"Thank you." Sam managed to get out as a whisper.

Frank only raised a hand as if to say 'De nada' and retrieved his duffle bag. Sam nodded when Frank motioned for him to follow him. They moved towards the front as they heard something break further towards the back. Sam worked the slide back and ejected another bullet. This time the slide slid forward and the bullet fed into the chamber.

Sam heard what he thought was the sound of canned food falling off a shelf behind them; this time closer than the last. Sam glanced behind them and saw what he swore was one the zombies jump from one shelf to the next. He lost the creature in the darkness.

"We're going to make a run for the cruiser. Don't stop for anything unless it's me. Don't lose the food and when you shoot; shoot to kill." Frank explained as the made it to the end of the aisle.

Frank looked left then right and slipped out into the store front. Sam heard the shot before he saw the body crumple to the floor. The second shot hit the woman standing next to the register. Sam followed behind Frank as they made their way outside.

Sam was in front of the register where Frank had shot the woman when he heard the noise behind him. Sam turned to see what it was and his heart sank. Sam could only watch as the man leaped from shelf to shelf in a mad run towards them.

Sam felt those eyes were burning with rage as he lifted his weapon to sight in on the man. Sam could see the green power shirt shift from aisle to aisle like a pinball trying to get past the flippers. Sam shot and it connected with the man's shoulder but it never slowed him down. One bounce after another as Sam shot again and missed. A glass bottle of what Sam thought was mayonnaise exploded in a barrage of glass. He pulled the trigger one more time and it caught the man in the left knee as he landed on another shelf.

The parkour runner was at an odd angle as he lost his balance and met the next shelf face first. Sam listened to the busting glass and crash of canned food, but jumpy never showed his face again.

"Come on let's move Sam." Frank called out behind him.

Sam turned and followed Frank out the busted window and they made their way to the squad car. Sam quickly tossed his bag in the backseat. Sam reached for the passenger door handle when he saw it crossing the road a few streets down. Sam motioned for Frank to look but it was already out of sight by the time he found out where he was pointing.

"What was it?" Frank asked.

Sam turned and shot. Frank turned and noticed how close the body was and opened the driver door. Sam turned to his right and saw the red sets of eyes making their way towards them.

"It was a truck. It might be more survivors." Sam said as he climbed in and closed the door.

Frank climbed in and put the key in the ignition. Sam thought what more survivors might mean. What it might mean if they were not peaceful survivors. Sam wondered if Frank was thinking about the same thing.

Sam hated to think that they had more to worry about than the damned. Things didn't seem to be going their way. Sam fastened his seat belt as Frank peeled out of the parking lot and set a path for Police HQ.

Part 5

Frank Peterson stood in front of the Shop and Save and had a bad feeling about this. Henry had insisted he take someone. Frank had thought that if Sam was going to learn anything about survival then he needed a test run. This was no time for people to crack under pressure. They needed to get all of them combat ready. Hard times bring out the worst in people.

If there were other survivors it was not going to be the helpful neighbor kind. Frank reached down and pulled his 40 caliber from its holster and made his way towards the front doors.

"I'll take point. You keep a watch on our six." Frank said as they made their way to the door.

Frank watched as the electric doors opened as if some magical word had been said. The emergency generators were keeping this place going. One good thing he thought as he stepped inside. Frank looked back at Sam and saw he had that 'deer in a headlights' look. He had seen that look too many times on the new guy that had rotated into their unit for the first time.

They always seemed like fresh meat for the grinder. Yet one by one the shock and awe would leave their faces and would be replaced by the cold blank stare. You either learned to focus on the task at hand, sort it out, or made a mistake and got sent home with the flag.

"Don't focus so much on what could happen and think more about what needs to be done. We have to get food for the others. There is nothing in this building that will keep us from that task. That's the first rule of survival. Failure is not an option." Frank said in a rather cold way he didn't mean, but it needed to be said.

Frank looked back at Sam and the boy gave him a solemn nod. He could tell he didn't have the stones for it. Sam stood there in his black rock shirt and his pale face. The boy had plenty of tattoos but he was no bad ass. Frank only hoped he could change that.

Frank saw a set of red eyes come walking out of an aisle about ten feet in front of them. He could tell by the way she dressed it was

Alecia the manager of the place. Some big corporation owned the building but she was in charge of the place. It only took her a second to realize they were there and she spun on them.

Frank watched as the woman bared her yellow teeth at him and hissed. He noticed the weird purple tint that had set up on her face. She was a decent looking woman for her age. Not so much anymore as Frank holstered his weapon and took a step forward.

The woman crouched in a lunge and started towards him. Frank could hear her heels tapping on the tile floor as he took another step forward. She was coming at him rather fast but it all began to slow down to him. She made a ragged swipe at him with her right arm and she reached him. Frank had a second to grab her wrist and brought his right knee up with all the force he could muster. His knee connect square with Alecia's abdomen.

Frank watched as the woman's speed coupled with the lack of balance from the heels sent her flipping into the air. Alecia's head connected hard with the floor before her back ever touched. The woman lay on the floor for a second before Frank put his left foot on the woman's throat. Frank placed his other hand around her wrist and jerked up hard. The sound of her neck breaking echoed through the dimly lit store like a tree limb breaking.

Frank looked back to Sam, who stared at him with his mouth open. Sam seemed to clutch the duffle bags even closer to his chest as Frank let go of Alecia's wrist. The arm fell lifelessly to the floor.

"Come on let's get those bags loaded and get out of here."
Frank said without emotion.

Sam only nodded his head and followed Frank as he made his
way down an aisle. Frank began to grab things from the shelves.
They grabbed food that wouldn't perish as they went along and the
bags began to fill up. They reached the end of the aisle and Sam had
spotted a large area of beef jerky. Frank began to fill his bag when he
heard a door burst open. "Show time!" Frank thought as he stood up
and saw the man. It was Rodney Perkins the butcher hissing like a
wet cat. He had always been an asshole Frank had thought. He
watched as Sam picked up a jar of pickles and heaved it at the
rushing man. The jar burst across the ridge of Rodney's nose with no
result.

Frank instinctively went for his weapon because he had no time
to silently stop this one. Sam froze as he sighted on the butcher's
head. Sam was almost in Rodney's reach when Frank pulled the
trigger. There was a bright flash, and like a wrecking ball the bullet
slammed into the man's head.

Rodney careened off course and slammed into the meat case.
Sam looked back at him and covered his left ear as if Frank had done
something but save his life.

"If you want I can let the next one eat you." Frank said in a flat tone.

Sam only shook his head. There was a great crash and Frank began to finish stuffing his bag with jerky and bags of nuts. That had to be the main window by his guess. Frank didn't know why the stupid things didn't use the doors. He zipped his bag and crouched down and watched as Sam stretched to see what was coming in. Frank listened to the footsteps in the glass and started making his way back towards the front.

"We are so fucked," Sam stated from behind him.

Frank glanced back at the boy with a bit of disdain. The boy was at the age to be a man. There was no more waiting on someone else to protect you this was time to take the reins. Frank turned and continued his creep towards the front. Glass began to break on both sides of them. He knew if this were to go sideways, and it would if it turned out to be a shootout; then Frank couldn't keep him safe. Well I guess it's up to you he thought to himself.

"You stay here and be quiet. If we start shooting we may get over run. I'll take care of this." Frank said as he set his duffle bag on the floor.

Frank crept up the aisle. He needed a knife of some sort. He began to scan the aisle and he crept forward. Hoping he would find a display of kitchen knives of something. Frank smiled about three quarters of the way up when he saw a butcher knife hanging from one of the display pegs. He stood up and retrieved the blade from the peg. Frank removed it from its packaging making sure to do so quietly. He listened to the dark as he made his way down to the end of the aisle. Frank made sure to stay in the shadow. He searched the darkness around the storefront. He saw none of the eyes peering in.

Frank crept around the front of the aisle and looked down towards the shambling corpse. It was knocking cans and jars from the shelf. Frank eased forward towards the creature before him. It seemed preoccupied with the ransacking to even take notice of Frank. The best thing to do was to kill it without a lot of sound.

Frank grabbed a bag of beans from the shelf to his left. Quickly Frank tossed the bag of beans in front of the monster. While it was looking down Frank covered its mouth and ran the blade across its throat in one quick slice. The arms flailed for a second, sending one lonely jar of sauerkraut to bust and the body sank lifeless to the floor.

"Oh Jesus," Sam whispered from the next aisle over.

Frank figured he may be in trouble. Quietly he climbed up the shelves before him. Frank saw the mountain of muscle making his way towards Sam. He watched as Sam pulled the hammer back on his weapon. "Don't shoot him it will be too loud," Frank wanted to say but he didn't want to give away his position.

"Frank?!?" Sam managed to get out in hurried tone

Frank thought he might be able to sneak behind him but the rather large man began to run. Frank climbed higher and lowered himself on the shelf as not to be seen. He would only get one chance at this. He counted the man's stride in his head like a drum beat. "One Mississippi, two Mississippi," Frank counted. He watched as he leveled his weapon at the man. "Fuck he's going to shoot him," Frank thought as the gun clicked loudly. That would be as bad as any situation would be to have a bad primer but 9 mm rounds were notorious for it.

Frank watched as Sam messed with the slide. He could see this was his opportunity. Frank leaped from the top shelf and tackled the large man. Both men went into the shelf opposite from the one he had been standing on. Frank sank his blade into what he hoped was the man's pancreas. The weight of both of them caused the shelf to flip on its side. It was followed with a thunderous crash of canned food and busting glass.

Frank never hesitated for a second and pulled his blade free and cut the large man's throat. Frank felt the hot black blood cover his right arm from the elbow down. A scream echoed through the store. "Yeah, that was loud enough to bring them running like a dinner bell," Frank thought to himself.

"Thank you." Sam managed to get out as a whisper.

Frank dismissed the boy's unneeded gratitude and grabbed his duffle bag. Frank motioned for Sam to follow him as he sneaked up the aisle in a low crouch. Frank heard things breaking occasionally behind them, but kept his eyes on the front. He hoped Sam would keep up his deal and keep his eyes on the back. When he reached the end of the aisle he stopped in the darkness.

"We're going to make a run for the cruiser. Don't stop for anything unless it's me. Don't lose the food and when you shoot; shoot to kill." Frank explained as the made it to the end of the aisle.

Frank looked left then right. On his right stood a elderly type man next to the magazine rack and a younger female standing next to the register. He stepped out of the aisle and shot; sending the man's brain matter all over the newest editions. The second shot caught the woman in the mouth. The bullet destroyed the brainstem at the base of her brain. The woman sank lifelessly to the floor. He made for the door in a brisk pace. Frank heard three shots behind him and a loud crash. Maybe the boy wouldn't be completely useless.

"Come on let's move Sam." Frank called out.

Frank jumped through the glass window and made his way to the squad car. Sam went running past him. He watched as the boy tossed his bag in the back. Frank reached down and was looking at the keys to the car. Sam motioned for him to look one way but when he looked there was nothing there.

"What was it?" Frank asked

Frank had a second to see the gun coming for his face. The boy had the drop on him and he would never get his gun raised in enough time. The muzzle flash from the 9 mm was bright in the choking darkness outside. Frank had a second to wonder if he was dead when he saw the body crash to the ground at his feet. See now, that was what the boy needed to do. No hesitation, all reflexes.

Frank thought higher of the boy as he watched the red eyed bastards start walking towards them.

"It was a truck. It might be more survivors." Sam said as he climbed in and closed the door.

Frank climbed into the vehicle and closed the door. Survivors were not what he wanted to see. He wanted to see the army or the marines. Survivors would be some mean, heartless bastards. Killing anybody they came across for what little they had. Parasites were all they would be.

He pulled the shifter down into drive and floored the vehicle. Frank peeled out of the parking and slid sideways. Frank barreled down Jackson Street towards the Police station. Henry would want to hear about this, he thought as he fetched a cigarette from his pocket and lit it. This was not good at all.

Part 6

Henry Myers stared out the window of the Jacob's Ladder police department. He felt like he had been staring for so long he couldn't look away. Frank had told them of their exploits at the grocery store. The fact that Sam had seen another moving vehicle meant there were others alive. Jimmy's first idea had been to seek them out and offer them shelter. Yet Frank had advised against it until they figured out who they were dealing with. Henry himself was a caring man and loved the community he called home, but he was not about to let a fox in the hen house.

" Frank I want you to go check it out. Think you can do this one by yourself?" Henry asked.

Henry turned from the window to see Frank sitting on the edge of the conference table. Henry wanted to know what the other survivors were up to if anything. There were many possibilities running through his head. He wanted a little light in this darkness. If these people were a threat he wanted to know before they showed up at the door steps.

"I want to know what they are doing. If they're a threat I need it dealt with before they find their way to us." Henry explained.

Frank nodded at Henry and stood up from the table. Henry knew what Frank was capable of. Henry had seen his resume and his military background. The man was a dye in the wool killer. He was glad Frank was on his side. Frank left the room without a word and was gone.

Henry felt the pain creep up his arm and clamped down on his teeth. It was going to be there for a while so he might as well get used to it. The weight of events and the stress of being the unvoiced leader was beginning to weigh on him.

Henry wanted a little guidance in all this. The nightmare he had about the angel had terrified him. He was trained to not be terrified. The zombies, if that's what he should call them, didn't scare him. Henry wasn't afraid of anything that could be killed. Henry was sure there were some forces in this that couldn't be destroyed. The way the angel had said it that surrender wasn't even an option. All it seemed to want was their deaths. Henry knew he couldn't lose hope but he hadn't exactly seen a whole lot to go with.

"That seems like a pretty deep train of thought." Sebastian exclaimed from the doorway.

Henry looked up at the well to do man with his ruined expensive clothes. The pale blue of his eyes seemed to go on forever. He watched as Sebastian grabbed a bottle of water and took a seat across from him. Henry looked at the man's face and saw no personality. The man's face was as blank as a fresh sheet of paper. If Sebastian was afraid it was nowhere to be seen. Sebastian twisted the cap off and took a drink of water. Henry watched as the man's gaze never left his own.

"Who are you really?" Henry asked Sebastian.

Henry watched as the dark haired man smiled. It wasn't one of those smiles that met the eyes. It was one of those cold smiles Henry was sure most villains would use on their prey. Henry felt his stomach go in a knot as the man continued to stare at him. He put his money on assassin. That was what he was.

"I'm no different than you officer Myers I assure you sir. I'm another old soldier without a flag to fight for anymore." Sebastian said

Henry had spent a lot of years learning to be able to tell if someone was lying. In his craft he had come to call it a blessing. As Henry watched the man take another drink of his water he knew he was telling the truth. So he was a military man as well. That was at least a piece of the puzzle.

"Then what brought you to Jacob's Ladder then? Was it to meet Pastor Clark like you said, or is there another reason?" Henry asked the man.

Sebastian reached in his pocket and pulled out a silver cigarette case. Henry only watched as the man took one of the cigarettes from the case and lit it. Smoke curled from Sebastian's lip as he continued to watch Henry. Henry was beginning to get unnerved by the man's constant staring.

"I came to your rather quaint town to indeed see Jimmy. Quite a good fellow that one is. I seemed to end up on the losing side of another fight that I didn't start." Sebastian said as he flicked his ashes.

Henry watched as the man took another large puff off his cigarette. Henry could sense there was an underlying point to that statement, but he didn't want to push that. Henry himself had been on the losing end of fights before. There were some wins that Henry counted as a loss because they had sacrificed too much for the win. There was a fine line between losing and winning in Henry's eyes.

"So what do you think is going to happen to us?" Henry asked the pale dark haired man.

Sebastian looked at him once more with cold grim eyes. The lack of emotion in them was rather startling. Henry had to look away after a second and glanced at the stitches in his arm. It was good suture work. Sebastian took his cigarette and snuffed it out on the glass of the conference table. Henry gaze traveled upwards as the Sebastian clasped his hands together.

"I know eventually these lights are going to go out one by one, and in the darkness they are going to panic. People will start dying like they always do. They are going to die unless we can keep them from that fate." Sebastian said in 'matter of fact' tone.

Henry let out a breath that he hadn't realized he was holding. The sad fact of it was he was already come to that realization. That was what the terrible weight he felt was; the knowledge that he wasn't going to be able to save them all.

Henry knew his first concern was his daughter but he knew these people. They were good people in this town, and his job was to protect them. It made no difference to him that social structures had broken down. The government had abandoned those of less notoriety. Henry would not leave them to the creatures in the dark.

"Well what do you think we should do?"

Henry watched as Sebastian leaned back in his chair and clasped his hands across his chest. He noticed that the quaint gentlemanly manner kind of melted off his face. There was something about this man that was not right. He could not see it as much as feel in in his bones. Sebastian was a wolf in sheep's clothing if he had ever seen one.

"These devils are only going to get worse old boy, Sebastian stated with a cold look. This is the only the first stage of this I assure you."

Henry leveled his gaze at the man's cold eyes. He couldn't see an ounce of fear on Sebastian's face. Henry had been around a lot of hard men in his years. Frank had been one of them. The boy had got lost in the bottle. Henry had watched him try and chase the demons away. All the bad men Henry had known in all his long years had shown wear from it. Henry didn't see that wear on this man. Sebastian seemed quite at peace with dancing with the devil.

"Who are you really?" Henry asked the man again.

Henry instantly wanted to take it back. That old knot he had forgot about for so long tightened up in his gut. That air around them seemed to grow cold as he saw the man smile. Those cold blue eyes seemed to twinkle with fire as Sebastian leaned forward in his seat. The smile seemed to grow to an unnatural width and it sent chills down Henry's spine.

"It's better the devil you know old friend." Sebastian said. "We should make preparations for what is to come. It will not be pretty but it will have to do."

Henry watched as the man stood up and made his way out of the room. Henry knew deep down the man was right. The man was probably more dangerous than any red eyed monster outside. Henry was still glad he was on their side because when the lights went out, they were gonna need people who weren't afraid of the dark.

Chapter 9: The burning man

Part 1

Frank looked through the eyepiece of the night vision scope at the group of men. He knew deep down they would be trouble. It had only took him an hour moving around town before he heard them. Automatic gun fire had a very distinctive sound once you heard it.

Frank recognized several familiar faces in the group. Local trouble makers with colorful backgrounds to say the least. So far they hadn't done anything too bad. The scream that cut through the night air had beckoned Frank to take another look. He felt a chill go down his spine.

Frank watched as one of the bulkier men dragged a female out of one of the low income housing apartments by her hair. The woman was putting up a pretty decent fight until the man hit her in face with the butt of his weapon. She sagged lifelessly to the ground. The man never missed a beat as he continued to drag her behind him.

Frank slid the bolt back on his rifle to make sure the weapon was loaded. He would have to be quick and precise if he was going to save the woman. Frank adjusted the distance on his scope and aimed it at the one dragging the woman behind him. When the scoped was zeroed on the large man's head Frank stopped.

"What the fuck?" Frank whispered to himself.

Frank could see deep discoloration on the mans face. He thought back to the store manager at the Shop and Save. The purple patches that had been all over her body. Frank had dismissed it as lividity at first. Yet now as he looked at it on the face of the living he could only think of one thing. If this reanimation was a plague like disease then it could be communicable as well. Which only decreased their chance of survival.

The woman's renewed screams snapped Frank from his thoughts. He focused on his scope recticle once more. Ray Malone, or Ray Ray to his biker brethren, was already tearing the woman's clothes off as the bulkier one watched. Frank scoped out the scene. His head count was three plus the girl.

Frank switched his cross hairs to bulky and sighted in on his heart. Frank took a small breath and held it as he squeezed the trigger. The concussion from the shell was deafening inside the small tool shed. His hand worked the bolt with remembered ease. Ray Ray was still trying to pull his pants up as Frank's next shot caught him in the neck. The arterial spray from dear Ray Ray caught man number three in the face on his way down.

The small Hispanic boy began firing his assault rifle in his direction. Frank worked the bolt again. The boy was in mid-turn to bolt for the truck door when the third shell caught him above the navel.

The Hispanic male left a smear on the truck bed as he hit and fell to the ground. The boy's death shrieks were gonna draw more attention than Frank wanted. He slung the rifle on his shoulder. He drew his 40 caliber pistol from his drop holster and eased the shed door open and scanned the dark. He saw several pairs of eyes making their way towards the noise the boy was making.

Frank made his way across the parking lot of the housing complex. The younger woman was still lying on the ground sobbing as he walked up. Frank leveled his pistol at the boy and pulled the trigger. The boy couldn't even be seventeen yet. The woman stared up at him in wide eyed horror. He had seen that face before. You wouldn't believe the violence some tribes in Africa would inflict on women. A lot of people had seen it in movies, but until you saw it with your own eyes, you couldn't fathom it. Frank reached down to offer the woman a hand up.

"Come on sweetheart," Frank said with the best smile he could force. "Let's get you back to the station and get you cleaned up."

The young woman reached up with a trembling hand and took his own. With little effort Frank had her on her feet. He removed his jacket and offered it to her. To give her some of her modesty back and began piling the attackers weapons on the truck. It would seem the would be pirates had managed to get a fair amount of supplies in their pillaging. "Waste not, want not" Frank thought as he climbed in the cab. The girl joined him, locking her own door once it was shut.

"My name is Frank. I am a deputy sheriff here in Jacob's Ladder. Don't believe I've seen you around," Frank tried.

He wasn't sure if she even could hear him. Shock worked differently from one person to the next. The only thing he could think of was to make her feel as comfortable as possible. He could see her shaking in the seat next to him. This incident would either make her or break her. Only time would tell.

"My name is Grace," the girl managed to squeeze out in a whisper. " I moved here two days ago."

Frank smiled for the first time since all this had happened. "Make her smile," he thought to himself as he cut down Jones Street. The roaming red eyed freaks were starting to multiply faster. Maybe they were attracted to the living. Was that why they kept coming? Frank slowed down to a stop beside his police cruiser.

"Okay Grace I'm gonna need you to be strong for me. " Frank started in a calm and reassuring tone. "I'm gonna get in my cruiser and your gonna follow me to the station okay. We're not gonna make any stops until we get there. You think you can do that for me?"

Grace shook her head yes in a solemn nod as Frank put the shifter in park. He surveyed their surroundings and slipped out the door to get in his cruiser. Things weren't as bad as he thought . Frank slipped the key into the ignition and pulled away from the curb. Grace fell in behind him as he cut down sixth avenue. Frank pulled a cigarette from the half crumpled pack and put it between his lips. The lighter was bright in the dark cab as the tip burned cherry red.

Frank had a half a second to react when the truck came out of the side alley and crashed into the front of his cruiser. Frank felt the impact down to his bones as he careened sideways into the **Simply Floral** flower shop. He caught a glimpse of Grace speeding by and the sound of automatic gun fire brought him to his senses. The window to his left exploded in a shower of glass. Frank had half a second to see the shadow beside him before everything went black.

Part 2

Felix's eyes locked with his wife's across the dinner table. He could almost taste her lipstick on his lips as she smiled over top her wine glass. She laughed that deep hearty laugh she always did. Felix smiled back at her. He felt the coolness of her hand as she laid it over top his. A familiarity to it he always longed for more than anything. Felix watched his wife's lips move. What did she say?

"You have to wake up honey," his wife said.

A loud ringing cut through the room. Felix watched as the wall paper he had hated in their home began to peel off the walls. The furniture began to shake violently. The wine glasses and their contents spilling across the floor. Felix reached for his wife's hand. In a flash of white light his wife was gone.

"Is he still alive?" A voice cut through the ringing in his ears, snapping him awake.

Felix opened his eyes to see Scarecrow standing over him checking his pulse. The sounds of gunshots echoed around them. The ringing in his ears was terrible. He reached up to touch his ears. Looking at his fingers he could tell why. Felix smeared the congealed blood between his fingers. His first though was his ear drums were busted. Felix raised up to his elbows and his vision swirled with black. He closed his eyes and tried to center himself.

"Welcome back to the world of the living." Scarecrow said as he pulled him up to a sitting position.

Felix glanced around at his surroundings. He felt bile start to creep up his throat. He was hurting everywhere that he still had feeling.

Scarecrow lifted him up and let his back rest on one of the parked cars. They must have made it to the parking garage. He couldn't make anything out from the dim lighting. The flash light Scarecrow was using to look around was bright. At least in comparison to the encompassing darkness.

Felix squinted as he tried to let his eyes adjust. He could see that Grifter ,the youngest, was badly hurt. Grifter's head was wrapped in a makeshift bandage that made him resemble a mummy from a 1930's movie. Felix could tell by the boy's facial expression he was in a lot of pain.

"Come on Jake you gotta pull it together man." Hades said in a hushed voice as he loaded the boys weapon for him. " Here you're locked and loaded."

Felix watched as the boy nodded and took the weapon. Even in the low light Felix could tell he couldn't grip it. Blood was finally starting to seep through Grifter's head wrap as he put his finger on the trigger. Felix could see the younger man's eyelids start to droop and the weapon sagged in his lap. Grifter wasn't going to make it.

Felix could tell the boy needed serious medical treatment from a skilled trauma team. His odds would still be slim. The gunshot beside him made him jump. The very sound set his ears to ringing again. He only heard the first one. After that it was all muzzle flashes casting eerie shadows on the abandoned cars.

"We're gonna have to find cover. We can't stay out in the open." Scarecrow said as he kicked the corpse he had shot down. "Fuckers are tough."

Felix's stomach turned once again as he looked down at the body lying a few feet from him. She would have been a decent looking woman before "this" happened. The half of her face that wasn't charred to a black flaky crisp was smooth. Except for the congealed blood smeared around her mouth. Her hair was long and dark. One of Felix's favorite qualities in a woman. Her rather perky breast protruding from her torn blouse would have even got the men looking. Now she was another one of the "claimed." Some spooky code name thought up by the media. He admitted it was catchy.

"Crow! Jake 's not breathing!" Hades exclaimed and started shaking the boy. "Come on Jake! Wake up! No one said it was quitting time!"

Felix could only watch as the man nicknamed after the God of death started to crack. He winced as Hades struck the boy hard to the face. It didn't even rouse the boy. Grifter was gone. Felix wanted to console the man. If only he still had his legs he would try and pull the man away. Some people got this way when they lost someone. The hysterics was commonplace in hospitals and funeral parlors. It was always painful to watch. No matter how many times you had seen it.

Felix jumped again as a gun shot rang out next to his head. Grifter's head exploded in a wash of blood and gore. Felix could only watch as the globs fell to the ground. Hades whirled around now, bits of blood and bone splashed across his face. Scarecrow stood to Felix's right. The proverbial gun still smoking in his hand.

"You know what was about to happen. You saw what Sandman did to him." Scarecrow said solemnly as he replaced the pistol in its holster on his chest.

He could only explain what he saw on Hades's face as pure rage. You could see it trickle across his face like magic. Felix came to the conclusion that Sandman had died and came back to attack Jake. That was easy to learn from the conversation. Yet he knew he still had a look of shock on his face because he realized his mouth was agape. Hades looked like he was coming around. Felix could hear his leather gloves crackling again.

"You don't know he would have been like that" Hades spat out as he stood up.

"You know as well as I do he would have." Scarecrow said calmly. He sounded almost robotic as he said it. One big hand going up to stroke his Rip Van Winkle beard.

Hades only shook his head as he began to strip his fallen brother of his ammunition and his weapons. They had lost a friend and a brother, but it was back to business. Felix felt remorse for the two men. What was a lifestyle to live that let you cut losses so easily. He closed his eyes as Hades took one last thing, a dog tag, with a quick tug.

Felix got that whole vision of a coffin with a folded flag and a crying widow. It had been all for him, and now that they were trapped here, it felt like for nothing.

"If we get to a roof we might be able to get a evac chopper." Hades said as he shouldered the extra rifle. "I wanna finish this."

Felix sensed a heaviness in the man's voice now. It had weight to it now. Like he wasn't sure if he could speak the words aloud. Felix lowered his head as a jolt of pain shot through his skull. He feared it might split his skull in two if it kept this up. Felix thought he had a concussion. He was sure it hurt. He knew that was true.

A feral scream echoed through the parking garage. His blood ran cold as he felt the hairs on the back of his neck stand up. The scream was met by another. This was had more of a baritone sound. It was obviously male. All around them Felix heard the screams matching each other. It reminded him a lot of how dogs would bark once they heard another dog bark. He felt very alone all the sudden. Even with the best the military had to provide on either side. Felix still felt terribly alone.

"Alright I'll carry him and you cover us." Hades said as he lifted Felix up and over his shoulder.

Felix felt the air whoosh out of him in a huff as he rested on the man's shoulder. Hades definitely had some muscle to him because he never even grunted. Felix knew his lower half was weak and feeble but he worked out at the gym 3 days a week. He took pride in his upper body. Hades waited a second to balance his weight and they were off.

Felix felt the man's shoulder grind into his stomach and it almost made him nauseous. The view wasn't much to look at. He could see Scarecrow' s feet in the occasional dash of light. Another feral scream echoed off the cold stone walls and it made him jump. This one was closer he thought as he tried hard not to throw up. The animal like howl sounded out again. This one with the bass to it sounded not to far away.

"We got company," Scarecrow said as his weapon sounded off in the usual machine gun fire sound.

The muzzle flash cast eerie shadows on the wall. Felix could hear what sounded like dozens of people running towards them and his heart sank in his chest. "We're never gonna make it," he thought to himself. Felix felt another sharp pain as Hades shifted his weight again to better balance the load. Another burst of gunfire echoed around them as Hades reached for something. The familiar sound of a door handle turned, shook, then turned again let Felix know they had made it to the door.

"It's fucking locked. You got to be fucking shitting me!" Hades exclaimed with an obvious hint of disdain.

Hades shifted Felix around again and put his weight into it. Felix heard the metal groan but he could tell the door and lock were sturdy. The weary soldier gave the door and exasperated retort from his fist. Felix felt Hades' shoulders slump in exasperation.

"Only way we're getting through this is to break the lock." Hades stated.

Felix could hear the desperation in the man's voice even if it wasn't clear. The thought of the breaking the lock made Felix very on edge. there would be no escape if the trio couldn't at least slow the reanimated. They would keep coming until their ammo was spent and that would be the end of it. Felix tried to maneuver so he could see around the man's bulky arms and at the door itself. A single gunshot cut through the silence that had been building between the men. The sound of the bullet hitting metal compounded with the closeness of it gave Felix a start.

"Only easy day was yesterday, " Scarecrow stated bluntly " only way is forward, there's no going back. Well get a few floors up and we can frag the fucking hole."

Felix felt his spirit renew at the thought of a new found game plan. It was brash and primitive, but the results would speak for themselves if they survived. Felix's head swam with the turn as Hades put his shoulder and weight into it this time. The metal door gave a brief creak and a groan and the pieces of the lock came crashing down to the floor. Two shots sounded off beside them followed by a swallowed scream.

Felix managed to twist enough to see in the dark gaping hole of the door frame. Through the dim lighting of the emergency lights he could see the carnage. It was scattered across the floor and stairs. Felix felt the knot raise up in his throat at the sight. The pile of mismatched limbs and gore smeared walls was enough to have stopped anyone.

"Holy fucking shit," Hades managed to get out in a whisper.

Felix could sense the weight of those three words by the sound of them. From his limited view point Felix could see it had been a bloodbath. These poor souls had tried to make a break for their vehicles and it was like lambs to the slaughter. He surmised the power failure had disabled the key lock. When the people had reached the bottom it was the end of the line. There had been no hope and no way out for these people and the dead had fell on them like hungry wolves.

"Stay frosty and let's move buddy," Scarecrow said in a reassuring voice. "There's nothing we can do for them now."

Felix groaned as Hades composure hardened underneath him. He felt the man's shoulders straighten as he readjusted his grip on Felix. He knew the soldier was trying to square himself away. He could only half see what Hades could and it made his skin crawl.

What they had been through in the last couple of hours had been enough to break most people. Felix knew that his spirit had been broken. He had no hope to survive this night. Even if they did manage to make it through today what would they do about tomorrow, or the day after that? This is a full scale extinction event.

Felix didn't believe man was meant to survive something like this. This was the rapture. This was Ragnarok. Those that survived couldn't hope to survive forever. Eventually mistakes would be made and lives would be lost. That would only add to the enemies numbers until there was nowhere to run and nowhere to hide.

" Alright let's get the fuck out of here," Hades said as he stepped over a severed arm and onto the first flight of stairs.

A loud burst of automatic gunfire almost made Felix jump off the man's shoulders. The second burst made Felix turn his attention from the front to the back. He could almost feel his heart stop at the sight. The rushing wave of black shapes with burning red eyes emerged into the faint light. Felix couldn't even start to count their number. It was too many to fight he knew that. In fast succession mindless shambling turned into full run. As another burst of gunfire cut down a few of their number.

" Up the stairs now!" Scarecrow shouted as his rifle sounded off again and again.

Felix felt the Hades's shoulder grind into his rib cage as they started up the steps. Hades huffed and he puffed but moved with fluid grace up the first two flights. Felix could watch through the jostling as Scarecrow stood his ground. Hades didn't waste the opportunity as they climbed higher.

The gunfire was deafening in the narrow enclosed space of the stairwell. With each burst of the rifle his eardrums felt like they would swell and rupture with the force of it. Felix had only a brief glimpse of the man who was aiding in their escape turn to run.

With a deafening **BOOM** the stairwell walls shook. The air pressure around them swelled and, like a giant heated hand, clasp down on them. The force of the explosion sent Hades careening into a wall. The force of the impact took all the wind from Felix and he tried to learn to breathe again. The dust and smoke he breathed in hungry gasps made him choke and cough even more.

Felix tried to squint through the cloud to see Scarecrow. There was so much soot and dust he couldn't make out anything more than a flight below them.

"Sound off if you're still with me brother," Hades shouted out into the gloom around them.

Felix strained his ears but the overwhelming ringing was all he could make out. He resorted to using his eyes instead and searched through the choking fog around them. The smell of burning flesh crept up around them and Felix almost gagged.

He waited to see the rushing forms come screaming up the stairs but there was nothing. Just dust hanging in the air. Felix's eyes began to water and he tried to blink it away as a form emerged into view. Scarecrow's blackened face had a smile on it. The magazine from his gun ejected out and he replaced it with another.

"You crazy mother fucker. " Hades managed to get out without much astonishment.

Felix could only guess that this wasn't the first time the man had survived something like this. It amazed him if no one else. The man's singed beard and face seemed the worse of his wear as Hades started up the next flight of steps. Felix felt a little hope rise in him as a feral scream erupted through the silence around them. Felix watched as Scarecrow's gaze drifted upwards to the origin of the sound. That little flame of hope he had stamped out as another scream sounded out. The definitive feminine sound set it apart from the first scream, which meant all too well that they still were not alone.

"Out of the pan." Scarecrow grumbled as he stepped around them to take point.

The bright flash of the soldier's tactical light cut through the smoke. They started upward once more.

Part 3

Jimmy Clark sat on the edge of Jacob's Ladder police department roof watching the night. He felt this darkness had an infinite weight to it. One that seemed to drag down your soul. He sensed the man before he heard him. He thought it was weird that he could feel someone like that.

"Are you the devil, Sebastian?" Jimmy asked without hesitation.

Jimmy had lost all care for civility at this point. The odds were definitely stacked against them. There was no longer a fear of death. Death would be coming for them all sooner than later. He might as well get his questions answered. Jimmy heard the strike of the man's lighter as Sebastian chuckled. The man thought Jimmy's question a jest, but he was serious as he could be.

"Do you want a lie or do you want the truth?" Sebastian called out from behind him.

Jimmy felt his heart sink a little bit with the realization. This man was the Lord of lies. The most evil thing ever mentioned in Bible. If he was on this plane then that meant the end was upon them. Jimmy felt hot tears begin to well up in his eyes and streak down his face.

He had never thought in his many years of trying to save people he would be the one in need of saving. Jimmy felt the man's hand clamp on his shoulder and give a reassuring squeeze. Jimmy sobbed and felt the tears begin to come faster. He had always been a faithful servant. He didn't understand why he was being tested this way. He had only lived to serve ever since he had heard the calling. Yet now in the darkest hour he only felt alone.

"You are not alone old friend." Sebastian said aloud. "Some of the hardest tests are reserved for the strongest believers"

Jimmy felt those words down to his soul. The fact that the prince of darkness was the one telling him this was disturbing as it was comforting. Jimmy reached up and wiped the tears from his eyes.

He had been a hard man all his life. Had his faith and desire to serve a higher purpose push his son away. He was not gonna let the apocalypse be the turning point. Maybe Sebastian was right. If he was still here then it was for a purpose. He was meant to show spirituality to these lost and hopeless people.

"Thank you for that......" Jimmy trailed off. "What would you like me to call you?" he asked.

Jimmy was not sure if the web he had spun was the truth. If what he said was true then all the the stories were not true. Then again that could be what he wanted you to believe. Jimmy heard the man let out a sigh as he walked around and took a seat beside him. He watched as the end of the man's cigarette burned bright, and the ebbing black sweep back in. The security light on the roof was the only thing shining anything in the darkness.

" You may call me Lucifer, Morning star, or Devil if you prefer." Sebastian started. "But since we are friends you can call me Sebastian. I do not care much for the old names. I have went by Sebastian for longer than you can know."

Jimmy thought he sensed a bit or tiredness in the man's voice. He couldn't begin to fathom his age. He didn't even dare try. In truth like any gossip, the stories he had read were not good. He wondered if the man was reading his thoughts. The chuckle that came from him in a puff of smoke let him know he was.

"Alright Sebastian." Jimmy said as he cleared his throat. "If you are indeed the devil. Why do you choose to help us? Shouldn't you be offering us deals for salvation? Why save Henry if these are in fact machinations from the realm where you are king?"

Sebastian took another drag from his cigarette. Jimmy watched him as he let the white stick dangle from his bottom lip like some old school movie star. The ones from back in the day when smoking was still hip in movies and television. Sebastian reached up and took the cigarette from his mouth. He flicked it off over the edge. Jimmy watched as the cherry end spun out of sight and into the black.

"I can make you a deal if you want." Sebastian said coldly. "I don't think you would take it."

Jimmy felt the bite to the man's words. Yet he was right. No matter what came out of that black he had a good idea where he was going. He didn't need salvation because he had received it years ago.

"These are no machinations of mine." Sebastian started. "I am no master of the void, or what your kind call hell. There is no lake of fire. No burning torments or little demons with pitchforks. Hell is what you see here. A cold and empty black where no light ever shines. You see in the beginning God, or what you call him by was a in every aspect a supreme entity of unbelievable power. Yet, as for every aspect in this world he had an opposite. The dragon, or beast, as he is referred to in Revelations. When God brought life and light to this black, he struck a chord with his twin."

Jimmy was drawn back from the man's words. He wasn't sure if he could believe the man. Yet he wanted to hear his side of the story. The Bible painted a different picture. Yet it doesn't mean it was the whole picture.

Sebastian let out of scoff of acknowledgement as he pulled another cigarette from his case. He gave it a tap on the container. The man placed the pale stick between his lips. Jimmy watched in awe as the tip burst into flame on its own. He could tell this man had immense power at his control. It scared him a little, but he knew it had a point.

"God........was not a fighter." Sebastian said as if trying to find words. "He created five angels to fight for him. I was the first, then Micheal, Gabriel, Raphael, and Uriel. In each one of us he bestowed a bit of his power. The same power from the creation. So that we may wage war against the dragon to save this world. You could call us elementals. We can control a key element as master. The Greeks and Romans worshiped us as gods ourselves. I control fire, Micheal light, Gabriel the air , Raphael electricity, and Uriel water."

Jimmy hung to the man's words as he paused to puff on his cigarette. He knew that religion had been adapted to each assimilated religion since its start. A lot of the aspects people followed were in fact adaptations of other cultures. It made assimilation easier. If you thought part of your beliefs and customs connected then you were more than likely an easy convert.

Jimmy thought back to the woman's tale of the warrior angel and the lightning. That had to be Raphael. Jimmy could see the smile spread on the man's face from the faint glow of his cigarette. The man nodded as if to agree with him and continued.

" We waged war against the dragon." Sebastian stated with a hint of pain. " For a lifetime it seemed, or at least a mortal lifetime. One by one our rank fell until it was but Micheal and myself left standing. With one last push we defeated him and locked him in the void.

Micheal, Raphael, and myself were able to heal our wounds. Gabriel was destroyed in the fight. Uriel survived but the battle had scarred him. We had been brother's, but the damage to poor Uriel and the loss of Gabriel changed Micheal. I think in the battle he had become tainted by the dragon."

Jimmy was trying to take in the words when he spotted two sets of headlights coming in their direction. He strained his eyes against the darkness. Trying to make out what kind of vehicle it was. Yet there was no way to see anything in this pitch black.

Sebastian seemed to follow his gaze to the approaching lights as well. Jimmy watched as the man brow furrowed and his cool blue eyes narrowed to slits. He let out a sharp breath as another set of lights could be seen approaching towards the path of the other two. At their current rate of speed it would be a collision.

That was exactly what number three was aiming. Time seemed to slow for Jimmy as the first car, oblivious to the third, was smashed in the side. It was sent careening into a store front. The second vehicle swerved around vehicle one, and three. It continued towards the Jacob's Ladder police department.

"I must intervene or all this would have been for nothing," Sebastian stated and he was gone over the side.

Jimmy looked over the edge and searched the darkness for Sebastian but he was nowhere to be seen. Jimmy sprang to his feet and started for the roof access. Something was coming their way. Was it survivors,or the military, or even emergency response? Jimmy knew he needed to at least warn the others. As terrible as their circumstances were. Was Sebastian right and it was trouble? He hoped he wasn't too late.

Part 4

Frank Pearson opened his eyes to the barely lit room. His head felt like it was four sizes bigger than it should be. The piercing pain that spread through his skull every time he blinked let him know that he had a concussion. It wasn't the first time he had felt that kind of pain.

Frank had been too close to a grenade in Baghdad once. The explosion had propelled him out a second story window. Luckily the combat helmet he had been wearing had took most of the blow when he had landed.

Frank's eyes adjusted to the dim light of his surroundings. He knew he was in a bad spot. The large man on the other side of the room wearing the blood soaked apron was a good sign of that. The man worked the large butcher's knife back and forth on the sharpening steel he held in his off hand. The sound of the blade going back and forth made that cold rock sink low in his stomach.

Frank wasn't scared of death. Hell he wasn't even scared of torture. He had been tortured before. It had been part of his training. His eyes began to search around him for something to use to free himself. Frank tried to flex his arms but the cable ties that had his hand strapped to the chair were well placed.

"You know me and Ray Ray worked at the Mill Brook Slaughter House since we were fifteen years old." The bloody apron man said as he stabbed the knife in the wooden bench he was standing in front of him.

Frank directed his sight towards the man as he lifted a large cleaver and began to eyeball the blade edge. Frank looked at surgical tray to his left. The surgical scalpel still had hunks of gore and hair smeared on its handle. That is what he needed. The question that presented itself was how was he gonna get to it?

Frank looked back at the man who was now trying to sharpen the blade of his cleaver. In the dim light of the man's lantern Frank could see the purple blotches on his skin. This absent member of Ray Ray's gang had the same sickness as the large man from earlier.

"As bad as old Ray could get, and it was bad sometimes," the man said in a cold absent tone. "He was always there for me. Even more than my old man ever was"

Frank twisted his arm as hard as he could. The cable tie gave a little as it cut into his arm. He felt the hot blood rolling down his arm as he twisted again. The tie gave a little more. The pain shooting up his arm made his head feel like it was going to come apart.

Frank cursed himself as he twisted again. "Should have made sure they were all dead," he told himself. Always make sure they were all dead. Frank knew he got careless because of the girl.

"Going somewhere Frankie?" a voice slithered out of the dark.

Frank looked up at the man. He had retrieved another knife and was sharpening it as well. His eyes searched the dim recessed of the room for its source. Sue Foster hung from a meat hook in one of the dark recesses to his left. The white bone sticking out where her left hand was made Frank grind his teeth hard. This man was a killer. One of those sickos you would see on cable television. "Should have made sure they were all dead," Frank told himself again. He twisted his arm again; harder this time. The cable tie finally gave enough for him to pull his hand out. Frank grabbed for the scalpel.

"Uh oh Frankie." the voice called again as a knife stabbed through his hand and pinned it to the tray.

Frank screamed as he turned to look at his attacker. The large man's face was only a foot from his own. The stink of the man's breath made him draw back as the the man twisted the blade. The pain was unimaginable as Frank drove his head forward and connected hard with the man's face. The man let out a scream of his own and stumbled backwards.

Frank knew this was go time. That's how First Sergeant had always described it to him. "The moment will come son when its either go or die. Don't worry you will know when," Sergeant had told him.

With all the strength he had he jerked hard with his left hand. The surge of adrenaline was what he needed as his other hand broke free. Frank glanced at the man, whose face was bleeding, and reached for the knife in his hand.

"I can help Frankie." the voice called again. *"Just have to ask."*

Frank disregarded the sound and jerked at the knife. Every time he touched the blade it made him want to throw up . Frank looked back to see the man's face. The pure rage that trickled across his face was unquestionable.

"You're gonna pay for that." the man said in a murderous calm voice.

Frank knew he meant those words. The man let out a feral scream as he lunged for him. Frank jerked hard on the handle of the knife and it came free. He felt the bile creep up his throat as his eyes narrowed in the" about to pass out" sort of way. The room began to swim as Frank tried to adjust the angle of the blade. He was only going to get one shot at this.

" Tick tock tick tock Frankie." the voice called again. *" All you have to do is say yes."*

Frank saw the look in the man's eyes as he tucked his own elbow to his side. The training had taken over and he was in auto pilot now. The man's fingers were almost around his throat when he stuck the large butcher knife into the man's liver. The man never faltered. Those thick blood stained fingers wrapped around his throat and began to squeeze.

Frank twisted the knife to the left and right. At least if he died here the man wouldn't be that far behind him. He jerked the knife free and stuck it through the man's neck. The man gurgled and Frank felt his grip on his throat lessen. He put all the strength he had left in his free hand and struck the man hard in the solar plexus.

" Oh Frankie you shouldn't have." the voice cooed.

Frank struck the man one last time and the man stumbled backwards. The black blood welling up around the blade and down the man's chest was satisfying. The shock was beginning to set in as the large man sunk to his knees.

Frank tried to clear his head and focus. He needed to get out of these restraints before anyone else happened along. He wished he would have remembered to pull the knife back out before the man had stepped out of reach. Frank untied the rest of his bonds and tried to stand. The whole room spun with bright dots as he fell backwards in the chair.

"Fuck off," he whispered to no one but himself.

Frank had no idea where he was or how many others there might be. He knew that if he didn't get to his feet the shock would kill him. He wasn't gonna die on his ass that was for sure. Frank pushed everything he had into his legs.

"On your feet soldier," Frank reassured himself.

The rustling in front of him made him fall back into the chair again . His large butcher attacker who a few seconds ago had been most certainly dead, sat read eyed and smiling at him.

"Too late now Frankie." The large man said with a chuckle.

Frank hadn't felt fear for a very long time. He spent his first few months in combat consumed by fear. So much that fear had been drained and replaced with nothing. An empty feeling that most people could never get rid of. A lot of soldiers were consumed by it. Now staring at the huge man with the red eyes pulling the large butcher knife from his throat. Frank was afraid once more. Yet it was a secondary emotion, a motor reflex. He could feel the scalpel between his fingers already. The training always kicked in when it needed to.

"Let's find out fuck face" Frank spat as he moved back to a standing position.

The large reanimated man continued to laugh as it stood backup in one fluid motion. It was unnerving to see someone move like that. It was a good thing he didn't need nerves anymore. Frank took a step forwards as the large man flipped the knife over in his hand.

This was a big guy Frank summed. The fluid grace he used to raise to his feet without his hand was a sure sign not to underestimate speed. Frank took another step towards the butcher man. The first thing he had to do was disable him. So first thing was to go for the major tendons.

Frank stopped cold when he saw another set of red eyes open to the left of the butcher. Then another pair opened on the right. One by one every dark corner of the room filled up with them. Frank gripped the gore stained handle of the scalpel hard.

" So which one of you first?" Frank asked as he pointed the scalpel towards the back corner. "You?" he asked again pointing at the butcher. "Or you maybe!?!" he shouted pointing to another pair to the left of the large man.

Frank waited for them to come at him. He imagined it would be all over quickly. Yet he swore that he would take as many of them with him as he could. Frank felt it before he saw it. The air seemed to grow thick and stagnant. The temperature around them seemed to be increasing.

Frank felt the singe on his face as if he was standing too close to a campfire. He heard what he thought was a clap of thunder and then the roof seemed to explode inward towards him. Frank raised his arm to shield himself as he fell backwards into the chair. He peered through the dust and soot. Sebastian stood before him. He could tell it was him by his black hair and blood stained suit.

<u>"This one is mine."</u> Sebastian's voice seemed to shake the very walls around them.

Frank heard a growl reverberate around them as the amassed eyes took a step forward. He could feel the temperature around them seem to rise still. The first bead of sweat began to streak down his face. It started with a crackle like the breaking of underbrush.

Frank could only watch as Sebastian lifted his pale hands towards the sky. Then one pop and another. He could only draw in a breath as fire erupted to his left and spread around them in a circle. It was like a wind was drawing it as the flame began to race around them in a growing wave. Frank heard words coming out of Sebastian's mouth but he could not place the dialect.

" You cannot help them now arch." the crowd said in unison. *"The dragon is coming."*

Frank thought he would die from the heat. He felt his eyes begin to water and burn as he lifted his arm to shield his face. The explosion ,when it came, was deafening. The air was so hot that Frank could no longer breathe. All around them the fire seemed to clamp down as if to squash them into the ground.

Frank moved his arm away from his face to see and it shook

him. In a circle for fifty feet there was nothing. Like a small nuke had carved a circle of emptiness into Jacobs Ladder. The scorched earth around them blackened and still steaming. Frank knew that his mouth was agape. He watched as Sebastian turned towards him. The man's eyes were solid blue as hot flame. He wanted to ask questions, but they alluded him. Frank could only stare at the man's face.

"Let us go." Sebastian said and reached to help him up.

Part 5

Felix Cherry stood and watched the two military elite men guarding him argue. Their whispered argument would have been made a hit on the internet; if it would have been under any other circumstances.

Yet, that was not the case at the moment. Felix had seen many well to do couples argue the same way before in public. Both men would have been red in the face if you could actually see their faces. The soot and and the smoke hid all skin color.

"I say we carry on." Scarecrow said as he pointed into the dark doorway. " There has to be another stairwell that is passable."

Felix watched as Hades milled the thought in his head and dismissed it. The man only shook his head no and continued to stare up the stairwell. Felix knew that way was a loss. They had already tried that route. Someone had tried to make a barricade by tossing chairs and desks down the stairs.

Scarecrow had only made it up halfway when he had double back. That route would take forever and it would leave them too bogged down if they needed to move fast. Felix was under the impression the man was not keen on a fire fight. At least not one in the stairwell anyways.

"I don't like it." Hades said. " But at this point we are out of options. "

Felix watched from his propped position against the stairwell wall. Both men reached in the packs and retrieved a long black cylinder. In what looked like a practiced movement they began screwing it into the end of their rifle. Felix could only surmise the were suppressors.

He had seen enough war movies to know that. At least the two men still had their act together. Being extra quiet would be the safest route. The less noise they made meant the less attention drawn to them. The dead were everywhere now. They had seen several on their trek to the roof. They would wander around their former cubicles. Trying to find the semblance of their lives in the ruins.

"Alright we do this quick and clean. " Scarecrow said with confidence. "I'll take point."

Felix swallowed hard as Hades picked him up with one swift movement. He was positioned in a fireman carry position. He was not happy with his limited field of sight but it was better than his other options.

Felix knew he had sustained several injuries. The parts of his body in which he still had feeling let him know that. He still had hope deep down that this was a bad dream. That any minute he would wake up at home in bed covered in sweat and this would all be over. Yet hope had been one of the few luxuries this new world did not offer. Felix heard the stairwell door open and into the black they went.

" Mother Mary......." Hades whispered and Felix felt the man inhale beneath him.

The smell hit him before his eyes had adjusted enough to see. The smell of urine and feces was so strong Felix almost gagged. He twisted on the large man's shoulder enough to see around him. What Felix saw in the dim light was almost more than he could grasp. The bodies were strewn in random awkward angles. Most them had looked like they had been torn limb from limb.

The rather large man that blocked their path ahead stood in a mass of entrails and blood. The large fire ax in his hands gleamed in the low light as he sunk the blade into another one of the corpses. The sickening thud it made as it buried deep made Felix have to swallow hard.

He was not gonna throw up he told himself as the man pulled the blade free with a jerk. Felix watched as Scarecrow took a step forward. The barrel of his rifle aimed at the man as he gave another swing. The cracking of bone was loud. He felt the horror begin to sink in as the man lifted the severed arm in his hand.

"United States Navy Sir!" Scarecrow said with an authoritative tone. " Put the ax on the ground and put your hands on your head."

Felix watched as the man froze for a second. He could tell the man was not one of the undead because his eyes were not glowing. The carnage that surrounded the man definitely said he was a threat.

Felix could tell the man was gathering what to do as he turned his head to glare at Scarecrow. The man's gaze traveled from Scarecrow to Hades and back to Scarecrow.

"I have to chop them up before they come back." the ax man as he raised the ax and swung it again.

The single shot from Scarecrow's rifle made a hiss as it hit the wall to the man's left. Chunks of plaster shot out and bounced off the large man's blue mechanic coveralls. The ax man spun around. Felix could now see the red patch on the man's chest. Steve it said in white letters emblazoned in red.

The look in the man's eyes made Hades tense up under Felix. Steve the ax man's eyes had that feral almost savage look to them. As if in all this carnage Steve's very mind had snapped. Felix could almost hear the man's grip tighten on the ax. The man definitely had murder in his eyes now. A kind of rage that could not be sated.

"There is no more rank and file boy!" Steve spat out. "There is no more government! It's us and them now!"

Steve's hysterics struck home for Felix. He knew the man was right. Whatever this pandemic was, it had shook the system down to its core. The government had tried to cover all contingencies. They had sent their best special forces to round up the elite doctors and epidemiologist. They had even launched missiles at their own capital.

This had all become a battle of damage control. Kill as many as you could and fall back to safety. Felix knew this man was a janitor or building maintenance. In the moment, the man had evolved into something he was not in order to survive. He was standing off with men that killed professionally. That little nit of survival he had embraced was drilled into these two men a long time ago.

"Put the weapon on the deck or I will put it down for you," Scarecrow stated in a robotic tone.

The man's savage face seem to melt away and replaced with a calm serenity. Steve the ax man was either having a moment of clarity or he was about to attack. The fact that the events had already caused the complete break down of human civility hurt Felix.

How were they supposed to survive this if the human race had crumbled so already? Humanity had survived the eons on their savagery, yes. Yet acts of compassion and kindness had also been one of the pinnacles of their survival. If they no longer cared about human life then they were no different than the red eyed monsters.

"Steve is it....," Felix cut through the tension. " Do as these men say and we can all get out of here together."

Steve leveled his gaze in Felix's direction. He could tell the man was milling the thought over in his head. His eyes would drift from Scarecrow to Hades. The man crouched towards the ground and placed the ax on the floor.

The man's large hands flexed and released as he stood back up. Steve the ax man seemed to tremble from Felix's obscured view from the back of the soldier. As if seeing other humans might have caused the shock to wear off a little. Scarecrow never lowered his rifle as the large man began to shake more visibly. The piercing scream that came from the stairwell behind them made Hades and Felix both jump.

"Stairs move now!" Scarecrow yelled as they all scrambled down the hallway.

Steve the ax man reached down and retrieved his ax. Felix heard no protest as Hades lurched forward in a slow jog. He turned around from his upside down perch and looked back. That brief second the stairwell entrance was empty lasted what seemed like forever.

The first one through the door tripped and crashed into the cubicle wall with a loud bang. One by one they came through the door in a wave. The silencer did keep the gunshot from sounding through the whole building. Yet the screams from the returned were loud enough that it didn't matter.

Felix watched as Scarecrow dropped his rifle, letting the sling catch the weapon as it fell. With fluid grace he retrieved his pistol from its holster.

"I need to reload!" Scarecrow screamed out.

The non-silenced pistol sounded out into the darkness its defiant **BOOM BOOM BOOM**. Steve started forward towards the damned. The long red fire ax dragging on the floor behind him.

Felix could only surmise by all the bodies in dismembered shambles around him. Steve had been here before. The large man never faltered or turned away in fear as the pistol mag shot out the bottom of Scarecrow's pistol.

With one quick movement the fire ax went from the floor through the air. Felix watched as it connected with the blonde woman's neck and sent her head flying off into the darkness. Like a bladed hurricane Steve waded into the mob that had come through the door.

Scarecrow had reloaded his pistol and was now reloading his rifle. Steve showed no mercy and no quarter. His large hand reached out and grabbed a small wiry man. The man's head looked small compared to the large man's hands. With one swift movement he smashed the creatures head into the wall. The second smash sent the brains exploding all over the wall.

"Move, move, move!" Scarecrow screamed as he began shooting around Steve.

Felix felt a sharp pain shoot through his head as Hades hurdled an overturned desk. He watched as ax man Steve ducked and turned to run. The shells from Scarecrow's weapon clattered along the floor. More dead piled through the door. Felix wished he could fight.

He so wanted to help them. These men could have left him for dead. They would have made it to safety by now if they hadn't been carrying him the whole way. He was only slowing them down. Yet they had been sent on a mission.

Ax man Steve slipped on some gore and stumbled. Scarecrow reached down with his free hand and drug Steve to his feet. The man never faltered in his resolve.

" Crow! Stairs!" Hades shouted out to the other two men.

Felix watched as the whole room spun as Hades turned to join the fight. He scrambled to get a view of what was going on. The damned continued to scramble through the door. The two men assumed a duck and run position as Hades's weapon reached out and laid waste to the enemy.

Felix only half saw the object that Scarecrow had in his hand. He had a good idea what it was though as the man threw the round object towards the door.

"Get down!" Scarecrow screamed as he dove towards the ground.

Steve the ax man hurdled over the desk as the explosion cut through the hallway. Hades ducked down behind the desk. The rushing heat and concussive force crashed into them with little mercy. Felix tried hard to breathe and get his senses back as the ringing once again resumed in his ears.

He twisted and tried to get a better look as Hades rose to a standing position. Felix squinted through the dust and debris hanging in the air. Steve the ax man stood up and gripped his ax. His body stood rigid against the light from the flames. His pose resembled that of a major league baseball player.

"Jessup?" Hades's questioned the fog.

Scarecrow form emerged from the smoke with the same cocky grin on his face. The screaming form that emerged from the fog and tackled him from behind made Felix's heart jump. Steve the axe man was already moving forward when Hades leveled his rifle.

Felix could only draw back at the savagery as the male pommeled Scarecrow's back like a primate. The combat veteran desperately tried to roll over so he could get free. Steve scrambled to clear the expanse. The red eyed monster only hissed as it seized the back of Scarecrow's helmet and smashed his face in the floor.

Felix felt his heart sink as the blade of the ax sunk deep in the chest of the red eyed male. Both Steve and the reanimated man disappeared into the smoke.

"Jessup get up buddy! We gotta move!" Hades shouted.

Felix heard the first taint of fear in the man's voice as he started over the desk towards his fallen comrade. Felix swung back and forth and lost his ability to see what was going on. He tried to adjust himself so he could see.

Felix listened as he heard Steve go to work on the man in the smoke. The sound of the ax sinking into flesh had appalled him at first. Now he felt a sense of satisfaction at the sound. It was like the sound of justice to him with each sickening thud. Felix swerved around enough so he see Scarecrow's form start to move.

"You okay buddy?" Hades asked his fallen brother.

Scarecrow reached out with both of his arms in a push up position. Slowly he pushed his upper body off the ground. The cough the man let out sent blood splattering the floor. Felix knew that creature had broken several of his ribs. Now looking at the mans face and the blood rushing down his beard he bet the man had been hurt a lot more than that.

Felix watched at Hades leveled the rifle at his friend. They had still not seen his eyes. There was no sure way of knowing if Scarecrow, or Jessup to his friends, was even still in there.

"Fucker broke my damn rib," Scarecrow managed to squeeze out.

Felix felt an overwhelming burst of joy spread through him as the man coughed again. The fine red mist that came out worried Felix from a medical view point. Yet the man still lived. That was what mattered.

Scarecrow made his way to his feet. The magazine from his rifle sounded through the hallway as it ejected. That hollow rattle sound of an empty can kicked across the floor. It was loud in the new silence of the hallway.

"Steve?" Felix called out into the smoke.

Felix wasn't sure why he cared about the ax wielding madman they had met. Maybe it was the way he had rushed in to save a man he didn't know. Was it the fact he was the only human they had seen since this had all went bad? Felix tried to see around the soldier and into the smoke.

The grenade had sealed up the doorway and had bought them a breather. Which he thought was definitely a good thing. Hades leveled his rifle towards the smoke and motioned for Scarecrow to move forward.

"Steve?" Felix asked again barely above a whisper.

Steve's form walked out of the smoke. The front of his coveralls had been ripped open. The scratch marks across his chest still had fresh blood seeping from them in streaks. The look on the man's face held an animal like rage to it. The man's eyes were his own but his brow was furrowed in a concerned way.

Felix's gaze drifted to the ax that he still held him his right hand. The veins in Steve's arm bulged and the grip he had on the handle had turned his knuckles white. The man didn't say a word as he stepped past them. Felix was glad they both had survived that fray, but it had been close. Too damn close.

"Let's get the fuck out of here" Scarecrow said with some effort as he stepped past them.

Part 6

Abigale Myers sat and watched as her father paced the floor. She was worried about the injuries her father had sustained. He looked like a mountain about to explode at the moment. Abigale watched as the heated exchange, between Jimmy and her father,continued on. "What exactly is he telling you?" she wondered to herself. As the thought entered her head Henry turned and started forward towards the door.

"You're in no shape to go out there by yourself Henry," Pastor Clark called after him.

Her father stopped in his tracks. Abigale watched as he clenched and unclenched his fists several times. The big vein that ran across his forehead was standing out now. She knew he father was fuming at this point. Something must have been wrong with Frank. Abigale watched as her father turned and faced the pastor again. She watched as the mix of emotions that were on his face faded away to cold blank stone. That was his warrior's face.

Abigale recalled the time she had broken her arm as a little girl. She had been brave when it came to the swing set her father had built her. Every time she would climb those steps by herself at her mother's protest. Yet her father would say she's gonna have to learn it eventually.

One day she had slipped climbing those steps. Her father had ran to her. She could see the concern on his face. Yet as he had scooped her up in his arms and he realized she was looking at him it had all vanished. The warrior face was there; stoic and stern as ever.

"If you think I'm gonna sit here and do nothing then you are mistaken." Henry spat at the pastor.

Abigale could feel the sting in those words. She could understand her father was frustrated. Hell she was frustrated herself. The current state of events seemed to have everyone out of sorts. The atmosphere here was already dry and all the needed was a catalyst and it would all burn out of control.

" Daddy listen to him." Abigale stated barely above a whisper.

She watched as both men turned to look at her at the same time. Abigale knew they both had good intentions, but the road to hell was paved with them. If something happened to Frank. IF. Then what could they do anyways? Stage some rescue attempt against these God awful things? That would only cause more danger to those left.

It was a sad thought to have. One she never thought she would have herself. Yet at this point they needed to think about survival. Frank was a warrior and they might need warriors right now. Yet, if they had gotten him then what chance did they have? Abigale tried to calm the sea of thoughts that were raging in her head.

"Baby I know you're worried but…" Henry started to say.

Abigale raised her hand. He of all people knew that he was the only one she had left. She wasn't about to sit by and let him throw his life away on a fool's errand. She rose from her seat on at the desk and started towards the two. She didn't know the whole story, but she knew what was outside. A darkness that wasn't going away and it had rows of teeth. Their had been stories of angels falling from the sky. Now one of their own had gone missing. That was enough for her.

"You're not going out there and that's the end of it." she said with an almost angry growl.

Abigale saw it for a second. That faint flicker of hurt that passed over her father's face. It was gone so quick you wouldn't have noticed it if you weren't looking close enough. She had seen it many times throughout her childhood.

Every time he would end up with a fight with her mother. He would stand there and try and state his point. Her mother was a kind soul but once she felt like she was on the losing side of the argument the claws would come out. You would have to look close to see it. Her parent wouldn't argue if they thought she was around or could hear but she saw enough.

"What's going on?" Sam chimed in from somewhere behind her.

Abigale turned and looked at her boyfriend. He had that concerned/bewildered look he often had from time to time. His blood shot eyes drifted from her to the people behind her. Sam had always been considerate to her needs from time to time. Yet she often placated his somewhat childish views on life.

"Your father believes Frank had an accident on his way here. Sebastian has already left to go check on him." Henry stated calmly.

Abigale watched as Sam's eyes went from her father to his own. The bewildered look left his face and it had become hard and stern. Abigale believed Sam knew the severity of the situation outside. Not with Frank but the "zombies" or "demons." Whatever they were it wasn't safe to be out there. Her father had already almost died once and she wasn't about to let it happen again.

"I'm with Abby on this one Henry." Sam stated. " If Sebastian is gone as well then we don't need to risk losing anyone else. He could already be gone. I don't think Frank is the type to want someone to get killed on his account."

Abigale turned and looked at her father. She could tell as his eyes moved from one person to the nextjk he was calculating his odds. He would still try to go and save Frank. Henry Myers was that kind of man. The thought of one of those things killing him made her chest hurt. She felt her face flush and her eyes became hot with tears. She didn't want to cry. She wasn't going to cry. He father locked eyes with her as she felt one of the tears burned a hot path down her cheek. She saw that faint flicker in his armor again.

"I think we should all settle down and give Sebastian enough time to get back here." Pastor Clark stated in that calm prayer meeting kind of tone. "They could already be on their way back."

Abigale reached up and brushed the tear from her cheek. She felt Sam's hand on her should giving it that reassuring squeeze. She had managed to choke back the tears. She was only giving up that one. She knew she had to be strong. Meek little Abigale was going to make it through this. No matter how she wanted to crawl in a corner and hide she wasn't.

BOOM BOOM BOOM startled her and made Abigale jump. She watched as the look of surprise spread like a waved to all their faces. The sound had been so abrupt in the silence of the police station. They all turned to search for where the sound could be coming from.

"PLEASE GOD HELP ME!!!!"

Abigale saw a brief look of disbelief cross her father's face as he turned towards the steps to the lower floor. That big structure of muscle that had gotten him the name Bear lurched forward. Like a running mountain he started for the stairs to the first floor.

"Someone's at the damn door!" he shouted as he started down the steps.

Abigale started after her father along with the others. Maybe it was someone she knew she thought to herself as she started down the steps. She counted them one after another. Part of her incessant compulsive disorder. She hated doing it but it gave her some pleasure to do it. She liked the uniform and order of mathematics. Its structure had always intrigued her.

Abigale let out the breath she didn't realize she was holding. Car headlights were shining in the windows of the lower lobby. The shadowy silhouette standing in the middle of the door framed in glass. **BOOM BOOM BOOM** echoed through the darkness again.

"PLEASE FOR THE LOVE OF GOD HURRY!" the shape exclaimed to them with much need in its voice.

Her father reached the door before any of them. Abigale knew that the size of Henry Myers had fooled a many a man in his time. You wouldn't think that a man that size could move that fast but he could. I guess if you spent enough time moving like your life depended on it you would too.

Abigale heard the jingle of keys on a key ring as her father searched for the keycard to open the door. The sound of the keycard as it slid through the lock and the red light flickering afterwards made her heart race. It looked like everyone was holding their breath.

Abigale turned to see Sam standing on the bottom step with the rifle aimed at the door. He glanced at her for only a second and mouthed the words "never know." Abigale turned to see her father trying the key again. Henry desperately rubbed the key card on his pants and tried it again.

"PLEASE LET ME......." the shape didn't get the rest of the words out its mouth when the door came open and a female landed in the floor.

Abigale had a brief glance at the woman on the floor when her vision focused back on the open doorway. The dozen of black shapes with red eyes shambling towards the now open entrance to new prey. She felt her her heart rise up in her throat.

The woman tried to get out of the way as her father began to push the heavy door closed. The movement of the woman trying to scramble to her feet was like a cat trying to take off running on ice. Abigale watched as pastor Clark grabbed the woman by the arm and tried to drag her out of the way. She knew the woman, who was trying to pull away from him and do it on her own, was only making things worse.

Abigale rushed forward and grabbed the woman by the other arm. With all her strength she pulled the woman backwards . She got the woman out of the doorway and sent herself backwards on her bottom in the process. She looked up at the door as he father slammed it shut. She felt the warmth drain from her as the piercing set of red eyes locked with her own. That brief second before the echoing boom of the door as it slammed shut.

.

"We will get you harlot oh yesssssss we will." the creature hissed from the other side of the glass.

Abigale felt a shiver go down her spine as the creature struck the glass in defiance. The new black silhouette framed in glass with red coals for eyes. The sickening sound of its voice made her stomach turn. All her thoughts of being strong had drained from her with those few words. As strong as she thought she might could be someday, those things took all that away from her.

Abigale looked down at the face that was close to her crotch. The sheer horror that was on that face mimicked her own.

"He said we…….he said we weren't……..gonna make any stops." the woman choked out as she started to cry.

Abigale looked up at her father who suddenly had that stone statue look on his face again. She hoped the woman was talking about someone else. Yet she knew like her father knew that she was talking about Frank.

Chapter 10: There came a pale horse

Part 1

The air around the black crater still smelled of charred meat and death. A few of the red eyes still roamed amidst the ash of their fallen comrades. The air still had a feel of heat to it even when the flames had disappeared as quickly as they had begun.

In the now infinite blackness that had consumed this world a hum began. At first it was at the level only dogs and animals could hear. The hum grew louder and louder. The attention of the red eyes now searched the darkness for its source. They looked for new prey to claim as their own.

In the very center of the black crater a ball of light cut into the darkness. At first no bigger than a golf ball. Now all the damned looked at the light as it grew in size. The golf ball sized orb of light had grown to baseball size, and then basket ball size.

The hum had only increased in intensity as the orb grew. The red eyed wraiths covered their own ears in pain. A single beam of light cut down from the sky and crashed into the basketball sized orb of light. The eruption of light that came from the orb cut through the darkness like a hot knife through butter. Many of the red orbs bounced in retreat away from the light to hide in corners like snakes and wait for prey.

A lone figure stood in the center of the crater now. The orb, now shrunk to baseball size again, swirled around the figure like an eager puppy with a new playmate. The soft white glow of it catching on the white and gold of the man's armor. Pale blonde hair covered the figures face as it stood there almost statuesque.

One eager set of eyes focused on the figure and made its way towards it. The tattered red of its stock boy apron bright in the darkness. 'Bill' the once white letters on the apron read. The pale warrior seemed to pay no heed to the creature as it stooped down. The white pleats of the man's fustanella touching the ash now. The figure placed a palm on the still warm black ground.

Bill the bus boy made a slow trek towards the white and gold clad figure. The stooping warrior had flipped his hands over now. Mashing the ash between his thumb and index finger. Bill stopped at the edge of the crater and watched the figure. The warrior still hadn't bothered to acknowledge its presence.

If one could see in the darkness, one could watch an eerie smile creep across Bill's slack jawed face. The creature crouched lower and continued towards the stooped warrior . The swirling ball of light still bounced around the man who didn't seem to acknowledge the stock boy either.

The red eyed former Bill was only a few paces from the man when the bouncing ball of light stopped bouncing. Those faint red slits had a brief second to widen when the ball shot up in the air. The creature turned to flee but it was too late. The ball of light had gown to basket ball size and crashed down with a force into the stock boy's back. The sound of breaking bone was almost deafening as the creature whirled on the ground.

The orb, now resting in the middle of the Bill's back, looked as if it was going to push its way through the creature. The creature let out a wretched scream as the white clad warrior rose to his feet. Bill clawed furiously at the ground as if he meant to escape. The other red eyes stood in silence as the pale warrior looked out from behind his pale tresses at them. The hunger on their faces plain but they dared not move.

The warrior began speaking in words barely audible, but the language long forgotten. The sound of breaking bone sounded off again in the night and Bill screamed again. The pale warrior continued to speak as the pairs of red eyes began to move forward. Their call to arms. The horrific screams of Bill the stock boy. Its body almost bent in half from the weight of the orb.

The blonde warrior never stopped his path towards the stock boy. With a flick of the man's wrist the ball shot up into the air again.

The glowing white orb shrinking again to baseball size. The warrior whispered and the ball shot forward in a streak of light. The stock boy tried to crawl its way forward but its lower half no longer worked. It could only watch as the dazzling ball streaked its halo trek around them in brilliance. One by one the sets of red went out until there was no one left to come to its aid.

"You are nottttttt allowed to interfeeerrrree arrkkk." the creature spat out sending a faint red mist into the air.

The creature watched as a pair of sandalled feet stopped in front of its face. It reached out in anger and seized the ankle with its hand. The blonde warrior stooped down and pushed the hair away from its face. A shining ring of light shot around the warriors head and held the hair back from his face. The creature looked into those bright blue eyes and felt fear for the first time. It released the warriors ankle and screamed in defeat

" I sound the trumpets vermin, and in so, I go where I please." Michael stated in a deep booming voice that shook the very ground. " Tell me where the morning star is and I will send you back to the void."

Bill the stock boy watched as the orb came back to its master and swirled around them. Bill, or the spirit that now controlled the body, knew there was no reasoning with it. There was no escape to be had. Micheal grasped it by the throat and lifted the Bill's broken from off the ground like it was a feather. The creature knew it was experiencing its last moments of freedom.

"I don't know masssster I don't knowwwww.....he wasssss here but now hessss gone.....please master please." the creature choked out.

Michael looked at the creature. Those pale blue eyes now glowing like the white orb that whistled around them. Even as this creature begged for its life the light intensified. The creature gasped and gagged as if something had caught in its throat. As Bill opened its mouth to scream a white hue could be seen coming from inside. The burning red of its eyes too began to take on the white fire glow.

Bill the stock boy grasped at its throat and struck Michael's arm with futility. The white slowly claimed the creatures eyes. The light's intensity grew tenfold as the creature squirmed. It even attempted to claw Bill's face to ribbons in a means to escape.

The light grew even brighter. The creatures borrowed veins lit up like little tracks of white across its face. The creature could only suffer as the light consumed it from within. In a brilliant flash it was over as iridescent dust spilled into the night like fireflies on the wind.

"What are you up to?" Micheal questioned nobody but himself.

Michael looked once more across the area as the orb began to spin around him in a bright rampant circles. He thought for a second he could sense him but it was gone. The warriors face,though firm but pleasant to look upon, now appeared grim.Michael whispered a word again in the foreign dialect and in a pillar of light he was gone.

Part 2

Henry Myers stared at the blonde woman sitting in the small chair before him. His eyes traveled from her face down to the jacket she was wearing. Bad thoughts were all that was going through Henry's head. He looked at the Jacob's Ladder patch embroidered on the front.

Melissa Grave's handiwork work over at **Seams and Stitches**. He didn't even have to look at the name patch to know it was Frank's jacket. The only question going through his mind at this point was where was Frank. Pastor Clark handed the woman a cup of coffee which she cradled in her shaking hands. She hadn't even attempted to drink it. She only stared at it.

"What's your name dear?" Pastor Clark asked.

Henry locked eyes with the pastor from his seat at the table. The woman only traced the ring of the coffee cup with her thumbs as more tears streaked down her face. Henry knew that she had no doubt suffered something bad since this whole thing had began. He also knew that she knew where Frank was. That would end up being the deciding factor in how this turned out for her.

"Where's Frank?" Henry asked getting straight to the point.

The woman looked up from the dark cup of coffee to look Henry in the eyes. He could see the fear. Hell he could almost smell it at this point. Yet Henry didn't care. Either she knew where he was or she had something to do with it. There was no way he would have left that jacket.

Henry had it made special for him when Frank got his last promotion. They were a small town. The city would pay for uniforms, but it usually was cheap. Henry had paid top dollar for it and Frank knew that. It had been a treasured gift to a friend. Frank wore it everywhere he went even when he wasn't at work. Henry kept his eyes locked on hers. Long enough to realize they were green and bloodshot.

" I don't know........." the woman started. "He had saved me from some bad men."

Henry watched her face while she talked. He had been a cop for long enough to know if you were telling the truth or not. He also had done his fair share of prisoner interrogations. Enough to tell when someone was lying by their pupil constriction. He knew she was telling the truth, but she wasn't telling the whole story. The best tactic to trip people up with their story was to throw in fake facts to see if they agree. You could torture people and get the truth sometimes. Most of the time they would tell you what you wanted to hear. Anything at that point was better than the pain you inflicted on them.

"So it was you that crashed in to him over by MacReady's?" Henry stated.

He watched as the woman's face twisted. That first hint of disgust and rage bubbling to the surface. Henry knew that he had struck a nerve. He was glad that he did. People will either tell you the truth or slip up when they get angry. If the woman started back-peddling he knew that he had her.

"My name is Grace!" the woman shout with an exasperated scream.

Henry watched the woman. He could see Sam standing in the doorway with that concerned look on his face. Henry knew that he was judging him. He knew they boy knew nothing about aggressive questioning. He thought he was badgering a poor distraught woman. Henry knew this was a necessary evil to get to the truth.

"Well ....Grace is it...can you tell us what happened to Frank?" Pastor Clark chimed in a soothing voice.

Henry wasn't sure if the pastor was playing good cop/bad cop with him or if he was trying to keep her calm. He decided to use it to his own end.

Henry stood up from his position at the break room table and grabbed his chair. He took the few paces to where the woman sat in the middle of the room. Henry sat his chair down in front of her. Henry knew that all eyes in the room were on him at this point. He sat down in front of the woman. He knew that his size intimidated most so this time he would use it to his advantage. The woman looked at him as he clasp both of his hands together.

"I live in the low income houses. The ones on Price Circle. I moved here like two days ago. I had seen the stuff on the TV. They told people to stay indoors. So I stayed indoors. I got up the next day and tried to turn on the TV and it didn't work. I went outside and it was dark. Then I saw those things. I went back inside. I heard a truck later on. I opened the door to see who was outside. Then I saw those guys with guns. I had shut the door and tried to hide but they got in. They beat me and drug me out into the street."

Henry watched as the woman paused. She had managed not to cry for this part. He didn't think she was lying to him yet. Grace seemed to be telling the truth.

"Go on Grace." Henry encourage the woman.

The woman stared deep into his eyes. He could see the abused dog look she was putting off. Henry did feel sorry for her. He had seen it dozens of times throughout his career. The battered wife that wouldn't press charges. You could feel sorry for them. You couldn't do this job without compassion. Henry had seen officers that had gone hard and cold. The stress of the job had burned them out.

"I tried to fight back. They hit me in the head......Everything got fuzzy. I remember one of them pulling my clothes off. Then I heard gunshots. Then the police officer....Frank was there. He gave me his jacket. We took the truck back to his police car. It has supplies in the bed. He told me to follow him....then a truck came out of a side street and crashed into him. I should of stopped.....I should of."

Henry watched the tears start streaking down her face again. Grace had started to shake and sob. It was a believable story at this point. The waterworks was helping her case. Yet Henry was more concerned with Frank than he was her. It was selfish to put someone before others in time like this, but he was Henry's friend. He knew that Frank would tread through hell for him and he wouldn't do any less.

"Is he still alive?" Henry asked the sobbing woman.

Henry was aware all the faces were on him now. He could see the shock spreading from the pastor to his son and finally his own daughter. They all thought he was a monster now.

"She's been through enough Bear." Sam stated with obvious disdain oozing in his voice.

Henry leveled his gaze on the boy's face. He knew that Sam only had a spine on occasion. Maybe he was right. Maybe he was taking it a little too far. He had the ability to make men cower but the boy stood defiant.

He wasn't going to protect these people if the shit hit the fan. Frank was the only person besides him that had seen real death. That had taken lives and lived with it. Sebastian was right when he said that they would panic. When the lights went out, and they would. That's when the real killing would begin. When you couldn't see what was eating your face. That's when you need people that don't run; they fight. The pastor had said Sebastian had went after Frank. Yet if the two never came back it would be up to him and who? Would the pastor be able to do it? Sam would run and hide.

Henry knew he would do what he could to keep his daughter alive. Down to giving his own life. He couldn't say the same about the others.

"Grace......" Henry started and had to clear his throat. " It's nothing against you but we need Frank. That's all there is to it. Can you tell me if he's still alive?"

Henry watched as the woman stopped crying. The emotional wreck she had been so far was justified. Hell he wasn't sure how they all hadn't went stark raving mad at this point. Yet the calm that came over her almost startled him. He felt the prickle of goose bumps as she those green bloodshot eyes looked him dead in the face.

"No.....I don't think he is officer."

Henry felt the weight of those words bear down on him like a mountain. The seriousness of the situation became all too clear. It was all up to him now, and he wasn't sure they had a chance in hell.

Part 3

Sam stood on the roof of the police department and looked out at the infinite blackness that had once been a good town. He had always hated it growing up. He was a firm believer small towns had small minds. Never open to change or new things. Now he wished he had it all back. The small diner that had burnt down. The grumpy old pharmacist across town that had tried to eat Henry's face off. Now it was all gone and they weren't gonna get any of if back.

The thought of it was terrible and made his stomach turn. He could use a drink right now. Abigale seemed cold and distant. Henry was becoming aggressive. He wasn't sure if this whole mess was making his post traumatic stress worse. He knew that they were all under stress.

Sam made his way over to the roof edge and looked over. The headlights were dying on the truck below. It wouldn't be long until the battery was dead and it would be of no use. He should let Henry know and one of them could sneak out and turn the lights off. Grace had said there was supplies in the back. What if it was food and guns? Those would be useful for sure.

Sam eased his leg over and seated himself on the edge. He caught a glance of a few eyes roaming in the dark. Those burning red eyes hovering in the darkness. The sight brought back the image of Abby's neighbor. Sweet old lady that she was. Those eyes and that twisted grin. Even now it sent chills down his spine.

"Jump and it will all go away…..no pain…no fear."

Sam almost slipped off the roof. His hands shot out and braced himself. What the hell was that? It reminded him of the voice the little old lady had. That sickening feeling was growing in his stomach. He searched the roof behind him and didn't see anything. He was sure that he was alone up here. The general creepy vibe had went up that was for sure.

Sam glanced back down at the street. A woman stood down below staring up at him. Her hair matted with blood. The curlers in her hair matted to her head. The fact that she was staring at him with that smile. It made his stomach turn worse. Sam didn't believe in angels and demons. None of this made any sense in the logical perspective.

"Let us take away your pain…..come be with us…you need not be alone."

Sam watched another form shamble towards the curls lady. Even from here he could tell it was horrifically burned. There wasn't much of its face left. He could see the glistening white of its teeth reflecting in the soft glow of the light.

"Your imagining things Sam." Sam stated to himself hoping for reassurance.

Sam noticed that he was drawing a crowd. Another form had shambled over to join the other two. This one he actually noticed. . His friend Mike was staring up at him now. The blood smeared across his face made Sam's heart sink in his chest. Poor Mike had always been an underachiever. Yet the two had been friends since high school. Now staring down at him the weight of the situation was almost unbearable.

"It will be so much easier Sam.....no need to fight it."

Sam almost thought the voice was right. Was it his thoughts manifesting into a voice? Had he finally cracked from the stress? Sam closed his eyes and tried to center himself. "You got this," he reassured himself. His family had a long history of mental illness. He had never been one to embrace those kinds of thoughts. He had always faced his problems the adult way. He drank and forgot about them until the next day.

"Why are you up here by yourself babe?" Abigale's voice called from behind him.

Sam jumped a little bit and had to steady himself on the edge again. The group below him had grown to five now. He couldn't look away from Mike. New age hippie he was he didn't deserve this. Abigale sat beside him on the roof edge. He heard the sharp sigh come from Abigale's lips. He wondered if she would be able to notice Mike. He felt her hand cover his own. It's comforting warmth made him feel more centered.

"Is that Mike?" Abigale asked.

Sam nodded his head yes. Hearing his name made Sam feel as if he was only hearing things. He knew the damned weren't talking to him. How could they? Then again they very well could be trying to get in his head. The fact that the dead were walking around trying to kill the rest of them, and warrior angels were falling from heaven. That was proof that the world was bigger than we thought.

"Come now SAMMMMM....come now.....JUMP JUMP!!"

Sam shivered and he felt Abigale squeeze his hand. This had to be those things trying to get him. It was the only explanation that came to mind. Like matters were bad enough now they could get in your head as well. The deck seemed stacked against them and that didn't seem fair.

"I feel like these thing are trying to get in my head." Sam said.

Sam looked at Abigale now. He could see the mix of worry and concern spread across her delicate face. If she would have said it to him he would have thought she was off her rocker. Sam couldn't expect any different a reaction from her.

"What do you mean babe?" Abigale asked.

Sam pointed down at the crowd that had gathered below. Where there had been five there were now ten. Some of the faces he knew. Some of them he didn't. He half expected to see his agent Roger down there. Sam knew that Roger was out of town. He had only been in town to renegotiate the contract and he had left for his office in Houston.

"When they started gathering I started to hear thoughts…not good ones."

Abigale's brow deepened and now the concern was real. He was sure of it. She thought he had gone bananas as well. He couldn't blame her at the moment. Yet if the thoughts were being forced in to his head then they were doing the same to others. He knew enough about zombies to know if there is something wrong tell someone while it was still you. Abigale looked down to where he was pointing. The sets of hovering eyes seemed to be fixated on him.

"What do you mean......bad thoughts..?" she asked.

Sam searched for the words to make her understand without thinking he was a total whack job. He wasn't sure how to even begin that conversation. There was no logical way to explain that and still not sound crazy. So he was going to go with it and hoped she understood.

"I was sitting here and they started to gather." Sam started. "Then I heard that creepy voice the old lady used on us in your house. It kept telling me to jump. It seemed to be coming from inside my head and not from them."

Sam felt Abigale give his hand a reassuring squeeze again. He knew it sounded crazy. It sounded even more crazy when it came out of his lips. Sam looked out over the black horizon. Man how he wished the sun would come up and this horrible thing would be over. That is what he wanted.

Sam saw a blink of light on the horizon. It streamed up from the ground all the way to the sky. It almost seemed like lightning, but it was straight. He pointed for Abigale to look but it was gone. He watched her look at the horizon. "Now she's gonna think I'm crazy," he thought.

"If what you're saying is true Sam we should tell the others." Abigale stated calmly. "I'm not saying it isn't true but if it is we have to watch each other. We don't know how this could affect people."

Sam nodded his head yes in acceptance. He didn't care if they thought he was crazy. Yet the possibility of it affecting the others and causing an incident; that had a high probability of happening. Everyone was walking that thin edge between sanity and insanity at this point. No one needed to wake up and find someone with a knife killing someone because the voices told them so.

" You're right babe." Sam said and squeezed her hand.

They both sat there and stared off into the blankness. The little crowd of the undead scattered. The realization that they were no longer the center of attention clear. In that moment Sam felt like things would be alright. He knew it was far from the truth but he could at least revel in the moment while he still could.

There were several unknowns on the table. Things were gonna get worse before they got better. Sam knew that. The streak of light flashed again in the distance. Sam felt the squeeze of Abigale's hand again and was followed by a little gasp. She had saw it that time. Maybe he wasn't crazy after all.

"We should tell your dad." Sam said and they both started for the door.

Part 4

Frank Peterson had seen a lot of things in his time. A lot of it he wished he hadn't seen. He still couldn't even begin to explain what had happened. There had been many times he had escaped his ass being handed to him, and it had been by the skin of his teeth. Frank knew the spill Dianna had told them had seemed like bullshit at the time. Now he was having serious doubts that it was.

"She was telling the truth." Sebastian said without hesitation.

Frank felt the strength go out of him again and Sebastian didn't even lose a step. He shouldered the weight like it was nothing and kept on going. They were only a few hundred yards from the police station now. The alley between the strip mall and parking garage was dark. Way too damn dark. Frank wished he had a weapon. He felt naked and weak without it. Even if he had some powerful creature dragging him down this alley. Frank was the dependent type.

"Are you an angel Sebastian?" Frank asked.

He already knew the answer to the question. Either he was one of the good guys or the bad guys. Frank didn't think he was a bad guy because why else would he save him?

"That is up to interpretation old friend." Sebastian stated.

Frank looked over at the man that was assisting him to walk. Frank had one arm thrown over his shoulder as they walked. Frank had felt better once he had got his bearings. It had taken a block before the shell shock had worn off. He wasn't sure he would live long enough to process all the information. Frank wished he had a flashlight at least. His eyes had gotten used to the darkness for the most part but your eyes can only process so much in pitch black.

"So you're playing for the opposing team then?" Frank stated.

Sebastian halted their pace abruptly. If Sebastian didn't have such a firm lock around his waist he would have toppled forward. Frank saw what he had stopped for. Two sets of red eyes hovered next to a car about twenty paces ahead. They hadn't seemed to notice them yet.

"I play for my side Frank. Which I hope is the winning side in this. If it is not, there will only be losers in the end. Wait here please."

Sebastian released his waist and started forward. Frank may be limping but he wasn't out of the fight. He didn't have to be handled with kid gloves. He had fought worse off.

Frank watched as the two undead finally noticed Sebastian. The pair let out a feral screams in unison and lurched forward. He could tell the mechanics of their attack was all animal. If you could imagine a lion as it starts after a gazelle; it doesn't think about how to be efficient in the kill. It plans on overcoming its prey with brutal force.

The first one to reach Sebastian was the unlucky one. It lunged at him with all power. The brutal force take down. It didn't realize that it was coming up against an immovable object. Sebastian struck the thing with one hand and sent it careening into a concrete pillar. The force of the dead hitting the pillar exploded the creature into a shower of gore and bones.

The second monster only had a split second to realize it had made a mistake. It was all power and not enough time to correct its course. Sebastian grabbed it by its outstretched arm and launched the thing up into the dark night. Frank trailed it up with his eyes but lost sight of it in the blackness.

Sebastian turned and made his way back towards Frank. Frank was still processing what he had seen. Frank knew that they needed more of him on their side. Sebastian placed himself under Frank's shoulder and began assisting him down the alley once more

" I can hold my own you know." Frank threw out there.

"I have no doubt about that on a good day Mr. Pearson, but you are not having a good day." Sebastian replied.

Frank smiled at that. It felt weird to smile. It had been a while since he had heard a snappy comeback after he had the shit kicked out of him. Frank wasn't sure why Sebastian had been helping them, but he was glad of it. He knew that he definitely wouldn't be considering any options at this point if Sebastian hadn't helped him. The sound of the body hitting the parked car next to them made him jump. It was Sebastian's turn to smile now.

"You're a decent soul Frank. These people needed you to make it through this." Sebastian replied to his thoughts.

Sebastian stopped again. Frank searched the darkness for its source but he didn't see anything. He couldn't see anything. Which was not making him happy at this point.

Frank felt the man go stiff and Sebastian turned abruptly in the direction in which they had come. Something had the man spooked all the sudden. Anything that would spook a man like this was not good.

"I'm not spooked Frank, but if that is what I think it is then we may be in more trouble than I thought."

Frank searched the blackness for what this man could be talking about. He saw a few sets of eyes off in the distance. Yet he knew a couple of scrappers were no match for this guy. If Dianna was telling the truth about earlier he didn't think a hundred would be a match. So what exactly is this?

Frank heard Sebastian start to speak. It was no language that he knew of, and he knew several. Frank felt the air stand up on his arms. Frank could almost feel a charge to the air. His stomach began to turn. The air around them began to shimmer slightly. Frank wasn't sure what what happening but he was scared.

Sebastian tightened his grip on his waist as the air around them began to get thick.

Frank could taste the electricity in the air now. Sebastian continued to speak in this foreign language. It was almost like Frank was looking through a frosted window pane. He could see through to the other side but it was blurry and out of focus. Frank raised his hand to touch the air and it sparked. The shocked traveled from his fingertips all the way to his toes. Frank felt every muscle in his body tighten up.

Sebastian increased his grip around the man's waist to sturdy him. Frank thought he was gonna pass out for sure. He watched a streak of light shoot up into the sky in the distance. Frank stood as still as he could. He had learned his lesson the first time. After a few seconds Sebastian stopped speaking. Slowly the foggy glass around them started to crack and then it disappeared like it was never there at all. Frank inhaled and didn't realize how fresh the air in his lungs felt until he took that breath.

"What the hell was that?" Frank choked out.

Sebastian looked at him and smiled. Frank could feel the hair standing up on his arms. The air still felt like it had a charge to it.

"That was a magic trick old boy." Sebastian said with wry smile. "A very old one."

Sebastian resumed his position under his arm and began to help him down the alley once again. Frank could tell a difference in the air now. The closer they got to the street through the middle of town the stronger the smell of death got. Frank knew that smell.

He had seen it too many times in Africa. That was the smell of dead bodies and not just one. Sebastian stopped at the end of the alley. Frank almost had to choke back his own vomit. The street was scattered with dozens of bodies. Frank could see the carnage first hand. The faint beam of a flashlight was reflecting off a store front casting an eerie glow on the scene. Frank recognized the store front. It was the **Sweet Tooth Bakery**.

"I guess this answers the question about the automatic gun fire we heard earlier." Frank stated out loud if only to himself.

Even in their mangled forms he recognized several of their bodies. The local militia boys. Good ole boys at heart. They were also the most heavily armed people in the county. There were several assault rifles and handguns scattered around the corpses. A few shot guns too. As bad as it sounded they needed to check the corpses and salvage what they could. He wondered why they didn't grab the stuff when the fight was over. Unless this was the last of them.

"I think you are right. We need as much as we can carry."

Sebastian mirrored his thoughts.

Frank was pretty sure the guy could read thoughts. Which had its pros and cons. It would be efficient in a fire fight. Not having to shout out orders. Yet it definitely ruled out getting the drop on him if shit went south. Damn it. Sebastian chuckled as he released him and started towards one of the bodies.

Frank started towards the next closest body. It looked like it might have something of value. Frank noticed the back of the man's head was missing. That would indicate he took a point blank shot to the head. It was either self inflicted or he had caught a stray round. Either possibility was open at this point.

Frank stooped down to roll the body over. His head swam and he thought he was gonna pass out for a second. His body was protesting every movement at this point, but he was still moving. That was a plus in his book.

With minimal effort he was able to roll the body over. He knew the guy. Gil Fitspatrick lifeless form started up at him. The small hole in his forehead let him know he had taken a round to the head not caught one.

Frank unzipped the tactical vest and began to ease it off his body. It still had a few magazines and a pistol mag in it. With much difficulty Frank eased the vest over his shoulders and zipped it up. Frank was glad it was armored. The weight of it was painful but not unbearable.

Frank spotted the man's rifle a few feet away. Poor Gil he thought to himself. He had hunted with the man a few times. He had owned the hunting supply store in town before the strip mall put him out of business.

Frank eased back to a standing position and made his way back over to the rifle. He knew the gun was Gil's. It had been his pride and joy. He had named it after that song that was on the radio. Coincidentally it had also been the name of his ex-wife.

Frank picked up the weapon and ejected the magazine. He could tell it was almost empty by the weight. You would be surprised what you could learn over the years.

He placed the magazine in one of the empty pockets of the vest and pulled out a fresh one. The sound of the velcro was loud in the quiet of the blackness. He tapped the mag twice on his chest and placed it in the weapon. Frank chambered a round and slid the strap over his head, letting the weapon fall to his side.

"We need a bag," he whispered to Sebastian.

Sebastian nodded and continued on to the next body. Frank glanced around on the ground hoping for and ammo bag or a duffel bag. He didn't see one in the immediate vicinity. He knew the **Sweet Tooth** used to have those cloth bags under the counter. They had handed them out last week at their customer appreciation day. Maybe they still had a few left that they could use.

Frank made it about two feet towards the store when he saw Sebastian raise up a hand to stop. Frank stopped cold in his tracks.

The natural tenseness his muscles took when the adrenaline started working. It sent pain down his body. Yet like that it was gone. Frank eased his hand down to the grip of the rifle. Frank scanned the darkness with his eyes. The light reflecting on the storefront glass had hurt his night vision, but not to the point he couldn't see. He was glad that they were in the light but suddenly realized it made them a huge target.

Then he saw it. On the other side of the glass that the light was conveniently shining on. Several sets of red eyes were watching them. Now Frank knew why the weapons were still laying on the ground.

"It's a trap!" Frank yelled as he began to move the gun to a firing position with remembered ease.

Frank had a split second to react before it all went to hell. The returned started pouring out of the store fronts like a flood of red eyes and gnashing teeth. The rifle was loud in the canyon the store fronts made down the street. Controlled bursts Frank told himself as the rifle cut the closest red eyed freak to ribbons. The one behind that one used the falling body like a vaulting board and launched at Frank. He managed to dodge it as it went sailing past him. Frank put a few rounds in its back and watched it wiggle and flop for a second.

"One more burst," he reminded himself as he cut another one down. The mag ejected and skittered across the pavement in a loud clacking sound. Frank had another mag and was putting in the rifle when he glanced up. He wasn't gonna make it in time he told himself. He had a split second before a body came flying out of nowhere and crashed into the one about to mall him. Both bodies sounded like and explosion of bone as they went flying into two more. Like bowling pins scattering on a strike. Frank riddle all four with bullets and started towards a store behind him.

Two more were hot on his his heels as he hit one with another burst from his rifle. He watched the top of its head explode in shower of brain matter and bone. He had a half a second to catch a glance of Sebastian, or where he should have been.

The damned had piled on him like a mound of ants pouring over a piece of dropped candy. Frank emptied the rest of the mag into the growing mound and bolted for the door of the store. If he could get the door closed he might be able to buy himself enough time to get a weapon. Frank dove through the door as the explosion ripped down the street. He felt the force of it down to his very soul. His ears screamed with that high pitch sound that let him know he was way to close.

" FUUUUUCCCKK!" he screamed as he he tried to get his bearings.

Frank couldn't hear his own words. He had a split second to get his bearings when one came through the door on top of him. The things face was horrific. Its entire lower jaw was missing. That one red eye it had left burning in the dark had only one thing in its sight and that was him. It took all his strength to keep that thing off him. At least with its lower jaw missing he didn't have to worry about it biting him. Unfortunately it was covered in blood and hard to keep a grip on.

Frank glanced to his left and right looking for a weapon as the thing thrashed and wiggled on top of him. It was trying to get an inch enough to get the upper hand. Frank kicked out with its leg and took one of its legs out. He heard the bone crack under the force. It didn't lose a step. Frank spotted Pete Winslow laying on his left. He could see the revolver left in his hand. It appeared Pete took the easy way out.

Frank freed up one of his hands for a split second. In that moment the thing finally got its hands around his throat. Frank felt the inhuman pressure as the thing squeezed. The blood it had dripped all over Frank from it's jaw had made him slippery enough. Seems Frank wasn't the only one who couldn't get a solid grip.

Frank could feel his head spin. The thing was pressing on his carotid. He had a few more seconds before the thing cut off enough blood to his brain to make him pass out. It would all be over quick then. Frank fumbled for the revolver. "Come on Frank not like this," he told himself. "You could have died a hundred times don't go out like this. Not down and out like a bitch. You're a warrior Frank. Be a warrior Frank."

His fingers finally found the barrel of the weapon in the fray. He gripped the barrel and brought the weapon hard into the creatures temple. It was enough to stun it. Frank hit the creature hard in the head again. This time he heard bones crack like snapping tree limbs.

The creature tried to retreat. It rose to the best standing position it could on that bad leg in an attempt to flee. Frank took both of his legs and drew them to his chest and kicked outward into the creature's torso. In mid motion Frank flipped the revolver over as the creature flew backwards into the night. Frank thumbed the hammer back and pulled the trigger. The weapon went click.

"Empty chamber," he thought as he thumbed the hammer back again. The weapon clicked empty again. Frank screamed in defiance and kicked the door shut with his feet.

"For FUCK'S SAKE!" he yelled in protest.

Frank could at least hear that. He was at least happy for that. He was not happy about being trapped in here with those things outside. The entire store front was glass. He looked over at Pete hoping the man had another weapon he could see. He did not and Frank cursed under his breath. He could see the creature outside the glass now. The returned beat its hands on the glass in defiance. That one burning red eye shining in the opaque glass.

"Keep a knocking but you can't come in!" he screamed.

He hoped the thing was stupid and didn't go for the front glass. The door was at least impact resistant for security purposes. The main glass was only weather resistant. One good impact on it would be curtains. Frank watched as the eye disappeared in the smoke. "Well shit," he thought to himself.

Frank heard a loud snap and a crash coming from the other side of the door. He thought if this was gonna be the end at least he still had the revolver to use for a weapon. Maybe old Pete still had some ammo on him. He looked over at the gray haired man sitting next to him.

Frank could see the smear of blood on the ceiling. The old man had ran out of ammo. That's why he used the last shot on himself Frank. He cursed his own rotten luck. A polite knocking brought Frank's attention back to the door. "Polite bastards," now he thought.

"Come now old boy. I thought I was always a polite fellow. Unless you're in Georgia. They don't think that well of me there."

Frank busted out laughing. He didn't even get the joke but it was good to hear his voice. Frank rose to his feet slowly. The adrenaline had wore off now and he felt like he had been run over by a car. A very large car and god he was tired. With a shaking hand he reached up and opened the door. As happy as he was he wasn't quite ready for the sight on the other side.

Sebastian stood there but you couldn't quite tell it was him. He was completely nude and covered in blood. His long black hair was matted to his head from it. Only those blue eyes glared out from all the red.

Frank looked past him to the carnage on the street behind him. Frank bet there was a movie director somewhere that would have sold his soul to have filmed this. Several of the storefront buildings were on fire. Bodies were torn to sunder and littered the streets. Some of them were still on fire.

"Let us go friend before this attracts more." Sebastian stated without much enthusiasm.

Frank watched at the man outstretched his arm and handed him another rifle. He smiled as he took the weapon from Sebastian. Frank believed he was starting to like this guy. Whatever he turned out to be. Sebastian only smiled as he turned and strolled nude across the street.

Frank glanced one more time around. He could only shake his head. He would have never have thought this would have turned out this way. He couldn't even count the bodies, or the smears of what was left of some of them. "Better them than us," he thought.

"Never have more truer words been spoken." Sebastian called after him. "Now let us be off."

Frank nodded in acceptance and shouldered the weapon. "Hoorah drill sergeant," he thought to himself and started across the street after him.

Chapter 11: Sounding of the seventh

Part 1

Harry Raines sat in his white Jacob's Ladder issued sport utility vehicle in sheer awe. He had been trying to make it back to the station. He had been doing good considering his condition; then the dash lights started flickering.

At first he thought it was himself and then the car died and coasted to a stop on the side of the road. Harry was having a hard time keeping himself awake. He was sure the amount of blood he lost was bad. Maybe the radio would work he thought. He tried to lift the mike and key the radio. The battery was too dead to do anything.

"Ah Hell." Harry stated to himself and then the darkness took him.

Harry woke up to the sound of gun fire. He wasn't sure if he was alive or dead. He watched a few of the boys he recognized as militia types shooting those red eyed monsters. They were looting the business part of town. They were a hundred yards from his truck. He reached up to sound the horn when he felt the weight of the vehicle shift. Something was on the roof.

Harry glanced up and saw a couple sets of those red eyes in his rear view mirror. Harry could feel his heart in his throat. Harry knew he didn't have long left. There wasn't any shame in at least warning them. Them things wasn't gonna kill him. Hell he was already dead.

Harry knew that to be the truth delivered down by the angels themselves. Harry slammed his hand into the car horn. His heart sunk when it didn't make a sound. The battery you damn fool. He didn't get a chance to protest.

The men didn't even know what hit them. The monsters came by the dozens out of the little stores. There was gun fire for a bit and then silence. Harry sat there and stared at the horror of it. He reached for his pocket; if he was gonna die he wanted one last cigar. Harry's hand never made it to his pocket before the darkness came for him again.

"Heck Harry you gonna sit there?" his wife asked him.

Harry looked over at his wife. He knew her face better than most. They had been married longer than most of the people in Jacob's Ladder had been alive. There had been a few of the old families left. Yet most of the elders had died off and it was just their kids left with the family legacy now. Harry sat there at the dinner table. He had done this every Thanksgiving since his kids had been in diapers. Now they sat at the table with their own kids in diapers and some of those kids with kids in diapers. There were three generations of Raines sitting at the table tonight. Harry put on his best "ah shucks" smile and started to carve the turkey. They hadn't broke the news to the kids about the cancer yet.

"Let's wait until the holidays are over Harry." she had begged of him,

Harry had agreed to those terms because since the day he had met her he had only told her no once. She had wanted him to quit smoking. He had tried through the years but he couldn't quit the cigars. He had stopped the drinking, the smoking cigarettes, and the womanizing for her. He loved them damn cigars though.

Harry wished she had been honest with the kids. She never made it to Christmas and they never saw it coming. Harry remembered the way they looked at him. How they blamed him for not going against her wishes. His son Roger still didn't speak to him. If he was in his boots though he didn't think he could blame him.

The sound of gunfire woke him up again. He had to shake the groggy out of his skull like a night of cheap wine. His stomach wanted to turn and spill itself out everywhere. Harry looked over the steering wheel and he actually knew one of these two.

Frank was one of his best deputies and he had walked into this trap. Harry tried to muster everything he had left to come to his aide but he was out of fuel. He watched as bad went to worse. It was at this point that Harry thought he was hallucinating.

He watched Frank fight like the devil. Then he watched those things pile on the other guy by the dozen. I mean they piled on him like a cheap wrestling match at the National Guard Armory. So many that he lost count. Which wasn't hard at this point because Harry wasn't sure any of this was real.

" Got damnit Frankie boy you neet to run." Harry whisper as the fog began to creep into his peripheral vision.

Harry had a half a second to see Frank dive into one of the stores. Hell the other boy had become snow crab legs at an all you can eat buffet. They had consumed him down to his toenails by the size of them things. He had only saw a flash of light when the explosion shook the vehicle. Harry felt the ringing in his ears down to his toes. Harry looked up at the bumper sticking through his windshield a mere two foot from his body. The windshield was all spider cracks but what Harry saw before him made him wake up good and proper.

The black haired fellow that had been with Frank, the one that had been at the bottom of the dog pile, now stood in the mass of burning body parts and twisted limbs wearing white armor. Like those Greek warriors wore in that spartan movie. The one with the spears. It was bright white in the darkness with black trim. Harry wasn't a hundred percent sure if he was hallucinating or he was witnessing a miracle.

"What in the actual hell?" Harry whispered into the dark.

Harry watched as the twelve plus red eyed monsters circled the armor wearing man. Half the bodies around him were burnt to a crisp and this guy is dressed in a skirt and armor. Yeah Harry was sure of it. He had died and went to hell and the only thing that was left was men in skirts and these red eyed bastards. It was at this point that Harry started paying attention.

He watched as the first one tested the waters and rushed the armor man. That poor fella had a half a second to realized he had tread the wrong water. The guy seized him up and flung him into the the roof of the **Sweet Tooth**. The creature exploded like a balloon.

Harry summoned all the energy he could and leaned forward. He rested his arms on the steering wheel and watched. The rest had learned the lesson of one on one and rushed this guy at once. It was a blur to watch. He saw the first one get kicked through the window of the saddle tack store across the street. Judging by the vibration it sent through Harry's bones he almost bet he came out the back wall.

The second one had a second to realize the jig was up when he used its body like a club to kill number three and four. Now number five was a brave fella that tried to bum rush him in the commotion of the fight. His face ended up a smear under the fellas foot without much of a debate. Harry was fixated on the fight, but his eyes were so heavy. He was so tired by this point.

The sound of the body striking his vehicle made Harry's eyes open up once more. All Harry could see were piece of bodies lying all over the ground. He could swear the armored man looked right at him when all was said and done. Harry watched as the black haired man made his way down the street. The smoke was thick but his front row seat still had a pretty good view.

The only one of the monsters that was left was beating on the door on the hardware store. It had been the pride and joy of Pete Winslow. Now, Harry had never cared for the man, he was too high in the saddle to care for anybody besides himself. The black haired man never lost a step. He seized the creature up by the back of its neck and pulled its head off like it was a tab on a pop can. Hell the blood was till shooting in the air when the body hit the ground.

Harry let himself fall back in the seat. He didn't have any energy left. His eyes were so heavy. Harry reached in his pocket and pulled out his last cigar. His hands felt like two lead weights. He fumbled with the lighter. His thumb wasn't doing what he wanted it to do. He tried to focus but he couldn't get it to work. His head slammed back hard against the headrest of his seat. Man if he could only get his thumbs to work. He closed his eyes at the flash of light. The cigar tip flamed to life on his own. Harry took a long drag and smiled.

Part 2

Felix Cherry sat and watched as axe man Steve stood watch over the stairwell door. Even in the dim light of the fire his form was menacing. The man hadn't even moved in an hour. Steve stood there with a two handed grip on his ax and waited.

Felix had hoped they had seen then last of them for now. One of Felix's elite military guards, Jessup the Scarecrow, was starting to worry him. Felix had tried to get Scarecrow to let him look at him and the man had refused. The man was tough as nails but there are only so many things you can walk off. Felix watched as Hades made his way over to the fire.

"He needs to let me examine him… I am a doctor." Felix proposed.

Hades shook his head no. Felix could tell by the grim look on the man's face he knew what Felix knew. The man didn't have long to live without medical intervention. Felix watched as the man pulled a black case out of his bag. It looked a lot like a briefcase but a little bulkier.

Hades touched a button on the front of the case. A little square lit up on the top of the case with a key pad on the screen. Hades began punching numbers into the case. Felix didn't know how the man could remember that many numbers. It would be impossible to memorize that by watching it. After what seemed like forever the screen changed from green to blue.

"Halo system authorization code accepted. Please state authorization status." a mechanical voice sounded from the case.

Hades looked at Felix. He had the look of a desperate man on his face. He could see the calm cool warrior look slide over his face like a mask. Felix knew this was a last resort. This was not something that was supposed to use unless all other means had been exhausted.

"Authorization.... Delta six command...Hunter Henders 324629754" Hades stated.

The realization that the man on the radio had been talking about Hades made Felix swallow hard. It had been his brother saying goodbye. He didn't know how much more of this he could take. This wasn't fair at all. How were they supposed to survive something like this? All this death and destruction.

"Halo authorization accepted Captain." the robotic voice stated.

Felix watched as the case clicked with a hiss. Hades opened the case and retrieved an ear piece from inside. A dim blue light from inside lit up the man's features. Felix believed the man hadn't slept in a week. Felix had guess the age of the man to be in his mid-twenties but now he was sure he was closer to forty.

A feral scream sounded out in the distance. From the sound it had to be from the street below. Felix wasn't sure how many of those things had died in the explosion. Felix looked out over the burning remains of the city. None of the classic DC architecture was there anymore. He couldn't even see the Washington monument anymore.

" Charlie actual this is delta six how copy."

Felix was dragged back out of his thought and looked at Hades again. The man was typing on a keyboard inside the case. Felix wasn't sure what this halo was. Was it some kind of communication hub? Would they actually make it out of here?

" Delta six this is command…go with traffic."

Felix watched as the relief showed on Hades' Face. He didn't realize the man didn't expect anyone to answer. Felix felt his spirits rise a little bit. They were gonna make it out of this after all. Felix glanced back at Steve. He still hadn't moved from his position at the door. Hades had told him to guard it when they had made their way out onto the roof. The man hadn't faulted in that resolve.

"Command actual this is delta command. Mission status critical. I have two KIA ....one critical.....precious cargo is still intact.....requesting evac at my HALO quadrants....cargo four....how copy."

Felix could feel the tension coming off Hades like an electrical buzz in the air. The relay of the message let him know that this was a please help or we're dead message. Felix closed his eyes and he could feel his own heartbeat in his head. Now he could feel the tension in his body.

Felix hadn't expected to make it this far. The fact that they had was only a testament to these soldiers resolve. Most people would have dropped him and run for their own lives. If he could run he would have too.

"Delta six that a no go....we have no birds on station for evac."

Felix heard the crackling of Hades' leather gloves again. They weren't gonna send help. Felix would say that was a surprise but it wasn't. Felix looked back in Steve's direction again. The man had turned around and was staring in their direction. He had heard the news as well.

"Command actual we are mission ineffective.....I repeat mission ineffective....I have a critical in need of medivac....." Hades stated harshly.

Felix could see the anger on Hades' face now. He couldn't say that he blamed the man. He knew that the two men knew this was a suicide mission when they accepted. Yet you could still expect a little help now and then. Was it so wrong to expect that at least?

" Delta six evac is a no go....we don't have assets available for extraction...over."

Felix watched as Hades' closed his eyes. This had been a desperate plea for help that was being ignored. Felix felt that little fire of hope that had sprung to life inside him, extinguish with that look. No help was coming. They were on their own.

"Romeo two three to Delta six over." An unfamiliar voice sounded over the com.

Felix watched that fire spring to life on Hades' face along with a little bit of confusion. This new player had brought a new spring of hope to the man. It was good to see some of that desperation leave his face. They had all been through so much at this point.

" Romeo two three this is Delta six go with traffic." Hades stated.

Felix could now hear the hope in the man's voice. Yes it was masked in the macho radio code, but he could still hear it. Felix could not hope against hope that a rescue was coming. It was still good to hear voices out there. Felix was at least glad someone else had survived all this death and carnage. He had been sure that they were the only people alive when they had met axe man Steve.

" Delta six I got two assets here from Georgetown fire willing to assist. We will make our way to your Halo ping for extraction...over"

Felix saw the makings of a grin tug at the corners of Hades' mouth. He felt that small fire start to spread inside himself. They were going to make it out of this alive. Felix looked over towards Steve. He had turned towards them again. He could tell he could hear the radio chatter too. Felix wasn't sure why he liked the man. Everything he had seen suggested the man had succumbed to a psychotic break. Yet the man had persevered in the face of overwhelming odds. That was a quality to admire if there was one.

"Command actual to Romeo two three. That is a negative on extraction...you are to sit tight and wait further orders...The area is too hot."

The shock Felix felt at hearing those words couldn't be described. They had people willing to help less than a mile away and they wanted to leave us to die. If he made it out of this. IF. He would definitely be having a words with the decision makers.

"Romeo two three to Command actual. You should let the people that stand in the fire worry about the heat. Delta six we'll be at your ping in 30 mikes…Romeo two three over and out."

Felix admired the camaraderie and brotherhood these people had for one another. There was no telling what was between here and there. He knew there was a high possibility that they wouldn't make it here at all. The fact that they were willing enough to try raised Felix's spirits.

Felix watched as Hades rose up and started towards Scarecrow. He was going to break the good news to his partner. Scarecrow was not looking the best at this point.

Felix could tell even in this light that his respiratory rate was elevated. That last thrashing must have broken a rib. Felix surmised he was looking at a pneumothorax at the least. Felix wished Scarecrow would let him at least examine him. Felix knew that he didn't have any equipment or medicine. He could at least do a physical exam for the incoming crew.

Felix watched as the two soldiers talked back and forth. Scarecrow finally nodded his head yes. The man was determined this was a fact. Even though Scarecrow looked like death he still had his rifle ready. To support Steve if something came through the stairwell door. Even now the man's finger tapped away on the trigger guard. Scarecrow was anxious. The man didn't seem like the type to be anxious, but the situation had everyone on edge. Felix wondered if it could be one of the first signs of shock. He hoped he was wrong about that.

Hades pulled out one of those metallic reflective blankets and wrapped it around his friend. Scarecrow had refused to sit by the fire. Said the light messed with his night vision too much. He also wanted a better angle on the stairwell door in case he needed to return fire. Hades squeezed the man's shoulder and made his way back over to the fire.

"I wished he would agree to let me examine him." Felix stated.

Hades shook his head as he sat down and took out his canteen. The man took a long drink from the canteen and handed it towards Felix. Felix shook his head no and the man replaced the cap and placed it back in his pack.

"He's not the kind to admit he's in trouble. Best not to press him about it." Hades stated without much excitement.

Felix had knew one too many stubborn men in his time. Even when he was still working in a hospital he had seen it. Men refusing to admit they were dying. The cruel thing about medicine is if they are still in their right mind there is nothing you can do. They usually end up dying and by that time there isn't a thing you can do to save them. You always tried to though. It was the only thing you could do.

"I hope it's not too late when the EMS crew gets here." Felix threw out there.

Felix watched as Hades' eyes met his own. He knew that the warrior understood what he was talking about. He could see it on the man's face from the dim light of the fire. These were proud men and there was a good reason behind that. He has seen the documentaries on the television. One could never understand until you saw it first hand. Yet Felix knew that it was no reason to throw your life away. If this was how it was gonna be then they were gonna need every able bodied man. It would be sad to see talent like that go to waste.

"He is too valuable to let pride take the wheel." Felix stated bluntly.

Felix knew that taking the bold route was not the best idea. He was grateful for what these men had done. He didn't wish any ill will upon them. Hades shook his head no again. Felix knew that he understood what he was saying. He wasn't ready to press the agenda yet with his comrade. The both of them would come to their senses before it was too late.

Felix looked over to Steve. The man stood so still he almost looked like a statue. The grim gargoyle was standing guard over them. Felix didn't believe the man expected to live very long. I guess none of them had.

" Godspeed Romeo two three." Felix whispered to nobody but the cold

Part 3

Raphael stood quietly on top of the Smiths Grove Mall is Stanley, Missouri. The people scurried back and forth below him without any knowledge of his existence. Raphael has tried hard to keep this group of survivors hidden from the damned. He had only intervened a few times on their behalf. Destroyed any large hordes of the damned that happened to get to close.

Raphael had only showed his face to three survivors. The rest of this group had only shrugged of their tale of a warrior angel as near death hysterics. Raphael liked it better that way.

"Sir what are you doing up here?" a voice called from behind Raphael.

Its funny that one of them had managed to sneak up on him. His moment of nostalgia had dampened his senses. It had been so long since he had to worry about those. Raphael would have scoffed on relying on his senses. When could something so minute sneak up on something so great ?It would be like a bug landing upon the skin on a lion. The lion would never even acknowledge its existence but to swat its tail. Now standing on the roof of this mall with this human but three paces behind him he could only laugh. It was a deep heartened laugh that he hadn't be able to do in a very long time.

"Simply enjoying the scenery." Raphael stated out loud as he turned around with his hands up.

The man that stood behind him with the twenty two caliber rifle aimed at his chest was young. Randal Ferell...age 20...football fan....hardly slept....greatest sin.. lied to his parents about his brother drug addiction. Randal had taken his brother's death harder than most. He had spent the last two days before the end of the world talking to a gun barrel. The boy had continued to drink whiskey and look at the gun without pulling the trigger. The news of the rapture had stopped him. The boy didn't want to die. His grief had gotten the best of him. Raphael wasn't sure why the boy was even here as his life played out before Raphael's eyes.

"Job is gonna wanna talk to you mister." Randal said with a shakey voice.

Raphael kept his hand's steady so the boy could see them. There was no need to escalate the boy's tension any farther. He knew he could be gone before the boy ever knew what happened but he didn't want to use that until things went south.

"Alright there fella. Just take it easy." Raphael stated in a calm and cool voice

Raphael felt it before he saw it. He had a nanoseconds to react.

Time seemed to slow down to him as he twisted his upper body. The shot came but Raphael was already moving forward when it did. He could see the look of astonishment play out on the boy's face.

Raphael moved behind him and jerked him close to his own chest. The movement had been so abrupt that the boy's pistol still hovered in the air. Raphael watched as the white orb shot past them so fast that it was a blur to even him. Raphael felt the impulses in the boy's mind firing for him to scream. He covered the boy's mouth with his hand.

"Be quiet child if you wish to live." he stated.

The orb came floating across the roof top slowly like an animal on the prowl. Raphael pressed the boy's form tighter to his own and he felt the boy become rigid against him. He had to act or the orb would find ba way to finish its task. The only way to do that was to call out its master.

"Show yourself Micheal...enough of these games."

Raphael watched as the air shimmered about ten paces to his left. The orb took off for its master in a brilliant streak. Raphael turned to face Micheal. If he could keep the boy close then he might survive this. The illusion faded like cracking glass and revealed the one thing that he wished not to see yet.

"Raphael dear brother.....it is good to see you." Micheal stated in a coy voice.

Raphael knew he was not happy to see him. He could feel that seething undertone in the air now. Raphael spoke quietly under his breath. He watched as a wry smile began to spread across his face. He knew that Micheal knew what he was doing. It was best to close off his mind now. It would give him a better advantage if this turned to a confrontation.

"It is good to see you brother." Raphael stated without emotion.

Raphael watched as Micheal looked from him to the boy clutched to Raphael's chest. He had seen that look coming from Micheal before. He knew when he had murder in his eyes. The sharp scent of urine was strong in the air. The boy had messed his self.

Raphael surmised that he would do the same if he was capable of such thoughts. Yet fear was not something they had even known. Not even facing the maws of the dragon.

"Your human seems to be afraid Raphael." Micheal stated followed with an arrogant laugh.

Micheal started to walk towards them now. His machination

circled around him in ever changing paths. Raphael felt the boy go limp in his arms. He felt the boys heart still beating within him. Randal had fainted. This was a small blessing at least. Michael wouldn't perceive him as a threat if he was unconscious. Then again this man had slain half of the children of Egypt while they slept.

"They are fragile creatures Micheal..and undeserving of this."

Micheal laughed again. Raphael lowered the sleeping form to the ground. He could tell Micheal was planning something. He wasn't sure exactly what it was at this point. It wasn't going to be good. They man got to much pleasure out of mass murder. Raphael glanced through the skylight on the oblivious forms below. Raphael looked back at Michael whose smile had grown too large. It was sickening to view.

"We are not to interfere Raphael. You know these are the rules. The human race had been allowed to pollute and corrupt this creation for to long. Their evil had tainted the very earth. They care not for the gift that was bestowed on them. Those that are worthy of him are gone. The rest will be judged as it was foretold. This is how it must be brother. You CAN NOT deny his judgement!"

That creepy smile hadn't left Micheal's face as he stared at him. What had happened to him?

"I cannot stand by brother......my heart will not allow it. " Raphael stated coldly.

Raphael began speaking in their language now. The language of creation. The mirage of clothing he had been wearing slowly fell away. The glistening white and gold below shining brightly. Even in the absolute blackness that his world had become.

The air around them began to crackle with charge as Raphael reached out. The electricity began to carve something out of the air. He seized the handle of the mace and let his arm fall to his side. Raphael's eyes had never left Michael. That sickening grin had grown wider if that was even possible.

"Neither can I brother....neither can I. I cannot stand by while they raise one on there kind to higher exaltation that God. I cannot watch as they let their love of money be greater than their love for him. I cannot let them put their own beauty on a higher pedestal than the world he created for them. While they crave to be with that beauty more than they crave to be with him. I cannot. I WILL NOT. Brother you see I speak the truth " Michael stated.

Raphael watched as the orb began glowing bright. Michael began to speak the language of creation. The orb continued to grow in size and intensity like a beacon in the darkness. Raphael heard a scream sound out in the distance. He could tell it was the sound of the damned. The light was going to draw them from every direction.

They had drawn the attention of the humans below. He could hear their terrified screams. Raphael's grip on the mace tightened as he turned away from Michael and started for the roofs edge. He could hear the footsteps in the distance. It almost sounded like a stampede of animals and it increased as he moved forward.

"This evil must be purged brother. It's the order of things."

Michael called after him as Raphael leaped from the roof.

Raphael glanced down at the humans as they scattered for defensive positions. The barricade of cars they had made around the glass front wasn't gonna keep these things out. They would rush over them like water over stone. The only hope he had was to keep them from the entrance.

Raphael landed a few hundred yards from the entrance. He could hear orders being shouted from the leaders. Raphael knew Michael hated the humans. They were supposed to be incapable of such things. They were not meant to hate. Raphael knew no other way to explain it.

Raphael could see the rushing masses now as he stood there at the brink. One could almost taste their hunger in the air. The haunting red of their eyes bouncing left and right with their hastened steps. They would be on them in less than a minute.

Raphael reached out with his mind. He began to coax the primal energies to life. One could hear the hum as particles separated and collided together around him. The charge at first was faint. If caught within the field it would have caused unease. As the electrical charge around him grew, strong arcs of electricity streaked through the air around him.

The damned were twenty yards from him now. He estimated their numbers in the hundreds. The humans behind him could only watch. He didn't think Michael would harm them yet. He would make it a test. Michael would get enjoyment out of that. They were ten yards away now.

Raphael reached out and pulled the positive charge out of the air around him. He coaxed the energy unit it built a bubble around himself. He manipulated the energy until there was but a thin membrane. A void of nothingness between negatively charged particles outside and the positive inside.

"Come now little devils and I will show you what power is." Raphael said as he swung his mace towards the bubbles edge.

With a speed and strength few had witnessed, Raphael crashed his mace into the bubble. The horrendous clap of thunder shook the ground. The arc of electricity that erupted when the mace broke the positive/negative membrane was bright in the darkness. The bolt traveled forward jumping from one form to the next. The poor creatures didn't have a chance to scream as the arc of electricity turned all it touched to ash.

Where there were hundreds only fifty were left standing. The howl emitted from those that remained standing was haunting. It came from all their mouths in unison. As if they felt the pain of those consumed by the energy.

Raphael gripped the mace with a renewed resolve and started forward. The first one that rushed forward was a fair haired woman. She was completely nude. She would have been beautiful in a past life. The creature that now inhabited her body made those days long past. The woman had deep cuts that ran down her face like war paint. She was clearing the ash field that had once been the Smiths Grove Mall parking lot with a grace that was inhuman.

Raphael prepared to strike the creature. They were all animal at this point. No finesse to their ability to kill. Only a desire to cause as much damage as possible . The creature launched in for the kill. Raphael waited until the creature could not change its direction and swung his mace. The speed of which he swung caused another clap of thunder as it traveled through the air. The creature was but a millisecond from its demise at Raphael hands.

The creature disappeared in a flash of blinding light. Raphael heard a scream come from behind him followed by automatic gunfire. One by one the remaining forms disappeared in the same flash of light. Raphael turned back toward the mall. The flashes of light inside the mall were a continuous strobe. Raphael glanced up at

Micheal who stood at the roof of the mall. The eerie large smile was still on Micheal's face.

Raphael cleared the expanse between himself and the mall. Even with his speed he knew he would be too late. The screams and gunfire had all but died out as he leaped the car barricade. He stopped cold in the entrance to the mall. The line of bodies standing in front of him among the remains of the survivors pained him. These people didn't deserve any of this. The rows of red eyes staring defiantly back at him. The same eerie smile on all their faces.

*"You cannot stop the legion arch. The trumpets have sounded in the void and we have answered their call."*they said in unison.

The laughter that boomed through the mall was that of Micheal. That arrogant booming laugh.

The damned piled on him like water in that instant. Raphael's anger fueled by lightning made short work of those inside. Those that had murdered the undeserving people inside the Smiths Grove Mall. Those that had come to extinguish all life from this world. Raphael's rage consumed him as he avenged them.

Yet as he stood alone among the remains of the murders and the murdered he felt no justice had been served. This should never have happened. These people were not to be judged. Their sins trivial and didn't merit this kind of divine punishment.

"MICHEAL!" Raphael's voice boomed through the mall shattering all the glass left intact inside.

Raphael leaped into the air. He tore through floors and concrete like paper. Anything in his path to Michael. He erupted through the roof of the Smiths Grove Mall in a shower of debris. Micheal had long since left. The damage had been done. He had proved his point in his own twisted way. Raphael looked at Randal's lifeless form at his feet. Michael had killed the kid for the fun of it. The hollow hole in the boys chest, where his heart should be, still seeping blood down on to the gravel beneath him.

Raphael looked at the words wrote in blood on the air conditioning unit behind him. The boys heart left like a trophy on top op it. Deut 30:25 in blood stained letters the message read. Raphael didn't know if he was powerful enough or even if he could. It didn't even matter if it damned him like the rest of the fallen. He would see that Michael paid for this in blood. If it was the last thing in this he did.

Part 4

Pastor Jimmy Clark watched as Sam covered Sebastian in a blanket.

Henry had been on the roof checking out a light Sam and Abby had seen when the automatic gunfire had started. It had carried on for a few minutes before an explosion had shook the walls of the police station.

Henry had come running through a few minutes later for the stairs. The sight that had followed was still stuck in Jimmy's mind. Sebastian had returned with Frank in tow. The fact that the man was nude had drawn looks from the rest. Sebastian had locked eyes with Jimmy as if to warn him about their agreement.

"What the hell happened to you Frank?" Henry asked as he handed water to both of them.

Jimmy looked at Sebastian who sat calmly in his blanket. Sam began to try and clean the blood of the man's face with a wet cloth. Sebastian's gaze had never left Jimmy's as the Sam continued to wipe away at the blood.

"I don't know Bear." Frank stated after a second. "I was coming back with the girl following me. There was a crash. I woke up in a room with one of those sickos about to cut me up. I must have missed one when I saved the girl. Sebastian here found me somehow. He came in guns a blazing."

Jimmy watched as Frank took a drink of water from the

bottle. Jimmy could tell by the look of both of them that wasn't the whole story. Some part of him knew that Frank wasn't telling the truth. Jimmy knew that much.

"We were making our way back here. Jesus those things are everywhere out there. We were over on east main when we got ambushed. They came pouring out of the stores like hornets out of a nest. I still don't know how we made it." Frank stated as he sat down in a chair.

Jimmy watched as Henry looked from Frank to Sebastian. The fact that the man was naked hadn't drawn a question yet. Jimmy knew that was coming.

"It was a mess that can be assured old boy." Sebastian stated calmly. " Frank here must have saved me twice in that fight if my count is right. He clipped a gas tank in the fray. As much for good luck as bad though I assure you. The side effect is my current lack of attire. I apologize for my state of dress. What the explosion didn't take I had to discard due to fire. I guess I can thank the stars I managed not to be burned."

Henry shook his head. Jimmy would be the first to say that the string of bad luck the world seemed to be having was incredible. That being the truth in the matter. It was mirrored by Sebastian's ability to save people from impossible situations. It definitely looked suspicious by all means. Jimmy knew he would not be the only to get to that conclusion.

"We're glad you're both okay." Jimmy stated in a hope to rally the crowd.

Jimmy watched as Sam and Henry both nodded their heads as if to agree with him. He knew that he wanted to know the truth. He could not call the man out nor would he. Sebastian had been good to them so far. Jimmy wasn't sure why, but a lot of blessings come in disguises.

"Where is the girl?" Frank asked as he took another drink of water.

Henry looked from Frank around the room. Jimmy had not seen the woman since Henry's harsh interrogation. Not that Jimmy could blame the girl. It had been rather uncomfortable for him and he wasn't even the one on trial. Henry's gaze finally fixed on Jimmy as if to answer the question.

" I haven't seen her since earlier." Pastor Clark stated. " She has to be around here somewhere."

Henry walked out of the break room. Jimmy watched as the man looked up and down the hallway. Henry shook his head as if disgusted and started off in the direction of the bathrooms. Jimmy knew that Henry was the last person that Grace wanted to see right now. His rather harsh treatment of the girl had not made her a fan. Jimmy watched as the light dimmed all at once. The gasps around the room echoed in the silence of the break room as the lights dimmed again.

"What's going on?" Sam asked with an obvious hint of terror in his voice.

Jimmy noticed that Sebastian was staring at him again with those piercing blue eyes. Every time he would meet the man's gaze he felt his whole life was on trial. As if those piercing blue orbs could take his soul.

"The generator is on its last leg." Frank stated with a sigh.

Jimmy knew that this insurmountable bad luck couldn't keep this up. Not handing them bad hands one after another. There had to be a break to this cycle. Jimmy watched as Henry came back into the room in a rush.

" I can't find her anywhere." Henry stated in huff.

Jimmy wasn't sure after all the damage and violence these warriors had endured so far how they kept going. Jimmy knew that he survived on faith. That would keep him going through this insufferable darkness. Yet he wasn't sure that his views were the same as the others. He knew Sam wanted nothing to do with God or the church. He had made that point obvious. In these trying times we should keep our faith. The lights dimmed again and this time they took longer to come back on.

"Sam find Sebastian some clothes. There should be something to fit him one of the lockers in the back. " Henry stated with obvious weight to his voice. "Hurry up before we lose the lights."

Sam nodded and took off in the direction of the locker room. He wasn't sure how long they had before the power went out all together, but Jimmy didn't think it was very long.

"What are we gonna do daddy?" Abigale asked with tears welling up in her eyes.

This will be a test of their faith. Jimmy Clark knew that deep down in his soul. Sebastian had taken to using the water to clean the blood off his face. The lights dimmed again and went out all together. A scream erupted from the hallway. Jimmy was sure it was Dianna Wheat. Jimmy heard a click then a bright beam of light cut through the new found darkness like a knife. Jimmy had to cover his eyes at its brightness.

" Everyone stay calm." Henry stated in his deep baritone authoritative voice. " We're still in here and they are still out there.

No need to start panicking yet."

Jimmy watched as the flash light shone around the room. The only two people that didn't look like they were scared were Frank and Sebastian. Even in the dark Sebastian's eyes almost glowed blue. He would assume after being out in the dark for as long as they had been they had become used to the terror.

"Ms. Wheat if you can hear my voice and see the light make your way in here with the rest of us" Henry called out.

Jimmy looked from one face to the other. He realized they were all staring at the door with anticipation in their eyes. The only one that didn't look that way was Sebastian. The man only had eyes for Jimmy at the moment.

"Ms. Wheat can you hear me?" Henry stated again as he started for the door.

Jimmy watched as Frank leaned forwards and picked up the Rifle from the table. He was picking up on the sudden bad vibe that was hanging like a cloud in the air.

"Sweet Jesus." Henry said from the hallway.

Frank was already on his feet and making his way towards the hallway. Jimmy felt the knot in his throat growing and he desperately tried to swallow it down. Abigale began to sob in the dark as Jimmy rose from his seat. The thought crossed his mind took his breath away.

Sam was in the dark alone. Jimmy felt the weight of those words sink down on him like a crushing weight. He struggled to compose himself as he looked around the door frame and into the hallway. Jimmy followed the path of light down to the fresh blood in the floor. Jimmy felt a pain in his chest. Henry followed the path of blood smeared on the floor with the light until it rounded a corner.

"Sam!" Jimmy yelled at the darkness.

Jimmy watched as Henry raised a hand as if to silence him. Jimmy felt a rush of heat to his face. How dare he try to silence him? If it was his daughter alone out there bleeding he would be concerned. A feral scream came from farther back in the police station. Jimmy was already around the door frame and starting down the hall. Henry grabbed him and held him against the wall. Jimmy struggled for a second but it was no use. He was too strong.

"This is not a time to do something stupid." Henry spat at him in a hushed whisper. "We will find Sam."

Jimmy looked over Henry's arm at Frank as the man made his way down the hallway. Jimmy believed they would find him. Either it would be his son or one of those "things." Jimmy felt the tears as they welled up in his eyes and burnt hot paths down his face.

"Go back inside with the others and shut the door." Henry whispered and pushed him back towards the door.

Jimmy walked back inside the break room and shut the door like he was instructed. Everything seemed so distant to him. It was almost like that time he had that high fever. He could remember things felt so far away.

"Ready to make that deal?" Sebastian asked without emotion.

(To be continued)